Table of Contents

Prologue

Parisians Want Love Without Locks

For years, lovers have come to The Pont des Arts or Passerelle des Arts, a pedestrian bridge in Paris, to profess their undying love by locking a padlock to the bridge, sometimes with their names engraved, sometimes with other poetic messages, and then they would throw the key into the River Seine. Unfortunately the bridge, which links the Institut de France and the central square (cour carrée) of the Palais du Louvre, has become the recipient of an estimated 700,000 locks, with more added every year, and the bridge cannot handle the weight. The mayor has asked that people no longer place the locks there and has started a #lovewithoutlocks campaign. In 2014, the grilles were removed so locks couldn't be attached.

Although Paris is known as the city of love, a little research into this tradition finds that Paris is not actually the origin of this loving tradition. The first notion of love locks appeared in a poem titled "Prayer for Love" by Desanka Maksimovic, a Serbian poet. The poem takes place before the First World War and is about a soldier

Hearts Locked in Time
Barbara Baldwin
Print ISBNs
Amazon print 9780228634959
Ingram Spark 9780228634966
Barnes & Noble 9780228634973
BWL Print 9780228634980

Copyright 2025 by Barbara Baldwin
Editor Victoria Chatham
Cover artist Michelle Lee

All rights reserved. Without limiting the rights under copyright reserved above, no part of this publication may be reproduced, stored in or introduced into a retrieval system, or transmitted, in any form, or by any means (electronic, mechanical, photocopying, recording, or otherwise) without the prior written permission of both the copyright owner and the publisher of this book

and young woman who were madly in love and secretly met every night at the Most Ljubavi Bridge in a town called Vrnjačka Banja. When the young soldier was sent off to Greece, he eventually met the love of his life. When his first love found out, she died of heartbreak. Out of superstition, local women started hanging love locks on that same bridge, the Bridge of Love, in an attempt to safeguard their love.

The popularity of love locking really took off after the release of the Italian movie "Ho Voglia di Te" (I want you) in 2007. It was inspired by the same-named novel from Italian author Federico Moccia, which was published in 2006.

The Mayor says that while the residents of Paris don't like the lock tradition, they aren't without sentiment for those who have tied their love to Paris, so sections of grille and boxes of locks will be auctioned off in the near future. That way, even if your lock no longer appears on the bridge, it may be out in the universe somewhere standing guard over another's love, or perhaps it has been melted down and incorporated into another artist's representation of love.

Chapter 1
Chicago, 2022

Jordan sauntered along the sidewalk, in no hurry to get back to the shop, even though the smell of deli sandwiches in her shopping basket made her mouth water. It was the perfect spring day in Chicago, a breeze off Lake Michigan keeping the temperatures cool. She lifted her head and inhaled deeply, fragrances of lilacs from the park to her right mingled with the city smells of car exhaust and asphalt, along with all the delicious whiffs of coffee and pizza and bread drifting from the open doors of the local shops.

She knew the neighborhood well, having grown up here, and although buildings had aged over the years, most of the shops in the neighborhood remained as they had for the last hundred years or more. The row homes had small stoops leading up to the front doors. A wrought iron fence lined the sidewalk on the other side of the street to offer a separation between the street parking and the spread of green grass and trees, the walking trail meandering through the park and around the curve of lakeshore. As always, old men sat on benches scattered along the path, some visiting and some sitting alone with a chattering group of pigeons at their feet. They were people her Gramps knew, and she wished she could get him to spend his days like those she saw, but he continued to run the antique store that had been in his family for generations, and to which she was heading, bringing him lunch like she did most days.

She waved at Mrs. Wilson as she shook out a small rug from her second floor window. At the beginning of the twentieth century, the row homes she walked past had been stately manors of the moderately wealthy of Chicago. Not the very rich industrialists with their grand gardens and gated grounds but she felt the area near the lake shore had much more character.

After the Great War and the depression, most of the businessmen who owned homes here had converted the lower level into their shops to save what little money they had. Her great-grandfather had done the same, giving up his large furniture showroom for the smaller shop here on Lakeview Street. Now her gramps kept only the more unique pieces, which were all now antiques, along with smaller fixtures and valuable jewelry he had for sale. There wasn't a great call for antiques today, but "vintage" housewares, jewelry and knick-knacks were in high demand and she had convinced him to carry more of that and less of the heavy cumbersome furniture of the past.

She opened the door to the merry sound of a bell overhead. "Lunch is here," she called as she wove through the chairs, buffets and dressers that created a narrow path through the store. Her gramps sat towards the back at a massive roll top desk that served as his office. He laid aside the paper and smiled when she approached.

"You should be fixing lunch for a houseful of babies instead of looking after an old man," he grumbled as she lifted a sandwich out of the basket she carried.

She ignored his comment because it was a conversation he started and ended the same way every day.

"Mrs. Wilson asked about you," she said instead.

He snorted. "Old busybody, always wanting to know what everyone's doing."

"I think she likes you," Jordan teased, although she felt it was probably true. Mrs. Wilson, a widow about her gramps' age, came into the shop almost every day. She rarely bought any of the candles Jordan made but always asked after her grandfather, and often peeked through the adjoining door when she thought Jordan wasn't looking.

"What did you do to your hair?" Gramps squinted at her as she laid out lunch.

"What do you think?" She fluffed the short bob as she spun in a circle. "Jaci

8

managed to get me in." Her friend had not only cut several inches off her hair, but had added blonde streaks to her plain brown and she couldn't be happier with the look.

He looked her up and down. "With that dress, you look like a flapper from the twenties."

She grinned, shaking her hips so the filmy dress swirled around her. She loved the sleeveless, drop-waist style and the strings of long beads. "I know! Carolyn has ordered in a truckload of vintage clothing. With Chicago having its Roaring Twenties Festival next month, everyone is getting into the action. Since we couldn't celebrate in 2020 because of the pandemic, they've planned a lot of extra activities and this year. You know," she tweaked his collar, "Carolyn probably has a nice vintage suit that would spiff you right up."

He laughed. "Honey, my entire closet is already vintage. Are we doing anything involving the festival?" Gramps had run his antique store all his life, and had tried to help the community by participating in just about every festival, campaign and youth organization fund raiser that was held. But he left the details up to Jordan.

"I'm working on it," Jordan said, although she really had no idea how to create a *1920's* effect in an antique store that was already full of stuff from well before 1920.

"Glad we don't run a bar or tavern," he said. "You know 1920 was the start of prohibition. How is the city going to handle that?"

"Certainly not by shutting down every drinking establishment," Jordan said with a laugh. "I've been hearing rumors about several local pubs posting doormen and you have to know the password to get in, like they did back in the day. People learn the password by following the pubs on Twitter." She frowned for a moment in thought. "You know, we should come up with some gimmick like that to get people into the stores."

"Do we have a Twitter account?" Gramps asked around a bite of sandwich. He still used a ledger to balance his books, though both Jordan and his accountant had tried unsuccessfully to get him to switch to computer. She had begun handling the social media for both his store and her candle shop when she moved back home. Before she could answer, her gramps changed the subject and handed her the newspaper, which he had folded back to the Editorial page

"Your favorite columnist is at it again."

Jordan didn't need to see the picture to know who had written the column, but her gaze flickered to the small photo anyway. Harry Gallagher flashed a smug grin and although the photo was black and white, his gaze boldly challenged anyone to argue with him. She knew because she had met the man on occasion and although he was intelligent and well spoken, he was also a bit on the arrogant side. But damn, he was handsome, she thought, not for the first time as she picked up the paper to see what his commentary was about this week.

She blinked, changing her focus to the article where today he blasted the mayor and city council for not doing more for the homeless. It wasn't that he had a "cause", but rather he liked to haranguer the local government about their lack of attention and support for certain sectors of the city. She had to give him credit, his facts were succinct and he knew how to use words that would not only raise awareness but cause people to actually do something. In this case she agreed with him.

Regardless of his topic, he was a favorite of every woman's auxiliary that had a cause in the city and was in constant demand as a speaker at monthly meetings. She glanced again at his picture, wondering if his knowledge was the sole reason he was so popular. Many of her friends had met him at various events and thought he was hot. She supposed...

Gathering the trash from their lunch, she cleared her gramps' workspace before bending down to give him a kiss on the top of his head; a daily ritual she knew he loved even as he fussed because a customer had come in.

"I'll be next door," she said, picking up his copy of *Antiquarian News* to read later that day. She stepped through the open doorway that divided her candle shop from his antique store. While the stores might appear disparate, they actually did a lot of combined sales. She took a deep breath, inhaling scents of lavender and strawberry, although lemon filtered through the air stronger than the rest. Her assistant, Alex, was in the back room working on the spring selections and she knew lemon was his favorite scent.

She glanced around the shop trying to decide how to package it. Although they often used jars with various tops or stoppers, she liked the bowls, cups and glasses she procured from her gramps' store. Taking an old jelly jar or flowered teacup and filling it with wax and a wick made a whimsical candle that sold faster than the pillars and plain glass containers and it made her store inventory unique. It also gave new purpose to some of the old but not valuable glassware that often came with a collective buy at an estate auction.

She gathered a set of lemonade glasses from the sixties off a shelf and took them into the back where they would be cleaned and ready for pouring. "I think these will be fun, don't you?" she asked Alex as she held up the glass which though clear, was decorated with sliced lemons and tiny yellow flowers.

"I was hoping you'd go with those," he replied with a nod. Alex and she had met in college, become friends, then gone their separate way for years. He had shown back up in Chicago almost the same time she had returned to take care of her grandfather. When she decided to open the candle shop in the vacant space next to the antique store, he had asked to come work for her. He hadn't told her much about his life, but she felt his secrets were his and she didn't question him. His creative flare blended well with her own, and that was all that mattered.

"Do some half pint mason jars also," Jordan said. "I'll work on the window display later." She left him to his work and re-entered the store, making minor adjustments to candle placement from where customers had picked up the merchandise and not returned it to its proper place. The antique tables and sideboards from next door were perfect to display the candles, just as her candles often set off a piece of furniture, such as a coffee table, in Gramps' shop.

it was Wednesday, the one day of the week they were closed to have time for inventory and for creating. It was essential to be open on the weekends as that was when the tourist traffic was highest, and she and Alex loved the mix of people who visited. They each had a story to tell and part of what she enjoyed the most was helping them choose a candle that matched their personalities.

She didn't feel like balancing the books today, so she opened a little gate to an alcove where she sometimes worked and where her pet project now stood. Several years ago, after she had read an article about the love locks on the Pont des Arts in Paris, she and Gramps had traveled to Paris for the lock auction. The grille sections, locks attached, or boxes of the locks had been auctioned off, the money to be used to rebuild the pedestrian bridge. Although Jordan understood the reasons behind the Paris Mayor's declaration and the auction, it seemed a shame as for every lock there was a couple who had pledged their love on that bridge. Would the selling of those locks somehow create crisis and lost love? Jordan's romantic nature felt sure the lovers would continue to exist, and she was determined to create a lasting memory for at least those whose locks were on the section of grille she had purchased.

She ran her fingers over one such lock, a pretty red and gold Yale with the initials BJN+TLVF etched onto one side. When she brought this section of grille back to Chicago, she had consulted a local locksmith. He gave her a basic set of tools she could use to open the locks. After all, she purchased the grille section because she wanted the locks intact, not cut open as she had found most of the locks in the boxes.

Her gaze slid over the four foot section of metal grille covered with locks of all different makes, colors, sizes and models that she had bought on a whim and really had no idea, at the time, what she would do with it other than she knew she needed to preserve it. What appeared to be the earliest locks, given they were linked directly to the grille and beneath other layers of locks, looked more ornate than the more recent locks in the forefront and it was those locks she really wanted to get her hands on.

She certainly didn't want to cut the fencing. After all, she wouldn't have bought them attached if she hadn't wanted the fencing also. It was as elaborate as some of the locks and quite old. At the top of the grille was a panel about eight inches high of ornate scrollwork that reminded her of the wrought iron railings in New Orleans. So while she had removed several locks using the tools her friend had given her, she realized she didn't want to remove them all. The entire piece was quite decorative by itself.

In the meantime she used the grille section as a window decoration, especially around Valentine's Day. Otherwise, it stood visible in the alcove where she would work on removing locks as she had time. She sat on a stool in front of the small section where she had managed to remove a dozen of the top layer of locks.

Some people had used the standard Master combination locks, which she felt defeated the purpose of locking your love and tossing the key in the Seine River, thus making the statement that your love could not be undone and would last for all time.

Combination locks seemed so...temporary; easily opened and removed to be used in some other manner. Like a person could go from loving another to loving their ten-speed or garden shed. Thus those locks were tossed into a basket and sold for a few coins at her Gramps as the combinations could easily be reworked to a new set of numbers.

The key locks were the ones she spent the most time on. Though most had a bit of rust, they were easily cleaned once they were off the grille. She sold quite a few even though they had no keys because people loved the story behind them. Some said they were going to lock them to a bridge back home. Others locked them straight away onto their purse or backpack handles. Regardless of where the locks ended up, Jordan felt the romance of it all continued and that was perhaps what she believed in the most.

Now, she maneuvered the grille around to work at it from the back side. One particular lock had intrigued her for the past week and she was determined to get to it, even though it was on the very first layer next to the grille. The metal of the grille was four by four inch squares so she could just manage to get her hand through the space, but in this case it didn't help.

The lock was an intricate scroll work of metal on both sides and it appeared that the locking mechanism was in the middle which made it extra hard to use the locksmith tools.

Short of cutting the grille, which she had sworn not to do, she would have to remove at least three other locks in close proximity. And those locks were layered beneath even more. She sighed, swiping her arm across her forehead and blowing upward to get her bangs out of her eyes.

Hours later Alex yelled from the back that he was heading out and the candles were poured and would set overnight. She yelled back to lock the back door on his way and she'd see him tomorrow. Her gramps had already called it a day and headed upstairs to his apartment, assuring her he could find his own dinner so she could keep working. That was the trouble with owning your own store and creating your own product. It was easy to ignore time and work much longer hours than planned.

In this case, she had told herself "just a little longer" more than once, but she had managed to remove four locks and the fancy one at the center of her attention was now more accessible. Not easily, but more so than when she had started. She had removed the lock directly beneath it and it now hung more directly down from the grille. It was then she noticed the etching on the back side, something that had been obscured by the other locks on the grille.

She tried to tilt it for a better look and realized how dim her work area had become. Holding the lock with one hand, she leaned over and flipped the switch on a small gooseneck lamp that sat on the table holding her tools, bending it toward the lock. Squinting, she could just make out some numbers but not the letters. She rubbed her eyes, realizing how tired and achy they were and decided she had done enough for the day. The lock winked in the light.

Just a little longer, she told herself, unable to give up on the prize that was so very close. She straightened in her chair, arched her back and tilted her head side to side until her neck popped. If she couldn't get it unlocked tonight, at least she could find out what was etched on the back. As she tightened her grip to turn it over, the lock jiggled about and the sharp edge of the scrolling cut into her palm.

With a yelp, she jerked her hand back to spy a small drop of blood just as she heard a light *clink*. She tried to find something to wipe her palm, and it was then she saw that the lock she had been so intent on opening, was hanging loose on the fencing. "Well, dang, all I had to do was cut myself and it opened right up," she muttered as she reached in with her good hand to slip the lock off the metal fencing.

The front door rattled and she glanced up to see Carolyn knocking vigorously on the glass. Jordan frowned as she wove her way past tables and shelves. Her friend knew the shop was closed on Wednesdays. In fact, she had seen Jordan earlier that day.

"Are you ready to head to the meeting?"

Jordan shook her head, confused. "Meeting?" She looked down at her palm, wondering if she needed a Band-Aid, but it appeared the lock made no more than a small scratch.

"The Chamber meeting," she said, inhaling and exhaling with gusto. "Lemon. My favorite. Is that Alex's work I smell?"

"Yeah. He's probably still in the back somewhere," she waved vaguely, knowing her friend had a thing for her business associate. Today, however, Caro waved her off.

"No time for that." She gave Jordan an overall look. "I'm glad you wore that dress today. It's great advertising for the shop."

Jordan shook her head. "I can't keep up with you." Her friend, normally energetic, today appeared overly enthusiastic.

Carolyn pursed her lips, took a deep breath and blew it out. "Sorry. I'm just super excited about this festival because Chicago is finally getting into the idea of promoting itself and its businesses. It's about time people recognize the arts and the many small independent businesses as versus the chain retail stores and the sports arenas.

"So yes," she continued, "I want this festival to be the biggest and best we have ever seen. And that means the young business owners, like you and me and Jaci and Ruben and the rest, need to make our presence known and our voices heard." She looked at her watch. "Are you ready? It's a great day and we can walk down to the Chamber office."

"Let me tell Gramps and Alex."

"You talk to Gramps; I'll tell Alex to check on him when he closes up." Caro wiggled her eyebrows suggestively and Jordan laughed.

It wasn't that Alex wouldn't check on Gramps because all her friends liked her grandfather and considered him their own. And it was ridiculous that Caro thought she needed an excuse to see Alex, but Jordan had never been one to get involved in other people's relationships. Especially considering the lack of any relationships of her own, although she didn't for a second regret moving to Chicago for her Gramps. After her parents had died, she couldn't have stayed in Colorado.

"Gramps, Caro and I are heading for the festival meeting," she said as she wandered to the back where he still sat at his desk. "Alex is still working, so check on him before you close up for the night, okay?" She knew her gramps often felt he didn't pull his weight around the shops, and Jordan always tried to reassure him that he was needed.

"And you told him to check on me, too, didn't you?" he smiled up at her, seeing through her ruse.

She kissed the top of his head. "Check on each other, then. I'll try not to wake you when I get home. I'm not sure how long this will take."

"Better grab the umbrella. There's a chance of rain."

Jordan glanced toward the front window where the sun shone brightly, but rather than get in a discussion on how right her gramps was and how wrong the weather forecaster *always* was, she smiled and promised to take care.

"Here, I brought you this to go with the rest of your vintage vibe," Caro said, as Jordan came back into the candle shop. She handed her a small clutch, incrusted with jet beads and hanging from a small silver chain.

"What fun it must have been back in the first Twenties. Always dressing up and going out on the town." Jordan dug through her shoulder bag for Kleenex, lip gloss, credit card wallet, a pen and small pad of paper, never knowing what she might need. "Grab an umbrella while I get my phone." She hurried over to the alcove where she had been working and grabbed her phone. The lock she had freed lay on her small worktable and for a moment, she wished the meeting could be delayed so she could investigate the intricacy better.

"Come on," Caro urged.

She sighed but grabbed the lock and tucked it into her clutch anyway. Maybe she'd have time for a closer look if the meeting droned on.

The evening sky was bruised in purples, blues and pale pinks although darker clouds hovered on the horizon. The Chamber, along with other city offices, was located in the refurbished Kirkland mansion on High Street. One of the things Jordan loved about Chicago was its history and the way so many of the old buildings had been restored or renovated so that you would never know that behind the brick and columns of an 1800's structure laid technology, stock exchanges and some of the major law firms in the city.

Just as they turned the corner onto High Street, fat drops of water began splattering the sidewalk. With a squeal, Caro tried to open the umbrella, fumbling with the clasp until Jordan took over, released the Velcro fastener and the umbrella popped open.

"Gramps said it was going to rain." She laughed as Caro hugged her arm tighter so they could both fit under the cover of the large umbrella. "Hurry." She quickened her steps but as they grew closer to the mansion, the crowd grew considerably.

"Is there a play performing?" Caro asked as they stopped just under the edge of the awning that covered the steps leading up to the doors.

"I have no idea but hurry out of the rain while I shake the umbrella and get it closed." Jordan stepped over to the edge of the sidewalk as a loud clap of thunder shook the air around them. Quickly, she slid the chain of the clutch over her arm and reached up to collapse the umbrella. Just as her fingers circled the metal slide, lightning cracked, the white light blinding her as a jolt of shock raced up her arm and down her spine. Her legs went out from under her and she felt herself falling...falling...into complete and utter darkness.

Chapter 2
Chicago, 1926

Henry paced aggravatingly in front of the Kirkland Mansion, muttering to himself about having to report on a ridiculous social event when he really wanted to be investigating the mobsters who were rapidly taking over Chicago. Stopping at the edge of the walkway, about to turn and pace the opposite direction, someone slammed into his back with such force he stumbled forward, barely catching himself on the brick railing running up the steps.

"Watch it," he hollered as he spun around but before he could say more, a body collapsed against his chest. He automatically grabbed, ready for a fight before realizing the form was female, and as his arms tightened around her, she went completely limp. Her head fell against his shoulder and he found himself supporting her entire body weight, which wasn't all that much.

"Hey, lady." He shook her slightly but there was no response. He swiveled, looking for somewhere to put her other than on the ground, which would be damp with the evening breezes coming in off the lake. Seeing a bench facing a small fountain and flowerbed, he adjusted his hold, reaching behind her knees to lift her and cradle her against his chest. He quickly shuffled the short distance to the bench, which sat in the evening shadows. Awkwardly he sat down and slid her to the side, being careful to keep an arm around her shoulders. The jostling seemed to arouse her as she murmured something that sounded like *Caro*. Just as he bent his head to try to see her more clearly, she woke completely with a start and began struggling against him. Not sure of her awareness, and not wanting her to fall off the bench, he tightened his grip, which only made her struggle more.

"Let me go!" She tried to take a swing at him but it was a puny effort and he easily caught her slim wrist.

"I'm not trying to hurt you," he said, his voice more agitated than he would have liked. "You fell into me; passed out. I was only trying to help." When she quit struggling, he added, "Although it's been awhile since I've had a dame throw herself at me."

Her eyes flared and she began struggling again. This time he loosened his hold, his hands hovering in case she teetered over, but not touching her. She looked wildly around then swung her gaze back to him. "What happened? Where's Caro?" Suddenly her eyes narrowed. "I wouldn't have expected you to be at a Chamber meeting."

Now it was his turn to be confused. "You know me?"

His question brought a snort. "Who doesn't? I don't know what happened but I have to go. Caro will wonder where I am." She stood too quickly, swayed and he grabbed her just before she fell again. He pulled her back down on the bench.

"I think you need to skip the festivities tonight and go home. I'll see if I can flag a cab." He started to rise but she grabbed his arm.

"I have to find my friend." She gazed up at him with damp eyes.

Whatever had happened to her, she was in distress, and he could not walk away. He turned back to the walk in front of the mansion. Spying a newsboy, he whistled sharply and waved him over. Digging in his pocket, he flipped the boy a penny. "Get yourself into that house and find a lady named..." He frowned and turned to the gal on the bench.

"Carolyn Johnson, but I really should..."

He ignored her and turned back to the newsboy. "You heard the name. Tell Miss Johnson that her friend isn't feeling well and I'm taking her home."

The boy tugged the front of his hat and nodded. "Yes, sir, Mr. Douglas, sir." He scampered off and Henry turned back to the bench where once again the woman was trying to stand. And once again collapsing.

"Stay here. Don't move," he commanded as he trotted the short distance to the street, whistling again sharply and waving his arm. Luckily, because of the number of people attending the Kirkland party, there were plenty of cabbies having just emptied their fares. The first one to stop was a horse-drawn carriage instead of the automobiles taking over the city, but he didn't care. He hurried back and carefully helped the woman to her feet. They shuffled to the curb. When she tried and failed to take a step up onto the cab, he managed to stifle his sigh, picked her up and stepped into the cab, depositing her onto a seat and sitting down beside her. She instinctively moved over.

"We'll wait a moment for your friend," he said, but after several minutes when no one appeared, he told the driver to go.

"Where do you live?" he asked. She turned and wrinkled her forehead in thought. "The driver needs an address."

She seemed totally confused by her surroundings, her gaze flitting hither and yon looking at everything and settling on nothing. Her hand reached out and hovered near the gas light on the wall, then gently touched the pulled back drape that allowed the night air into the closed box of the cab.

"Miss?" He hadn't even gotten her name, but at the driver's thump on the roof, that wasn't his priority. "Your address."

"124 Lakeview Street, I think." She turned back to the window, staring into the night. When the cab set into motion, she finally looked at him.

"Why did that newsboy call you Mr. Douglas? That's not your name."

"How do you know my name? Better yet, what is your name? After all, I've held you in my arms and carried you into a cab. I should at least have a name to go with the dreams that will find me tonight."

That brought a slight smile. "It's no wonder all the ladies want you to speak at their meetings. Your tongue is as smooth as the words you write to convince people to your way of thinking."

Henry would have asked her more but the cabbie had stopped. He reached across to open the door, hopped down and turned back to assist the woman. The instant she stepped to the street, she stopped and gasped.

"This isn't right," she whispered.

He glanced her way, her eyes once again glazed and confused. "This is the address you gave me."

"Yes, but it's not...it's the same but it's not." She had grabbed his arm and he was surprised at the strength of her grip as she pulled him back toward the cab.

"We need to get you inside," he tugged her forward slowly. "Something happened to you and you need to be looked after; perhaps seen by a physician."

She stumbled as he walked her up the steps to the door, clutching him tighter. "No, I can't go in there." She pulled back and tried to turn, but at that moment the front door opened and a woman of moderate age stepped onto the stoop.

"Jodelle, where have you been? Your trunk was delivered from the train station hours ago. I had instructed your mother to have you come directly here upon your arrival."

Instead of answering, the woman he now knew as Jodelle, pulled back even further, almost hiding behind him. "I can't stay here, Harry," she whispered urgently, her words muffled against his suit coat. "Don't leave me here."

She knew him, and even the nickname only his family used, but he had no idea who she was or why she seemed so reluctant to stay at an address that she had said was her own.

"What is wrong with you, girl?" the woman asked, followed quickly by, "And who are you to be escorting my niece about without so much as an introduction?"

"Henry Douglas, ma'am," he said politely, "and it's purely by accident that I bumped into your niece at the Kirkland mansion. She seems to have taken a fall or something and is slightly confused."

"Confused?" the woman repeated before gasping. "The Kirkland's?" Her gaze swung to Jodelle. "I take it upon myself to help my sister out by allowing you to come stay here and the first thing you do – before even letting me know you have arrived – is get involved with that group of new age riffraff and their black magic friends?" Her voice had steadily risen until she was practically shouting.

Henry felt Jodelle's clutch on the back of his jacket tighten. Trying to do a simple good deed, he had no desire to get in the middle of a family squabble and sought a fast way out. He reached behind him and gently tugged Jodelle to his side before pushing her forward.

"Look, she gave me this address and so I brought her here. She seems confused, but that is not my problem. I was trying to be helpful."

The supposed Aunt narrowed her gaze at him. "I know who you are and you have no business being around nice people. All the trash and misinformation that comes out in that newspaper of yours; how they support the criminals that are taking over our city. How—"

"Good evening, ma'am," he interrupted, "I hope your niece recovers." As gently as he could, he tugged himself free from Jodelle's clutches and hurried down the steps to the cab. Whatever awaited Jodelle inside that house, perhaps he shouldn't have left her there. At the same time, he wanted no part in someone else's family drama. He slammed the door of the cab, signaling for the driver to take off. His last glance of the stoop at 124 Lakeview would become branded on his brain.

Brown eyes, liquid with tears, and one hand reaching out to him, beseeching him not to leave her.

* * *

Jordan watched Harry Gallagher walk away, leaving her in this world that was not hers. All the way here, she had viewed the scenery with detachment, thinking she was either in a dream or watching a movie. The horse drawn cab they rode in was similar to the ones roaming the streets of Chicago, taking tourists on a historic tour of the city. She had watched the city go by, the buildings and pedestrians obscured by nightfall to the point where she couldn't distinguish details to determine exactly where she was.

And now, the row house she had lived in with her gramps for years, the one at 124 Lakeview, felt at once familiar and foreign. The woman tugging her into the front foyer and shutting the door behind her was no one she knew. Her ears rang and whatever the woman said only sounded like the "wa-wa-wa" of adult voices in a *Charlie Brown* movie. The door slamming behind her jerked her to awareness.

"I can not believe you have been in the city for less than a day and have already caused so much trouble!" The woman *tsked* as she secured the lock and removed the key, hanging it on a hook to the side. "To try to get into the Kirklands for that spectacle they are holding with that horrible Houdini, and then to be accompanied home by Henry Douglas, who everyone knows is a philanderer of the worse sort. Well, it's all beyond my understanding."

The names ricocheted inside Jordan's head like billiard balls on a hard break, and she felt her legs go weak. Somewhere in the recesses of her brain grew an idea of what exactly had happened to her, but she was nowhere ready to confront it. She collapsed onto the stairs, grabbing the banister to keep from tipping over and squeezed her eyes shut. Upon seeing her distress, the woman softened her tone.

"Well, apparently you have had some distress," she began.

You think?

"I suppose we can leave the questions until morning, but you will tell me what is going on, young lady."

Young lady? She appeared to be the same age as Jordan, but she couldn't really ask, now could she?

"Your room is at the top of the stairs on the left. Your trunk is there, also. I don't expect Maddie to do your unpacking; she is not to be at your beck and call. I will, however, have her bring you up a cup of tea, even though the house should have been abed long ago."

"Where is Gramps?" He would straighten out the confusion Jordan suffered.

The woman shook her head, again with a *tsk*. "My sister was right sending you to me. You are in dire need of not only discipline but proper etiquette. You will address my father as Grandfather or Sir. Likewise, you will address me as Aunt Beatrice, not Auntie or Bea."

Jordan's shoulders relaxed slightly knowing, regardless of who this woman said *she was*, that her gramps was here. If she could get through the night, she would wake up and all would be right with her world.

She wearily rose and turned to tackle the stairs. Her feet felt heavy and her steps thudded loudly as she slowly took one step at a time. She ran her hand along the wallpaper which was new; or at least different than the smooth painted walls her gramps preferred. The front foyer, the stairs and banister, all were the same as she had always known, although they had been the upstairs at her gramps because the first floor contained the shops. She closed her eyes, pulling forth a picture that hung on Gramp's office wall. It looked exactly like the front of this row home when the cab had pulled up. The outside steps led to the front foyer, actually the second floor, as the first had been the kitchen and living quarters of the help back in...the 1920s. She stumbled, griping the banister tighter.

She opened the door to her room; the same room she had slept in for years and felt a shock similar to what she had earlier at the Kirkland mansion...in the rain, she recalled, but it wasn't raining now. She felt electricity vibrate the air, a faint undercurrent of buzzing from the overly bright lights attached to the walls. Once again, things were the same but not. The basic furniture-- a bed, nightstand. chair and highboy dresser were the same but again there was floral wallpaper with matching draperies on the window, both a rather loud pattern with huge red roses on a mossy green background and something she would never have approved. The closet stood open and empty, and there was a trunk on the floor at the end of the bed. But there were no bookshelves or small desk with a computer. Her jewelry box was not on top the dresser, or anything else for that matter. It was a sterile, unlived-in room, devoid of even a picture or photograph on the wall.

"Excuse me, Miss Jodelle." A timid voice from behind her had Jordan turning quickly. She started to say that Jodelle wasn't he name but thought perhaps to get some information from this young girl instead.

She moved to the bed and sat, motioning to place the tea tray on the nightstand near where she sat. "What is your name?"

"Maddie, Miss." She kept her eyes downcast.

"And my...my aunt; is she nice to work for?" From the interaction already with her so-called Aunt, it might be rather difficult to get along with her.

"I'm not to speak with guests, Miss."

"Well, I'm not a guest if I will be living here, right? Perhaps we can become friends."

The tray rattled as she dropped it the last inch to the table. "Oh, no, Miss. Never. It's not my place to have friends, especially those who employ me." She backed up, hands behind her back. "Will there be anything else?"

"No, and thank you for bringing me the tea." So much for getting any information, at least not for now. She might need Maddie's help at some point and there was no sense alienating her from the start.

As the maid closed the door behind her, Jordan let out a sigh and turned to the tray. A small china teapot, cup and saucer and a dish of cookies captured her attention. She added a spoon of sugar to the cup and poured the hot tea. She was normally level-headed and practical, given to flights of fancy only in her work, but nothing in her present circumstances could explain why she was here in familiar, yet foreign, surroundings.

As she sipped her tea and nibbled on a cookie, she tried to make sense of her predicament, starting with the only relatable thing, or rather person – Harry Gallagher. Why had he used the name Henry Douglas? She recognized him; why had he not recognized her? After all, they had been in dozens of social and business situations together and had conversed on occasion. She grabbed another cookie, her anger mounting. Why had he left her here with people she didn't know, in a situation she didn't understand and certainly had no immediate control over?

Something was very, very wrong, but Jordan couldn't seem to pinpoint the exact what, or who, or where of it. If Caro were here, she would know what to do. *Caro!* She looked frantically around, spying her clutch on the chair by the other side of the table. She didn't remember dropping it there, but then she didn't remember a lot of what had happened tonight. She jumped up, dizziness hit immediately, and she grabbed the arms of the chair to steady herself. Clutching the bag with one hand, she kept the other on the furniture as she shuffled back to the bed and sank down. With shaking hands, she opened the bag and sighed with relief to see her cell phone nestled in among the other items she had added before the meeting.

Swiping to open, hoping the battery hadn't died, she grinned when the screen lit and a cover shot of her and her best friend popped up. Speed dialing, she held it to her ear but there was no connection or dial tone. She checked the screen where no bars or service were indicated. "Of course not. Why would there be something as easy as a phone call to figure this out?" Perhaps it had gotten knocked out when the lightning struck.

"And there you have it," Jordan muttered as she dropped the phone back in her purse and snapped it shut. Closing her eyes, she recalled the moments before everything went blank. They had arrived at the Chamber offices as the rain started, thankful for Gramps' reminder to take the umbrella. As she had struggled to close the oversized protection, thunder had shaken the ground and then lightning struck. She remembered the streak of shock running up her arm and could only assume the lightning had hit the metal tip of the umbrella and traveled into her body.

She looked around the room again. "So I'm either dead and taking one last look at my home before heading into the unknown, or I'm laying unconscious in a hospital somewhere reliving some piece of my life long forgotten." What else would explain all the familiarness and yet the unknown things that she had experienced in the last few hours?

She kicked off her shoes, pulled her dress over her head and crawled beneath the covers on the bed. There was nothing she could do about anything in the middle of the night. So her practical self told her fretting self to sleep, hoping that in the morning she would wake up in a hospital bed. The alternative was not an option.

Chapter 3

"Is this how you spent your days in Iowa, sleeping away and expecting people to wait on you hand and foot?"

Jordan groaned, recognizing the voice though she had only heard it for the first time last night. She opened blurry eyes to see the woman called Beatrice setting a fresh tray on the table by her bed. The starchy smell of her black dress wafted across the short distance.

"Then why are you here?" she asked before thinking better of it.

"I had thought to have a civil conversation about your stay here, but I can see that is not to be. So I will tell you this. You will follow the rules of this home, you will not take advantage of the staff, your grandfather, nor me and above all, you will not sass your elders."

Jordan hid a smile as she scooted up in the bed. Beatrice looked to be about her age of thirty, although the frown lines on her face made her appear older.

"If I may ask, how much 'elder' are you than me?"

She gasped. "It is so improper to ask a lady her age, even from another female! Although your mother is older than me by five years, I am most certainly older than you and shall be respected as such."

Respect is earned, Jordan thought, but was respectful enough not to say so. Until she figured out what was up in this topsy-turvy world she had entered, she would keep – try to keep—her mouth shut. Remembering the alternatives she had concluded last night, she could still be dead and living a life in hell, given the actions of her current "jailer". After all, what did she really know about the hereafter? Or she could be in a drug-induced coma in the hospital because the bizarre events she experienced certainly lent themselves to hallucination by drug injection.

She pinched herself, the sharp sting making her realize she was awake. That didn't leave her with a very likable alternative. There had to be something she didn't know.

"I am sorry."

Beatrice *harrumphed*, crossed her arms over her chest and glared at her. "I will give you today to settle in, but then you must seek employment for I won't having you freeloading. At eighteen, you are well old enough to be working; contributing to the household income."

Jordan choked on the sip of tea she had just taken, coughing into the napkin she had thankfully picked up. Whoever Beatrice thought she was, she certainly wasn't an eighteen year old! Although the thought that she *looked* eighteen pleased her a lot, until the woman spoke again.

"You have not aged well. Tanned skin and freckles are not a fashion statement here in the city. We shall have to get you some bleach wax to reduce all that brown." She turned to leave. "I see you have not unpacked your trunk, which means your dresses will be wrinkled beyond wearing. I shall send Maddie up to gather something for you to wear today, but you must hang the rest of your wardrobe so the wrinkles shake out. As I have said, the household staff has many duties, none of which, at the moment, are to cater after you."

"You don't appear to want me here, so why am I?" Jordan should have known she couldn't keep her mouth closed.

If she thought her question would cause an explosion, she was surprised. Beatrice's face fell, her eyes filling with tears. "After you left to travel here, your mother was put into a sanitarium, leaving you with no parent to supervise you."

Jordan gasped, momentarily caught up in the story. "Why? She...I would have taken care of her."

Beatrice shook her head. "She has an acute case of dementia, as they call it. You had last written that she had become quite irrational and...hurtful. I spoke with her doctor and it was decided that an asylum would be the best place for her."

Jordan's heart went out for Jodelle, wherever she was, for having to abandon her parent in her time of need. She would never leave her gramps, no matter what health issues he had. And that begged the question, where had Jodelle gone, for she apparently hadn't arrived in Chicago? Jordan's shoulders ached with the weight of everything that pushed down on her, but her first priority had to be herself. Still, she felt sorry for Beatrice, and would try to be more agreeable.

"I will unpack immediately. I have something to take care of in a bit, but I will certainly begin looking for employment at the first opportunity."

"Something to take care of? You have only been in the city a day. How could you possibly have business to attend?"

What to say? There wasn't any answer she could give, because honestly, she wasn't sure exactly what she was looking for outside the doors of 124 Lakeview. When she didn't immediately answer, Beatrice turned to leave.

"Dinner is promptly at seven."

The minute she closed the door, Jordan jumped up and hurried to the end of the bed where Jodelle's trunk sat. She lifted the heavy curved top and locked the lever that held it open. On top of dark wool material, possibly a coat, lay a white velum envelope.

In eloquent black script were two words --
Aunt Beatrice.

Jordan rocked back on her heels. This wasn't good. Why would Jodelle put a letter to her aunt in the trunk to Chicago if she intended to arrive with said trunk?

A knock on the door and a tentative, "Miss", had Jordan frantically looking for something with which to cover up, for she had slept in her undies. She threw things right and left from the trunk until she happened upon a robe. Hoping Jodelle was close to her size, she grabbed it and slid her arms into the soft cotton, tying it closed as she walked over to open the door.

"Good morning, Miss." Maddie walked in and stopped. "Oh, my."

Jordan turned back to the explosion of material on the floor, but Maddie was already moving in that direction.

"Anything you want is always on the very bottom, would that be right?" She said and Jordan could hear the smile in her voice.

"I am sorry and I fully intend to put it all away. I needed a robe."

"Not to worry. Miss Barrister said I was to iron you something fit for job hunting, and you've made it much easier to see what is here."

Jordan laughed out loud. "You are quite a treasure, Maddie."

"The bath is down the hall if you would like to freshen up. While you do, I'll pick a

shirt and skirt for you to wear and set the rest
to rights."

"No, you will not. My aunt made it very
clear I was to take care of myself."

"Then we won't tell her." Maddie raised
a brow as she glanced at her over a shoulder.

Jordan left the room with the conclusion
that at least she wasn't dead and in hell,
because no one as nice as Maddie would
have been relegated there. And if she were
dead and gone to heaven, she would have
surely met her parents by now. As she sank
into a tub of warm water, she contemplated
the other not so far-fetched idea – a coma.
How did one test for being in a coma? A pair
of vibrant green eyes came to mind and she
recalled the man who had helped her last
night. Harry Gallagher, or Henry Douglas as
he called himself, might just have the
answers she needed.

Maddie had made good on her promise
as Jordan found the room spotless when she
finished with her long soak in the tub. A long,
navy skirt and white silk blouse lay across
the bed, along with a white slip, and even a
bra and plain white cotton panties. The room
looked a little less sterile as there were two
books on the night stand and a vanity set of
brush,, comb and mirror on the top of the
dresser. Apparently things Jodelle had
packed to come with her. Which brought her
to this, Jordan thought as she pulled the
envelope from the pocket where she had
stashed it when Maddie entered earlier.

Sitting in the chair, she nervously pulled the letter from its envelope. She had to open it and read the contents if only to understand her position better, because at the moment she was impersonating Jodelle. She slowly unfolded the letter to find a single page, only half filled with writing.

Aunt Beatrice,

I know you expected me to arrive in Chicago today but I cannot. I am heartbroken that you saw fit to send my beloved mother to an asylum the moment I purchased my train ticket for what I thought would be a happy visit. Had I known that was to be your decision, I never would have written to you about her condition in the first place. Now, they won't even let me see her, much less take her home again. I will not forgive you, nor will I come to Chicago and give you an opportunity to inflict similar cruelty on me.

I can no longer consider you family.
Jodelle Foster

"Harsh," whispered Jordan as she stared at the letter, although she would have probably done the same thing. Trouble was, Jordan had seen the anguish Beatrice tried to hide when they spoke last night. A conversation between the two might have averted the present situation, but it appeared too late for that. She folded the letter and hid it beneath the mattress. Did she feel bad, keeping Jodelle's letter from Beatrice? Perhaps a little because the words would have pierced her heart. If any good could be had, the circumstances at least gave Jordan sanctuary until she figured out how she fit into all this.

* * *

Jordan held her breath as she slowly opened the front door, almost afraid of what she would see. Bright light and fresh air slammed against her senses and she steadied herself, back against the now closed door. She knew the phrase kept reverberating in her brain, but things looked familiar and foreign at the same time. Cars drove slowly down the street, but they weren't today's SUVs and trucks, but rather early model Ts and the trucks were more like flatbeds with wooden siderails.

A few women walked along the street, their fashions much like what she wore. That should have been her first clue when she dressed because her skirt was long and her blouse very plain and unadorned, but she had thought perhaps Jodelle's family was Amish, or of some other religious sect.

It dawned on her now where she was. Chicago, yes, but not her Chicago of 2022. For whatever reason and by whatever happenstance, she was in Chicago from many years ago. And it couldn't be because she lay in a coma and dreamed all this. The details on the cars, the fashions; she wouldn't have known that, conscious or not.

She realized her breathing was far too rapid, lightheadedness overtaking her. With conscious effort, she inhaled deeply and held her breath to an eight count, then slowly exhaled. Again and then again, until her heart quit thumping so hard and her ears quit ringing. There had to be a logical explanation, if only she could think logically. Where could she go; who could she ask? No one would believe her if she told her story; no one could possibly understand.

And then she remembered there was one other person here that she knew, if only slightly, although he pretended to be someone else. She pushed off the brick side wall of the stoop where she had been leaning, waited a heartbeat to make sure she wouldn't faint, then cautiously walked down the steps to the street. She would have to retrace her steps from last night and hope she could find the man because it would appear he was in the same situation as herself and she could only hope he knew the way home.

* * *

She spied the tall man in an ill fitting suit once again loitering in front of the Kirkland Mansion and rushed to confront him.

"What are you doing here?" she asked. She didn't understand how she came to be in this era, but for another person from the twenty-first century to also be wandering the streets? "You can't be here."

"Believe me, tell it to my editor," he said with a sigh, tipping back his fedora which allowed thick locks of black hair to fall across his forehead. "I'm looking for a good investigative story about crime bosses and he sends me to a sissy society party with a hokey magician."

His gaze narrowed on her. "You're the dame from last night," he said in recognition. Snapping his fingers, he pointed to her. "Jodelle." He flashed her a grin but she waved away his friendliness.

"What is the date today?"

He frowned at the question. "June 24th?" he said as though he weren't quite sure.

"The year! What year is it?" Her voice rose in demand.

"You don't know what year it is?"

"Just answer my question, Mr. Gallagher. I'm trying to understand what you and I are doing here, but I don't even know when 'here' is."

At the mention of his name , he pulled the fedora lower on his forehead as his gaze made a furtive sweep of the surrounding area. "You are mistaken. My name is Henry Douglas. And the year is 1926. Why?"

Dizziness struck her again and she swayed, grabbing his coat to steady herself.

"Hey, you okay?" He took her elbow and looked right then left before guiding her across the street. He seemed anxious to get her off the street. Was it any wonder? She could only imagine what people would say if they overheard the two of them discussing time traveling from the twenty-first century.

He pushed her into a booth at a cafeteria she didn't remember entering. She looked around. It might have been Gabby's for all the old fashion vinyl booths and the Formica counter running along one side. Gabby's, an historic landmark in Chicago, had not reopened after the pandemic, however when the waitress, dressed in a neat dress and pressed apron, came to their booth she handed them a menu that did, indeed, say "Gabby's – good home cooking".

She groaned, crossed her arms on the table and laid her head on them. Too many images flashed across her mind and she couldn't piece anything together to understand why they were here. She had been sitting in her studio removing locks from a section of grille. One in particular had caught her fancy, its shape almost heart-like and the edges and face of it made from filigree metal instead of smooth.

She had cut herself, she recalled and sat up, turning her hand over to search her right palm. Only the faintest of marks ran across the tender pad below her thumb.

"Here you go," the waitress said, setting glasses on the table along with napkins. "Enjoy."

Jordan turned her attention first to the drink,, which looked to be a Coke, then to the man sitting across from her. He had set his fedora aside and his green gaze grew more intent the longer their gazes locked.

"1926?" She whispered the date, watching closely to see his reaction. All she got was a single nod. "Why are we here?"

His lips quirked. "I figured only to offer you a refreshment as you seemed to be in distress."

She waved away his comment as she sipped her Coke, which had a flavor unlike any she had recently tasted and definitely better than diet Coke. When she looked up, his gaze had turned flinty and he no longer smiled.

"Whatever misconception you may have, Miss, I am not who you think I am. I don't know where you came up with," he paused, then continued in a low voice, "the name you spoke, but it's not me."

Jordan frowned. "You work for the *Chicago Tribune*, right?"

"*The Daily Journal.*"

"You write about the gangsters and mobs that controlled Chicago in the early 1920s, right?" Her gramps had all his books, many of which were considered celebrated histories of the many gangs and violence of the time. "If you're chasing gangsters, you're probably better off with a fake name. Harder to find you and kill you."

He grabbed his hat and slammed it on his head, pulling it low. Reaching across the table, he pulled her forward with a very tight grip at her wrist as he leaned in close, speaking in a rough whisper through clenched teeth. "I donna write books. I am no' chasing mobsters and I am no' the name you keep repeating with little care for the consequences." There was a lyrical undertone to his words she hadn't heard before but didn't have time to place before he continued. "I have acted the gentleman with you twice. I am givin' you warning I willn't do it again. Leave me be." He threw a dollar on the table and slid from the booth, walking away without a backward glance.

Jordan sat in stupefied silence, his words ringing in her ears. *Irish*. That was the accent in his voice when he spoke in anger; not the carefully modulated accent she had otherwise heard. The Irish weren't the most favored sect of immigrants in Chicago in the early twentieth century and many had changed their names in favor of anonymity over chaos.

She glanced out the window to see him disappear around the corner. He looked exactly like the grainy picture at the top of his column every week in the *Chicago Tribune*. She had met Harry Gallagher on occasion and could recall having a few conversations with him, yet none of those had indicated he came from Irish descent. And she had gotten the impression, perhaps from his columns, that he was more sophisticated and cultured than the rough speaking, carelessly dressed man she had just angered.

What had he said; that he worked for the *Daily Journal*? She knew that newspaper hadn't been in existence for any number of years. Jordan swallowed as realization hit her hard.

Henry Douglas might be an ancestor of the famous columnist, for they looked strikingly similar, but Harry Gallagher hadn't traveled through time as she had done. She had no ally to help her navigate in this unknown time.

Why had she accidently been transported back to this time?

And more importantly, *what* was she to do about it?

Chapter 4

Henry stood at the shore of Lake Michigan angrily throwing stones into the water as waves splashed ashore. He was normally an easy going sort of fellow for he had learned long ago that anger only got him in trouble. As a young sprout, he had been on the puny side, which meant he got picked on, a lot. His brother, if close by, had always come to his rescue, which hadn't helped matters, as the boys in the neighborhood would find times when Sully wasn't around, then they would chase him until he ran home to his mum. Even then, the name calling never stopped.

Now, at over six feet tall and muscular, he could fend for himself, but rarely chose to fight. Words were his weapon of choice, and over the years, he had learned to wield them like the finest King Arthurian sword. Which brought him to his current predicament – his angry insults to Jodelle.

He had instantly been fascinated by her when she bumped into him last night. With her cute bobbed hair and Pixie nose, she had reminded him of faeries from the homeland.

He had never seen her around town and thought to get to know her better, but at that time, some mishap she suffered had left her rather confused and the best he could do was to see her home. He had kicked himself later for not getting more than her first name. At the time he had wondered if they might bump into each other again and then, sure enough, she had come upon him today. And what had he done but gotten angry and walked away.

What she said about him had struck a chord of fear, which in turn made him angry. He was extremely careful with his investigations into the gangsters and mobs that were running and ruining Chicago. He had yet to have enough information to write the kind of expose that *The Daily Journal* would publish and what he had found out so far, he kept close to the vest. Yet she said he was publishing books about gangsters?

So he had lashed out, his words containing a healthy dose of Irish accent, as they always did when he became angry. He had tried throughout his growing up years to speak properly and to hide any indication of his Irish background. He wasn't ashamed of his heritage, but in Chicago, if you were a man and Irish, you were automatically considered part of the North Side Gang, which meant you were either feared or hated. That is what had gotten his brother, Sullivan, killed, and Henry considered it his life's work to avenge his brother's death. The only way that could happen was to keep his heritage secret.

If this woman knew more about him and his writing than what was published in *The Daily Journal*, he needed to find out. The only way he could do that was to seek her out, even though he said she would not see him again. He knew her first name, and he did know where she lived, although he hesitated to confront the dragon lady who have met him at the door last night.

And before he could ask her for information, he would have to apologize. It wasn't just his words, but his mum had not brought him up to manhandle ladies and he deeply regretted having done so.

"Psst, HD." A young, tinny voice had him spinning around, automatically aware of his surroundings and mentally thumping his head for having let his mind wander.

"What's up, Eddie?" He'd known Eddie for a couple of years as the kid hocked papers for *The Daily Journal*. He reached down and tugged the flat cap straight on the small newsboy's head. At least today he didn't wear it backward. What kids today thought was fashion, he would never understand.

Eddie looked this way and that and Henry tried to hide a grin. Eddie thought himself a spy and could often be found lurking around corners in the most unexpected places. They had formed an alliance of sorts the first time Eddie offered him information on an upcoming raid by local officials on *Marge's Still*. That information had given Henry a story for his paper that scooped any other news rag in the city. Unfortunately, neither the raid nor his story had much of an impact, for the speakeasy became even more infamous and continued to do a healthy business. Henry often wondered if the coppers put up a front with hokey raids so it looked as if they were in control of the bootlegging in the city, where in actuality Al Capone's *Outfit* controlled both the bootlegging and at least part of the police force. Still, Eddie's information often led Henry to information he wouldn't have obtained otherwise. Now, they had an unofficial pact where Eddie fed him information and Henry paid him well with the understanding that Henry was his only "client".

"I seen AC go into the Congress just a bit ago."

"You on the up and up?" One of Eddie's quirks was he never called anyone by name, instead using initials or some slang term that it had at first taken Henry time to decipher. Eddie was adamant about not saying certain names out loud, convinced that would keep him in the clear from anyone thinking he was a snitch.

"Pos-i-lute-ly." He nodded vigorously.

Henry wondered what Al Capone had going in the middle of the day, for even though he ran the *Chicago Outfit*, as his mob was known, he kept a low profile. He turned to stare across the lake, noting the waves had become more aggressive, dark clouds now hanging low on the horizon. A storm was coming in, which would preclude him hanging around Congress Park, across the way from the hotel, to see what might transpire. He could opt for lunch at the hotel restaurant, although ritzy, and he knew his editor would never agree to pay for it. Maybe he could just loiter around the lobby until they kicked him out.

He dug in his pocket and flipped a nickel to Eddie which made the boy grin widely. "How's your mum?" he asked, knowing the boy's mother was too sick to work, one of the reasons her eight year old son wandered the streets, often at night. The same reason Henry gave him more than required for his information.

"She doing a might better now she can rest more and not be working in the factory."

"Good. Keep getting me information and I'll see to it you have a little extra for Sunday supper." Eddie wouldn't accept charity; Henry had tried. Thus his agreement to *buy* information from the youngster, which had turned into a great arrangement because Eddie not only knew his way around the city, he recognized important people. Newsboys like Eddie were invisible to the people walking the streets until they shouted their wares. Even then, most barely acknowledged their existence, which often allowed them to overhear things better left unsaid.

"Anything else happening?" Henry asked, still undecided which direction he should go – downtown to the Congress or over to Lakeview to find a certain female.

"Naw," Eddie replied. "I ain't got nothing til the evening edition hits the streets. It's a slow day for spying." He shook his head.

Henry laughed at the soulful expression on his grubby face but it did make up his mind. Digging in his pocket for another coin, he flipped it to the boy. "I need you to mosey over to Lakeview Street – 124 to be precise – and keep an eye out."

"What I'm looking for?"

"A lady. A young lady, not the old one."

"You want me to watch a skirt?" His face broke into a grin. "You carrying a torch all a sudden?"

"No!" Henry denied a bit too fast because it made Eddie nod in apparent agreement while his lips twitched and eyes danced with amusement. He was quite street-wise for only being eight.

"I just need to know she's all right," he said. "We had a disagreement and if I know her itinerary, I can approach her at the proper time to apologize." Why on earth was he explaining his dilemma to a child?

"Sure you are." Eddie nodded sagely. "Betty at the flower shop says when a man comes in for flowers, if she knows he had an argument with his gal, she doubles the price.

And they pay it. Maybe you ought to buy some flowers; just don't say you had a row."

Henry cuffed the kid gently. "I'm not buying flowers. Now get on with you and let me know where she goes."

The kid hurried through the loose sand and back up to the walk. Henry's stomach growled and he decided, expense account or not, he would treat himself to lunch at the Congress.

* * *

"I didn't order this." Jordan stared at the plate the waitress set in front of her. She realized she didn't have a cent to her name, so no way could she pay the price of a hamburger.

"The gentleman ordered for the both of you," she said then seemed hesitant to add, "before he had to leave? So I didn't bring one for him." She reached down and scooped up the bill Harry had left. "This will cover it."

"A dollar?" she said in surprise.

The waitress blushed. "I suppose you want change?"

A hamburger, fries and a Coke for a dollar, with change? Even though she might need money, Jordan couldn't begrudge the woman her tip.

"No, you keep it. I would like a drink refill, if you can."

"Sure." She grabbed the glass and turned then stopped. "Is your fella coming back? I

58

can bring his hamburger." She didn't sound enthusiastic about it, for it would mean she lost her tip.

Jordan glanced out the window. "No, he, um, he had urgent business to see to."

"He's that newspaper fellow, isn't he? He comes around quite a bit but I've never seen him with a gal. No offense."

"None taken." If this waitress knew Henry, maybe she would offer information that would help Jordan out. Yet how did one ask questions to better understand being in 1926 when that person should already know about the year in which they were living? And if she were having lunch with Harry, wouldn't she already know about him? That would certainly raise suspicions so for now Jordan decided to keep her thoughts to herself.

When the waitress returned with her Coke refill, she commented, "Aren't those hamburgers grand? I sure don't know who invented them, but they're selling like hotcakes ever since we started serving them a few years ago."

"McDonald," Jordan said without thinking.

"Really? I didn't know that."

Jordan choked on her bite, not knowing whether to laugh or cry. McDonald's was the first thing she thought of but she didn't know the history of the hamburger. Once again, she cautioned herself to keep her mouth shut. She continued chewing, using that as an excuse not to talk and the waitress soon walked away.

The hamburger was exceptionally good and certainly a step above the fast food chains of her time. She had noticed in her walk down here that much about Chicago also seemed a step above, being crisper and brighter than the twenty-first century. There was some smog from the factories, but everything else was so...new, relatively speaking. What a difference a hundred years made!

She made her lunch last as long as possible, but soon was the only person left in the cafeteria. It made her stand out, which was the last thing she needed. What was she to do now that she had discovered Henry Douglas wasn't Harry Gallagher and there was no one she could relate to in 1926? How could she find out why she landed here, because she felt there had to be a reason she was cast about in history instead of just getting struck by lightning and left for dead.

A woman came through the door, hollered a hello to Alice, the waitress, then began tucking flyers into the metal clips that held the menus at each table and along the counter.

"Still looking for help?" Alice asked.

"Always," the woman replied. "Do you realize that over half the people in this city now have telephones *in their homes*? It was hard enough to maintain connections when we only had call boxes every other block or so. Now, everybody and their sister acts so pretentious, as if it's the epitome of uptown to have an exchange number."

The woman shook her head in consternation and Alice nodded in agreement. Jordan slid from the booth, snagging a flyer from an adjoining table on her way out the door. She needed to get back to the house, hopefully before Beatrice came home so she wouldn't have to answer questions about her activities. Glancing down to quickly scan the flyer gave her a moment of hopefulness. In bold black lettering, she saw that Illinois Bell was hiring telephone operators.

Surely she could do such a job. With a master's degree in marketing, she knew how to talk to people. How hard could it be? Her step lightened as she turned the corner onto Lakeview Street.

"Paper, Miss?" The squeaky young voice had her spinning around.

"Da...ng," she stumbled over the swear.

The youngster grinned, teeth flashing in a grubby face. He was polite enough not to comment on her faux pax. "Paper?" he repeated.

"I'm sorry, but I don't have even a penny to give you." She really had to find some money.

He shrugged. "That's okay. These are going in the trash bin anyways as I gotta get back for the evening edition." He folded one in half and held it out. "One less I gotta carry back."

"Well, thank you. One day I will have a job and pay you back."

He shrugged as if it were no big deal. "You should go to the telephone exchange. They's always looking for skirts to work there/"

"Skirts?"

"Dames. You know; your type." He ducked his head.

"I see." She had to smile at his discomfort. "Well, thank you for your advice." She turned to the steps.

"You live here?" he asked.

Her heart pounded, feeling it was a lie to claim she was someone she wasn't, but knowing no other way to get by for the time being. "For the moment, I suppose."

"HD didn't say you'd be a looker." The moment he uttered the words, his eyes got wide and he started scrambling backwards. Quicker, Jordan grabbed him by the collar.

"And just who is HD and why would he have you here looking for me?" Good lord, she had only been in this century a day, knew absolutely no one, and yet someone was making comments about her? Had someone keeping an eye on her? Who?

"Why is Henry Douglas having you spy on me?" It was the only explanation.

"Sh," the kid said urgently. "We can't use names. Never know who's listening or wants to do harm."

"That doesn't answer my question." She didn't have time for his spy nonsense. She lightly shook him by his collar. "What are your initials?"

"What's that?"

"The letters for your name."

"Eddie."

"That's not initials, that's a name."

"Don't got no last name. Can't just go by 'E', now can I?" He gave her a side look, quit struggling against her hold and stood there scuffing one shoe against the sidewalk.

"You know how to spell your name?" He was a street urchin, perhaps not homeless because he sold papers, but no doubt unschooled.

Her question got his shackles up. "Course I can spell. I can read, too, every bit of this paper if I had a mind. Which I don't cause I gotta get back to get my bundle for the evening. If 'n I'm not on time, I lose out. Then me and my mum get no supper." He clamped his lips, scowling as if angry for giving away too much information.

She let him go. "Again, I'm sorry I can't pay for the paper." She took a step up before turning back because it dawned on her the intent of all that he had said. Butterflies fluttered in her stomach. "When you see HD, tell him that JF is perfectly fine and entirely capable of taking care of herself. He need not have you spying on me."

The little boy flashed her a grin, happy that she seemed willing to join in his game and she smiled, not so much for his antics but because Henry had sent him. Henry Douglas was concerned enough about her that he had someone looking after her. Even if that spy was only like eight, and even if she had told said spy she didn't need his concern, she felt comforted.

"Good evening, Miss," Maddie said as she closed the door behind Jordan. "Dinner is in twenty minutes and you'd best not be late. I've taken the liberty to lay out a change of dress for you. If we hurry, you can manage."

Jordan remembered Beatrice's admonishment that morning about not being late for dinner. She really wasn't hungry and had so much on her mind, but knew she couldn't be absent.

While Maggie helped her change into a pretty, dropped waist linen dress in pale blue, she told her a little about her day, feeling she could trust the maid.

"Is Mister Douglas as good looking as my friends say?" seemed to be the takeaway from everything she said.

"I suppose," she murmured even as her heart beat a little faster. "But what am I to do for money? I didn't even have a penny to give the newsboy outside the house."

"What newsboy? Those boys hawk their papers down in the loop. Mr. Barrister holds a subscription to the paper, so it is hand delivered right to the door."

Not wanting to get him in trouble, she shrugged it off.

Maggie handed her a brush and headed for the door. "I must get downstairs for serving. If you speak the right way, your grandfather will see that you have funds. He is a gentle soul and would not want his grandchild doing without. Regardless what you hear, he does hold the purse strings."

Chapter 5

In the approximate three weeks she had been in 1926, Jordan had stuck very close to the Lakeview house, as it was the only even slightly familiar thing in this world she had been tossed into, and without her permission at that. After meeting her "grandfather" for the first time, an instant bond had been formed as he reminded her so much of her real gramps. He ran his furniture showroom during the day, but in the evenings after dinner, she would join him in a game of cards. As much as she could, she would ask him about things in this time; her excuse being that she was from farm country in Iowa and things were not the same as in the great city of Chicago. As Maddie had predicted, he gave her some money to "see to her needs" although Beatrice had at once admonished him for doing so, stating she should get a position and help with the household expenses.

Of course, Beatrice didn't work but she felt her volunteer work was her purpose in life and she simply had no time for anything else. She left the house almost daily but Jordan never knew where she went or what she did.

The time or two she had ventured outside for a walk in the small park across the street, she thought she had caught a glimpse of the little newsboy, but the moment she turned his way, he disappeared behind a shrub or corner. The thought that Henry Douglas had the boy watching her at first gave her some comfort, but as the days passed, it began to irritate her. Why was he watching her? Henry had said she would not see him again, so what did he care about her?

She wasn't used to having so much time on her hands and although she tried to offer her help to cook and Maddie, both assured her it was most certainly not her place to be in the kitchen or to handle a dustmop. So she had dug out the flyer from the telephone company, put on her most reserved dress, and walked into the Illinois Bell offices, walking out an hour later gainfully employed. Until she discovered why she was here, and hopefully find a way home, she would have something to occupy her time.

Just as she rounded the corner onto Lakeview, she caught a glimpse of the little spy hiding in the shrubberies and staring up at the house. Quietly walking up behind him, she said quite loudly, "Hello!"

"Gore, lady! You gave me a fright!" His voice squeaked as he spun around, stumbling backward into the sticky hedge. "Youch!"

She had to laugh at his confounded expression, even as she put a hand out to help him. Bending down to his level, she said in a stage whisper, "Tell your boss, HD, he can stop spying on me for I am now employed and I don't need his concern." She tried to make her voice threatening but simply felt too good, something she hadn't felt since arriving in this time. But today, she had accomplished something rather spectacular, given her circumstances.

Apparently trying to save face, Eddie blustered as though not believing her, "What kind of job you get?"

She straightened, deciding in that instance to play a little game. "If you are such a great spy, you find out." In the back of her mind, she hoped that he would and that he would tell Henry so that he could see her again, even after he had espoused no desire to do so. Sometimes things were said in the heat of the moment and later regretted. She hoped that was the case with one Henry Douglas, not only because she had found him attractive, but for whatever reason, she had felt safe with him in an unknown world. Perhaps landing a job had given enough of a boost to her morale that she wanted to take a step in her personal life, too. If she weren't to drop into a sea of depression, she needed to somehow live in the times.

After a week of training and another of very long hours, Jordan hurried out of the telephone exchange and quickly walked the two blocks to the drug store. She had woken that morning with cramps and knew she was within a day of starting her cycle. All she owned at the moment was what Jodelle had packed in the truck and after digging through everything Maddie had stored away, she could not find anything resembling what she needed. She knew this particular problem would not be as easy to solve as in her time, but she was thankful when she found a fairly recognizable item at the pharmacy. Tucking the brown bag under her arm, she left the store, trying to decide whether to walk home or hop the EL and explore the city.

"Excuse me, may I have a word?"

Jordan stumbled to a stop at the sound of a man's voice but didn't dare turn around. She pulled her hat lower on her brow and tried to take a step forward but her feet refused to move her along the sidewalk. The sun was shining; it was barely four in the afternoon and a warm breeze wafted across her cheeks. The voice she heard had begun taking over her dreams and she had begun to wonder if he was real and whether she would ever see him again.

She slowly turned, knowing the confrontation was inevitable. His black hair fell across his forehead as he swept off his hat. He wore a light suit, slightly rumpled, and she wondered briefly if he had no one to look after him. His intent green gaze swept across her face, stopping briefly at her lips which she knew were open in surprise. He fiddled with his hat and she glanced at his hands, the long fingers sliding along the brim. As his stare turned uncomfortably long, she wondered if it had only been the Irish in his voice that she recalled and he was not the same man at all. She finally let go of the breath she had been holding.

"I beg your pardon," he said when she finally acknowledged him with a slight nod. "I saw you exiting the Illinois Bell Telephone Exchange and thought to have a word."

"Did you have to pay much for information on where I worked?"

He grinned. "Eddie said you were spunky, as well as being the berries."

Not a word she had heard before, she decided to let it pass. "What can I do for you, Mr. Douglas?"

"Call me Henry and I hoped to ask you some questions about the phone calls you receive."

"Absolutely not," Jordan stated immediately, glancing around to see if anyone had overhead his request. Talking about her job, or what happened therein, was paramount to termination on the spot.

"Please. It could be a matter of grave importance." He held a hand out when she started to turn away, but pulled back short of touching her. "First, let me apologize for my behavior the last time we met. I should not have spoken so harshly, nor laid hands on you. I am sincerely sorry."

"That will not change my answer."

He smiled at her stubbornness and the tweak of a dimple caused her heart to flipflop.

"As you seemed to already know, I'm trying to gather information about some mobsters in this city. I don't care about the bootlegging and speakeasies; I'm after one in particular because of a murder."

"I'm sorry, but I really can't help you. I'm simply an operator and I don't know anything about any mobsters." She noticed others exiting the Exchange, one of whom was her supervisor. The woman would gladly see Jordan fired for even the slightest infraction because Jordan was very good at her job and had corrected the woman on more than one occasion.

She noticed Henry also carefully took in their surroundings and the people walking by. Without changing his cheerful expression, he swept her a bow and put out his hand. "Hello, hello I say. I told your father I would make every effort to give you his greetings if I saw you in my fine city." His mannerisms exaggerated, his voice became overly loud with the silly greeting. When she narrowed her gaze at him, his eyes shifted downward to his hand, still extended, and she realized he knew she didn't want to make a scene.

She wasn't wearing gloves and the warmth of his large hand shocked her, especially when his grip tightened and lasted a bit longer than might be deemed polite. She cleared her throat. "Why Mr. Douglas, how nice of you to find the time to say hello."

He leaned close. "I should know your full name," he whispered, still shaking her hand.

Whatever he wanted from her, she knew he was already very good at deception and ferreting out information. But in this case, Jordan had become just as adapt at hiding secrets. With a smile, she disentangled her hand and shifted her purchase under her arm. She watched as her supervisor continued down the sidewalk, no longer interested in any byplay between the two of them.

"There is no need for me to say," she said before adding sweetly, "my *father* already knows my name." Under other circumstances she would have laughed at the look on his face. She turned smartly on her heel and walked away, not wanting to appear easy, but hoping he would follow.

He finally tugged her to a gentle stop in front of a café. Even at this hour of the day, several of the outdoor tables were occupied. "Let me buy you a cup of coffee," he said, "and tell you what I need. Then you can summarily tell me to go to the devil." He gave her another of his dimpled smiles. "Or you might decide to tell me something else."

Jordan should have known better, but part of her was a bit curious as to what he could possibly want with her. And to tell the truth, her life was an utter bore right now. She worked long hours at the telephone exchange and she longed for the fun she and her friends had once had. Not that there weren't speakeasies here, but she didn't dare frequent them alone. The dance clubs were a different story, but even at those where no liquor was served, many of the men who came thought the women in attendance were there to do more than give them a dance, or so said the girls in the break room.

Giving herself a mental shake for being such a dullard, she decided she had nothing better to do at the moment, and Henry Douglas was easy on the eyes, so sitting across from him for a cup of coffee couldn't hurt.

* * *

Henry pulled out a chair at a table off to the side and away from foot traffic. Once she sat down, he went inside to order, hoping she wouldn't scare away in the few minutes he was gone. He had been surveilling the telephone exchange for over a week since Eddie had told him she had taken a job there. As he watched the shift change, ladies emerged, chatting gaily in groups of three or four. He knew somewhat of the rules enforced by the telephone company, for there had been plenty of articles in the *Daily Journal* as one of the best inventions of all time had taken off and expanded more rapidly than anyone could have imagined. Leaving work meant they could once again laugh and talk to each other after a day of speaking only over a headset to disembodied voices.

He had singled out Jodelle because he needed a loner. What he was asking couldn't be bandied about in the break room or after hours and women who were friends tended not to keep secrets well. Jodelle, on the other hand, came to work and left by herself, although she spoke with the other women once in a while. She didn't appear to have made friends yet and tended to be solitary, but not lonely.

He had known he wanted to see her again, even though he had protested otherwise. Something about her fascinated him and it wasn't just her help that caused him to seek her out. The drab black dresses that were apparently somewhat uniform among the operators didn't detract from her delicate figure. She only reached his shoulder in height but from her voice to the grip she had shown when they shook hands, there was much more to her than met the eye. He hoped that *something more* would help him gather information he needed.

He returned to the table with two cups of coffee, sugar and cream in small porcelain pitchers, and a small plate of domino cakes.

"I didn't know how you took your coffee," he said as he set out the table. She seemed surprised that he would wait on her and he found it wasn't just so he could get information out of her. He enjoyed taking care of a woman, and it had been far too long since he'd had the pleasure.

She quietly added a dollop of cream to her coffee, stirred it and took a sip. He waited; impatient but knowing he couldn't just jump in with both feet or he didn't stand a chance at gaining her cooperation.

"Jordan Foster," she finally said, and at his frown over the different name, she added, "My aunt calls me Jodelle but I've always hated that name. I prefer Jordan. While I thank you for the coffee, I can't tell you about the telephone exchange. It's against all the rules."

He nodded. "I know the rules of your employment but when it's important, perhaps those rules don't necessarily apply."

"Then why don't you simply walk in and speak with the owner, Mr. Atkins?" She raised a brow in question.

"Rules don't *necessarily* apply, Miss Foster. That's not quite the same as *never*."

She tilted her head to the side. "How do you know I'm not married?"

He grinned. "It's an Exchange rule. Besides, I'm looking for someone who's not...entangled," he ended for lack of a better word.

She narrowed her gaze. "And you saw me as a lonely, single woman who could be easily seduced to do your bidding?"

He tried to look shocked, but her sassy attitude was exactly what he wanted. "Certainly not seduced," he said in a hasty whisper. "There is no seducing involved, on that you have my word." Even as he said it, his heart pounded a little harder than usual.

"Cake?" He held up the plate of tiny frosted cakes to cover his embarrassment at her forthright manner.

She frowned for a moment; looked from him to the cake plate and back; then her red lips parted with a smile that led to a delighted laugh as she took a cake and popped it into her mouth. He hadn't chosen this woman for strictly business reasons and now found himself even more fascinated by her every movement. And yet he began to rethink his choice for it might not do to mix business with pleasure.

"You haven't lived in Chicago long, have you?" he asked simply to get a conversation going.

"No, not long," she replied, taking a sip of coffee.

"And before that?"

"In a place quite different." Another sip and she glanced at him, brown eyes twinkling.

She was playing him, but he couldn't fault her. She had no idea from their two brief conversations if he was a good guy or not just because he said he worked for a newspaper. The country was still in the middle of prohibition and many had found the benefits of *looking the other way* were more lucrative than a news hack's or a copper's salary. He couldn't clean up his city by himself, but he could ferret out the underhanded and unlawful and write to expose the truth.

Before asking her to gain information for him, he needed to find out if certain information was even attainable. After all, he had no idea how the telephone system even worked. The automobile engine, he could understand, but the telephone system was another technology beast as yet a mystery.

"Do you find the work hard? The photographs I've seen of a switchboard appear complicated. How do you cover such a large area?"

"Each operator has only a finite section," she replied, "and the mechanics are quite simple really, especially when the calls are made within the same exchange."

"The same?"

"Local calls, such as Mrs. Roberts calling the butcher, whose number she most likely has either memorized or has written down on a note beside the telephone. One of the disks on the board falls, and her number is displayed. I take up a plug which fits in a hole, asking 'What number, please?' If the number is of the same exchange, what happens is simple." She proceeded to give him a detailed description of the mechanics of connecting telephone calls and he only hoped his eyes didn't glaze over.

"...but when the talk is over and the receivers are hung up, another lamp glows," she said in conclusion.

"You make it sound quite easy," he said when she finished her monologue.

"It can get quite hectic," she said with a shake of her head. "While perhaps only half of the population have telephones at the moment, those numbers change almost daily. And even with so few telephones, I may have as many as one hundred twenty-five calls an hour. Mrs. Roberts, who I mentioned earlier, has the only telephone in her neighborhood, so although it is one phone, there are many calls from the neighbors that go to and from that single number in a day."

"It would certainly be easier on me to call in a story if there were telephones everywhere," he said. "Or imagine if I could somehow carry a telephone around with me and plug it in to a switchboard type socket anywhere in town."

She choked on the coffee she had been drinking, her eyes watering. For a moment he thought he might have to assist her in some way, but she soon set herself to rights. Only then did he continue his careful questions, because she hadn't told him what he needed to know.

"Do you know who is calling whom?" This was a key point for what he wanted from the pretty telephone operator.

"I know many of the local numbers, but for things such as the hotels and many businesses with several employees, I only connect to their switchboard." She tilted her head to study him. "Why is it important to know who is calling?"

He wasn't ready to give her his reasons. Besides, if she knew who he was searching for and she happened to hear that name, she might very well give away the game.

"If you could just write down any names you happen to hear, that might help immensely."

Her face paled and she shook her head before he even finished his sentence.

"I can't do that. We aren't allowed anything at our stations. If I wrote down names *while on duty,* I would get fired."

He watched her carefully as she took a last sip of coffee. Was her intonation on certain words a slip of the tongue, or was she making a suggestion?

"How good is your memory?"

She stood and he knew he would get no more out of her today. She slipped her handbag over her wrist and tucked a package beneath her arm, then put out her hand. As he took it in his, her handshake was firm, her skin warm and smooth as silk. "I have an excellent memory, Mr. Douglas. And as memory serves, you have promised me coffee and another of those delicious little cakes two days from now." She smiled, tilted her head in a nod and left him with a goofy grin on his face.

* * *

Jordan couldn't believe she had flirted with Henry, handsome though he might be. And she had even been so bold as to suggest he buy her another coffee in just two days. And his comment about carrying a phone with him? She could have suffered a heart attack at his reference to what would be a cell phone. How could he possibly know of such things. Things were not quite on the up and up with Henry Douglas and even though he requested something that could land her in trouble, whatever he was up to piqued her interest.

Two days after their first meeting, he was not waiting for her outside the telephone exchange and she had to admit her disappointment. She decided to walk home, but instead turned at the next corner where the coffee café was located. She tried to keep the smile from her face and almost turned around but knew he saw her; immediately standing at the table where coffee and cakes had already been ordered.

And thus began a friendship which was quite unconventional but to which she looked forward. She never gave him a paper with any names on it; he never asked her direct questions, but throughout their conversations three to four times a week, she managed to convey any specific names she had heard throughout the day. She told herself that if she didn't write anything down; didn't actually hand him a list, that she wasn't violating any of the numerous rules of the telephone company. There was nothing to trace back to her. She was very careful in that regard.

Sometimes he would wait for her outside of work and they would walk down to the quay and sit on a bench watching the sailboats glide across the water. Other times they would have coffee; sometimes at Gabby's or various other luncheonettes along the street. She was always back home by supper time. Although he didn't walk her home, she always had the feeling he watched her from afar to make sure she arrived safely.

They talked about everything. Well, not a lot about what he was really after with the names she gave him, but she had determined it had something to do with the mob and the bootlegging that ran rapid in the city. He had still never said who he was after and she did not ask, but certain names or places piqued his interest over others.

When he asked personal questions about her life, she tried hard to stick to the truth as much as possible. She had come to live with her grandfather after her parents were killed in an accident in Colorado, leaving out the word 'airplane' for obvious reasons. She figured he would have no call to find out she was supposed to be from Iowa and had a mother in an asylum. She really gave him very little information and as boring as it sounded, that had been her life, up until two months ago. After that were secrets she would not discuss with anyone.

She found out he had been born here within a year after his parents immigrated, yet he didn't say from where. It seemed they both had secrets. His father had been a carpenter but he hadn't wanted to follow him into trade.

"I wanted adventure, and I grew up in a rough neighborhood, full of those who would do most anything for a pint or two. I was too small and skinny for a boxer but I was fast so for a while I was a runner, until I realized the men I worked for weren't exactly doing something legal. My mum made sure my brother and I learned to read and it opened the world for me. I decided there was adventure to be had telling stories without breaking any laws."

"What was your very first story?" she asked.

"I wrote up an interview with the Wright Brothers," he said, "when I was thirteen."

"You've met the Wright Brothers?" she asked in awe, momentarily forgetting that all the people famous for inventions in the early twentieth century were still alive, not living in the history books of her youth.

He nodded. "I sneaked on board a train and rode clear to Dayton to see their factory after having read a report about their flying machines. I had read stories about the dirigibles and gas balloons, but controlled flight? I was intrigued that something like that could actually occur, and what the ramifications of such a feat could be."

"You were only thirteen."

"I had a very active imagination," he replied with a grin. "The entire train ride, I daydreamed of flying in their airplane, seeing the world from above. Perhaps even flying across the great Michigan lake to get back home to Chicago. Wilbur and Orville were very friendly and let me visit the entire afternoon, showing me their sketches for an even larger aeroplane, and talking about the dynamics of flight. Can you even comprehend that something heavier than an automobile can actually be kept aloft?" He gave her an embarrassed grin. "Sorry. I tend to get long winded when I talk about something as intriguing as flight and how it might impact our future."

Oh, if he only knew what the future held, Jordan thought. She laughed. "Perhaps one day we'll fly to the moon." At his look of disbelief, she mentally cautioned herself to be mindful of what she said. "Please continue."

"Their sister Katharine brought lunch to the factory and they invited me to stay the night. The next day when they found out I was actually from Chicago and intended to hop a train, they insisted on purchasing my ticket."

"And so you came home and wrote a story for the newspaper about the newest invention in history."

This time, he laughed out loud. "If only it had been that easy. I couldn't sit to write for a good few days after my mum blistered my fanny for not telling anyone where I was all night and for hopping a train."

She smiled, trying to picture him at thirteen. "As well she should have."

"Once I wrote my story, sort of a cross between news and commentary, there wasn't a newspaper or magazine in the city that would even let me in the door, much less read what I had written. So I had my brother, who was five years older, take it 'round and not only did the *Daily Journal* publish it, but they actually paid my brother and wanted more of the same kind of articles. Sullivan wasn't exactly the scholarly type, so I would write the articles – about people and places in the city – and he would sell them to the newspaper. When I got older, I got a job with the paper, writing the news, but once in a while would still do a commentary piece."

He turned toward her on the bench they shared. There was a hint of moisture in the breeze, along with the always prevalent hint of fish this close to the water. The day was warmer than usual and he had removed his suit jacket, rolling up his sleeves to his elbows. While his story fascinated her, she was just as intrigued by the man himself. As he crossed his leg over his knee and grabbed his ankle with his hand, she noticed the ripple of muscle in his arm and the light sprinkling of hair. His nails were blunt cut and clean and she had a fleeting thought as to what that hand would feel like in her own for longer than a brief handshake. He had never really touched her except for the slightest nudge of her elbow when they turned a corner, or the accidental touch when he held a chair out for her.

"Jordan?"

Her name startled her. She could feel her face heat at her wayward thoughts.

"I asked what you thought about going to supper one night," he said. "That is, if you aren't too tired after your workday, or if you don't have other plans, or if I'm not being too forward."

"Do you wish me to choose one of those excuses you have thrown out so freely, or may I simply say yes?" She gave him her best smile.

"No. Yes," he corrected hastily. "That's swell. Is tonight too soon?"

Her smile slipped. "I should probably give Cook some notice that I won't be there. And heaven only knows how Aunt Beatrice would respond. Perhaps we could plan for Thursday. That is my last free night before I go on the night shift at the Exchange for two weeks."

"You must work at night?" He looked quite surprised and she laughed.

"Would you believe people make telephone calls at night as well as during the day?"

His eyes narrowed in thought but when he finally spoke, it was only, "Thursday will work great. May I pick you up at your house around seven?"

She hesitated, but realized she needed to quit living in fear that she would be found out.

"I suppose," she said with a sigh, "it is time for a proper introduction to Aunt Beatrice."

* * *

On Thursday, after an uncomfortable but brief conversation with Aunt Beatrice, Henry had taken Jordan to *Henrici's*, known for its seafood. Their conversation, as always, have flowed freely and he found himself more interested in her than in what she was doing for him through her work. He listened carefully to the names she repeated whenever they met, but the few of interest were never mentioned. She had an aura about her that most women of his acquaintance lacked. She seemed amazed by the most ordinary things and made comments he often didn't understand. Like when he had told her about the flying machine and she had said perhaps one day men would fly to the moon. To the moon – what a pack of baloney, he had thought but had been too polite to say out loud.

As he dropped her off at her residence, he thought perhaps it was a good thing that she had switched to the night shift. After all, most nefarious activity was done at night and if he was to get any leads, she might hear something more relevant at night. He walked her to her door and hesitated in saying good night. Even with everything on his mind, his one prevailing thought was how much he wanted to kiss her.

"Thank you for dinner," she said shyly as she turned to him. "Aunt Beatrice detests fish, so I rarely have the opportunity of tasting it." She reached for the doorknob at the same moment as he and his hand encompassed hers. She looked up, startled when he gently circled her wrist and brought her hand to his lips, lightly kissing her palm.

He held her gaze, not saying a word. When she didn't pull back, he placed her hand on his chest and stepped closer, pulling her to him as he bent his head down for a kiss. She sighed into his mouth and softened in his arms and it was all he could do not to take the kiss deeper. Forcing himself to release her, he stepped back. He wasn't ready to leave, yet he didn't dare continue to touch her. There was something about her that tugged on his heart. From the first moment he had met her, it was as if they had known each other forever. "I don't suppose I will see you for a while."

"I would say perhaps, but if I work all night, I may spend the entire daytime hours in my bed." She glanced quickly away, as though embarrassed at what she had said. But Henry had instant visions of her curled on her side, sleeping as the early morning sun slipped between her curtains to caress her soft skin. He tried not to groan.

He reached in his pocket and pulled out a card, pressing it into her hand. "Here is my telephone number," he said. "If you need anything, please call me." He didn't want to ask her to keep collecting names for him. He didn't want her to think that was the only reason he sought her out. Not after their kiss.

She nodded with a smile, took a step forward and kissed his cheek, then quickly disappeared into the house, the door closing silently behind her. It took a second for him to regain his bearings and even so, his step was lighter as he wandered down the street to the boarding house he claimed as his residence.

Henry spent the next several days running down stories about the upcoming elections. Things were heating up and all the mayoral candidates were slinging mud fast and furious. Every statement required phone calls and more interviews to verify. He often made his calls at night with the hope of hearing Jordan's voice when he rang for an operator. She wasn't always the one to answer his calls, but when she did, he made sure he used his name, just to let her know he thought of her. Though she didn't give any indication she knew him, she said his name – Mr. Douglas – in such a way that he knew. It was a minor victory in his day, because everything he was investigating in secret seemed at a standstill. The city appeared quiet on the surface, but he would bet his paycheck something big was about to happen.

He kept an eye on the Green Mill Cocktail Lounge, a purported favorite of Capone's and stopped daily for a visit with the desk clerk at the police precinct, who would conveniently leave his post long enough for Henry to check the police blotter for recent activity. He was probably wasting his time on Capone, who was basically protected by friends, the Outfit, and even other business people in the community, not to mention having police in his pocket. In fact, he was beginning to think the entire prohibition battle was one in which the country was doomed to failure, as there weren't enough legitimate law enforcement to cover all the illegal stills, much less controlling the contraband being sneaked in at night by the various mobs.

He had no real beef with Capone although he didn't condone what he did. He wanted to find and bring to justice those individuals who had gone beyond the import business and were responsible for several deaths. It was one thing to import whiskey for resale. It was another entirely to shoot those suppliers in order to take over their business. Or to shoot innocent bystanders like his brother.

Chapter 6

Jordan woke midday to some delicious aroma wafting up from the kitchen. Looking at the small clock on the dresser she saw it was after two in the afternoon. Her shift from eight to six meant she often slept the morning away. Now, she quickly washed and dressed, trying to decide what to do so that the day would not be a complete waste.

"Something smells wonderful, as always," she commented as she walked into the kitchen.

"Thursdays are for baking," Cook replied. Why she was never called by a regular name, Jordan didn't know, and Maddie didn't either.

"Are they Toll House cookies?" She saw dark bits in the dough and thought they were chocolate chips.

"Haven't heard of a cookie by that name," Cook replied. "Is that something you ate in Iowa?"

Jordan cringed, quickly turning her back to made her way to the teapot. Having no idea when that type of cookie had come into existence, she quickly grabbed a cookie and took a bit so she wouldn't have to reply. As she waited for the kettle to whistle, she thought of all the things not invented yet; things she took for granted. She would have to be careful as she had no idea if what she did, or inadvertently said, would cause someone else to do something that would change history.

At the same time, perhaps she should look at the stock exchange and see if there were companies she knew would make money. She could become a millionaire! That is, only if she bought stock and only if she made it back to her own time. And if she survived the depression. The thought of being here in 1930 depressed her and she happily accepted the plate of cookies from cook, and set them on the tray with a teapot, cup and saucer, which she carried into the sitting room.

Since her grandfather was at work and her aunt went -- wherever her aunt went most days and several evenings a week – she enjoyed the solitude of the house, although her thoughts turned to her real gramps. Would he think her dead? Did her body get struck by lightning and lay on the sidewalk and she was inhabiting someone else's body in 1926? Was she in a coma as she had originally thought? Had she just disappeared without a trace? All her conjectures about what happened that evening in 2022 did not help in the least for figuring out how, or if, she could get back to her old life.

A flash of movement caught her eye and she rose to peek out the front window. Quick as a wink, Eddie disappeared behind a shrub across the street. With a smile, she wrapped several cookies in a napkin and opened the front door, descending the steps, walking across the street to stand directly in front of where she had last seen him. Not a twig twitched.

"I know you're there. Why are you still spying on me?"

Still nothing.

"I have cookies," she sang, peeling back one corner of the napkin. Twigs snapped as he scurried from his hiding place.

"What kind?"

"Does it matter?" she asked as she walked the short distance to where a park bench nestled beneath the shade of a giant tree. The late summer heat was unbearable when one was used to air conditioning. She had heard that a few buildings and the Congress Hotel were air conditioned but it was unheard of in homes and most other establishments.

She sat, placing the cookies on the bench beside her. Eddie cautiously sat on the other side, and the minute she unwrapped the napkin, he snatched a cookie and ate it in two bites.

"Why are you still spying on me? Don't you have better things to do? Like go to school?"

"Ain't no school in the hot months," he said, his mouth full. She raised a brow and he didn't speak again until he had swallowed. "Ain't any school," he corrected.

"You don't have friends to play ball with?"

He shrugged. "I can make more money selling papers and spying for HD. Besides, I gotta watch out for my mum. She can't do well by herself."

"Your mother isn't well?"

With another shrug, he eyed the cookies left in the napkin. She nudged it toward him. She knew very well that Henry was aware of her schedule, so perhaps he had the youngster watching her as an excuse to give him money. Eddie appeared very self-sufficient for a kid his age, and probably wouldn't take kindly to charity.

"And what have you found out for Henry lately?"

"Sh." He looked quickly around, as though expecting other spies to pop out from behind the trees. Then she realized she had used Henry's name.

"So besides HD and myself, JF, what are other secret initials you know?"

"I ain't telling." He sounded quite indignant that she would even ask.

"What about you? You should have a secret name too." She thought for a moment. "Your name is Eddie. What about Mr. Ed?" The moment she said it, she started laughing. "Oh, no, no. That won't work at all."

Eddie scowled. "Why not? Mr. Ed does sound important and what I do for HD is just that."

She tried to control her giggles as she shook her head. "It was the first thing that popped into my head but no," she giggled again, "it won't work." At his crestfallen look, she explained. "Back when I was very young, there was a television show called Mr. Ed, but it was about a talking horse!"

"A talking horse? I ain't no horse!" he exclaimed, followed quickly by, "What's television?"

Crap, she had hoped he wouldn't catch that slip of the tongue.

"Um, it's like the nickelodeon?" She hoped movies had been invented by this era.

"I've never been to the nickelodeon, but I sneaked into a Vaudeville show one time, til they caught me and dragged me out by my ear." He rubbed the offended lobe as though it had just happened.

"Perhaps we can go someday," she said, thinking every kid should have a childhood that included more than work and she rather liked this particular one. She heard a noise and turned to see August Barrister, her supposed grandfather, climbing the steps to the row home. It was later than she thought.

"I have to go." She stood and started to gather up the napkin, but instead of taking it with her, she held it out to Eddie. "You should take these home to your mother, EB, or I'll get fat eating them all."

"EB?"

"An actor on tele...nickelodeon movies...was named Ed Byrnes. He was quite handsome." She watched a grin split his face.

"EB," he said, throwing his shoulders back. "I think that will do me right fine."

* * *

Jordan had time for supper with her grandfather and Aunt before changing into her longer skirt and long sleeved blouse and leaving for work. Fortunately, the evening air had cooled somewhat and she enjoyed the walk to the EL.

She did not equally enjoy working the night shift but she had no choice if she wanted to keep her position with the telephone exchange. With the rapid expansion of telephone service, more operators were constantly needed, and those new employees were always started on the night shift as it was less hectic and easier to train them. As Jordan had excelled at her job in the time she had been there, she had been called upon to do the training. That meant long hours at the switchboard showing a woman on both her left and right how to connect the calls.

In the beginning of training, she listened in until the calls were connected so she managed to catch a few times when Henry called and it always made her smile. She liked him quite a bit and the kiss he had given her had both shocked and delighted her. She didn't know why she had been thrown into this era but had decided to enjoy it while she could. If she were somehow able to stay awake more, she might have tried to see him during the day, but the unfamiliar night shift wore her down to the point where once it was over all she longed for was her bed.

During her second week, she was back at her own board with a new girl working on either side of her just in case of a problem. A call came through from the Casa Marina Resort and she assumed it was the hotel operator placing a call for a guest. It surprised her to hear a male voice on the other end of the line.

"Connect me to Al Capone." The name, along with the voice, which was cold and curt to the point of rudeness, had Jordan's hand shaking and she missed the socket, the patch cord automatically retracting. She knew this would cause a beep on the caller's telephone although she was still connected to him.

"Hello, are you there?" He growled.

"I'm sorry, sir. Do you have his exchange number?"

"Hell, no. That's your damn job."

"Just one minute." She found the number for the Congress Plaza Hotel, deciding that would get him to another operator, and inserted the plug. The light flashed, showing the two telephones were connected but her hand stilled over the switch that would close her headset to the call. She held her breath, not wanting to give away that she was still on the line.

The tinny ringing of a phone was interrupted as someone answered. "Congress Plaza Hotel. How may I direct your call?"

"This is Tommy O'Connor and I want to talk to Al Capone."

Jordan quickly flipped the switch on the call, dropping her hands to her lap. She had listened longer than she should have and hoped the supervisor hadn't noticed. She clutched her fingers together to stop the trembling but cold shimmered up her spine and across her shoulders until she was shaking like a leaf. A light on the switchboard blinked but she could only stare at it. As it continued, the girl at her side quickly connected with the call. She turned to Jordan.

"Are you all right? You look quite pale."

"I...I," she shook her head. The minute the lights from the call blinked off, she jerked the plugs from the board as if that would also disconnect her from the names she had heard. She knew Henry was looking into mob activity, not so much because he had told her, but from his total lack of interest in any of the names she had given him so far.

The trainee had signaled for the supervisor, Miss Grant, who was less than sympathetic as she stood to the side of Jordan's station. "You don't look well, Miss Foster." She glanced up at the clock on the far wall. "There are still three hours on your shift so you'll be docked the night's wages, but I suggest you go home to bed. Be sure to call early tomorrow if you continue to feel ill."

Jordan hurried home, unable to enjoy the unusual quiet of the city in these hours before dawn. Usually, the sun was up by the time she came off her shift, but that didn't kept her from falling into a deep sleep the minute she closed her bedroom door. Today, however, she was too wired to sleep. She knew who Al Capone was and although Henry had never spoken the names of the men he sought, Capone had to be on his list. And now she had a new name; one she hadn't heard before, but one she thought would be of interest to Henry if only because of the call to Capone.

She had to dig through her dresser drawer for the card he had given her and then she realized she couldn't call from the downstairs phone. She had only his work number, which would necessitate her calling through the exchange and giving his name to the newspaper switchboard. She did not want to do that through the Barrister's telephone, as it would easily appear at the telephone exchange. Any operator answering that call could easily identify her voice and not only was she supposed to be ill, but she was calling a man. It would be her job for sure.

She laid down on the bed and managed to doze despite her anxiety. When she awoke at six, she hurried down to Gabby's where there was a phone they allowed the public to use. And it was certainly closer than the newspaper offices, which were clear across town and she couldn't even be sure he was there.

It took several minutes for the exchange to connect with the *Daily Journal* and for her call to be routed to the appropriate desk in the newsroom.

"I need to get a message to Henry Douglas," she said immediately when a woman answered the telephone.

"I'm sorry but he hasn't come in yet."

"I know, but this is the only number I have for him."

"If you will give me your name and telephone number, I will get him a message," said the woman politely.

Because she knew exactly how telephone exchanges worked and the fact that anyone could be listening in at any moment, Jordan didn't want to leave her name. In addition, she certainly couldn't leave the telephone number for the cafeteria or the Barrister's.

"Please tell Mr. Douglas it's important to meet JF at the usual place at the usual time."

She knew she sounded overly dramatic, but it couldn't be helped.

"I don't understand," said the woman on the end of the line.

"You don't need to," Jordan replied, "but Mr. Douglas will."

She gave the passing waitress a few coins for the telephone call and wearily made her way back home. It was barely seven in the morning and she had been up all night. She hoped a warm bath would help her sleep.

* * *

Jordan managed to sleep until mid-afternoon and would have continued on if not for her aunt pounding on her bedroom door.

"You have a visitor. I told him you were sleeping and he shouldn't wait but he insisted. So he is down in my parlor and now I can't get a thing done for I certainly can't continue my correspondence with a man sitting there."

Jordan groaned as she sat up in bed, brushing the hair from her eyes, which itched from lack of sleep.

"Perhaps give him a glass of lemonade and set him on the front porch," she muttered as she gathered clothes to dress.

"He is not *my* company, missy. I suggest you make him aware of your nocturnal activities." Aunt Beatrice was adamant about her having a job, but she didn't like the night

101

hours any better than Jordan did, even though dear Auntie was often out at night.

"It's my job," she said tartly. "I told you I had to work nights for two weeks."

"Nevertheless, it's simply not the thing." Her voice trailed off as she tromped down the stairs, leaving Jordan to dress in peace.

She chose a sleeveless, drop waist dress in bright pink as the warmth of early morning promised a hot afternoon. She carefully rolled on her stockings, gartering them above the knee and slipping into her brown tee-strap low heels. As she combed her hair before the full-length mirror, she scrutinized her image. She actually liked the dresses of today. Mid-calf was the fashion rage at the moment and she enjoyed the freedom from the full length skirts required for work. She never quite understood the Exchange dress requirements as no one saw them behind the switchboards. They were disembodied voices at best.

Henry jumped up the moment she reached the bottom stair, striding toward her with a determined stare. A brief tip of his head indicated her aunt's presence, for even if she couldn't *get anything done*, she had remained in the parlor.

"Shall we walk outside?" she asked.

"It's not so hot today," he replied. She almost giggled at their inane conversation, just so her aunt wouldn't overhear anything of importance.

"I'm sorry I called the newspaper office. I would have looked for Eddie, thinking he could find you quickly, but for once he wasn't sitting in the shrubberies."

Her comment made the deep furrows across his forehead soften and he smiled. "He thinks you are the cat's pajamas, by the way."

She laughed out loud. "The what?"

"You know, like the bee's knees."

Although the expressions were new to her, she understood. "Awesomesauce," she said with a nod.

That had him frowning, but he quickly shook it off. "Anyway, thank you for playing along with his game, although now he insists I refer to him as EB."

"It's far less than you do for him, paying him to watch me when you know very well exactly my schedule." Her offhanded praise seemed to embarrass him and he quickly changed the subject.

"You quite befuddled the newsroom receptionist with your coded message, and the fact you are female. She grilled me repeatedly when I would not tell her about you."

She quickly covered a yawn, but not before he noticed.

"I am sorry to have woken you but I couldn't wait until six to meet you at the café. Something is going down tonight."

"I thought as much, which was why I wanted to tell you the names I heard today," she said. "I took a call from a Tommy O'Connor--"

He grabbed her arm, spinning her around. "Who?" he demanded.

When her eyes widened in surprise at his tone, he quickly released her. "Sorry."

"The caller was a Tommy O'Connor trying to reach Al Capone."

"Damn!" He paced away from her and then back, grabbing his hat from his head and banging it against his trouser leg.

"Henry, please tell me what's going on; who you're after. I could help more if I knew more."

He shook his head. "Knowing could also get you in trouble."

She put a hand on his arm, stilling his movements. "Please."

She watched as his face completely changed, first from anger to deep sorrow. Although it pained her, she waited for him to speak.

"If you're a male of Irish descent, you're automatically assumed to be part of the North Side Gang, whether you want to be or not. That makes you an enemy of the Chicago Outfit, again whether you want it or not."

She had heard a hint of accent in his voice every once in a while, and assumed there were reasons he chose not to acknowledge his heritage. Whatever the case, now was not the time to question him about it. She gave a brief nod that she understood.

"Long story short, my older brother, Sullivan, was in the wrong place at the wrong time back in '21 and was shot by Tommy O'Connor."

She gasped. "You're sure?"

"There was a knock-down on the south side late one night involving both mobs. My brother was a physician, coming home from a hospital visit and got caught in the cross-fire."

"You can't know it was O'Connor then."

"You're wrong. I've spent five years investigating. There are plenty who knew Sully and who were part of the North Side at that time. Sully tried not to get involved with any gang activity, No one knew he was Irish so being a doctor, he was often called on because of the gang activity. When you're shot, you're not so particular who patches you up."

"You're sure that was the name you heard?" he asked her now.

"Of course, I'm sure. Why would you even ask?"

"Because Tommy O'Connor disappeared the same night my brother died. He hasn't been heard from since '21. Why would his name pop up today?"

"And if he and Capone are rivals, why was he trying to contact him?" she wondered aloud.

He looked at her as though she had told him the location of the holy grail. "Exactly, which means what you heard and what my police contacts are saying could be a set up. Either way, something is happening tonight and I have to go."

"Henry, you're not the police. Please, you don't belong in the middle of a gang fight." She panicked at the thought of him getting hurt. He had become her only link in this time and she definitely didn't want to be set adrift in a time where she didn't belong. More so, she worried about him getting hurt because she truly cared for him.

He gave her a cocky grin. "But I am a newsman. Whatever is up, it will be a scoop for the *Daily Journal* if I'm there for the details." His face turned serious as he gently cupped her shoulders, pulling her slowly closer. "Can you call the exchange and say you're ill? I want you safe, and I have no idea what will happen when, or how widespread it will be within the city."

At his words, her heart thumped harder but she shook her head. "I was sent home sick last night, or rather this morning. I can't afford to take off another day." Besides, she would know more about what happened at the exchange than sitting at home waiting.

"Please?"

She barely heard the soft plea as his lips descended on hers. The kiss, a gentle caress at first, quickly escalated to demanding and possessive and she reveled in the warmth as his arms wrapped around her. She melted into his embrace but at the distant sound of an automobile horn, he quickly released her and stepped back.

"I am so sorry," he stammered. "That was totally uncalled for."

She smiled. "Oh, I don't know." She stepped close again, "I didn't ask for it, but I certainly didn't say no." She stood on tiptoe, grabbed his lapels for balance and swiped her lips across his.

"I've got to go." His words belied his actions as he gently cupped her cheeks.

"Okay," she whispered, still holding on to him staring into his sexy, green gaze.

"I don't know when I'll see you again."

"I understand." She smiled. "I get off at six."

With a groan, he smashed his hat on his head and turned to leave. "Of all the nights for this to happen."

She grabbed his arm to stop him. When he turned toward her, she whispered, "Please stay safe."

He touched a finger to the brim of his hat, gave her a wolfish wink then turned and left.

Regardless of how she happened to get to this century, in that moment she knew her heart belonged to this true gentleman of 1926.

* * *

Jordan could hardly sit still through dinner. Her grandfather talked about business as usual and the market exchange. Aunt Beatrice was quiet and Jordan realized that lately it had been her mood more often than not. She no longer nagged Jordan about every little thing, and she had been spending a lot of time away from home. When questioned, she simply said it was not her business and just because she had no proper friends, that didn't mean Beatrice was alone. Jordan got the impression her aunt didn't care for Henry, which only gave him a leg up in her estimation.

The air was electric as she walked into the exchange and she barely had time to hang up her hat and store her bag before Miss Grant hollered at her to get to her station, something was going down. For awhile the activity was sporadic, but just after nine, the disks started dropping non-stop and there was no time to even take a breath because one call rang on top of the next. The police precincts were well known exchange numbers, as were several call boxes and those calls kept all operators very busy. Jordan listened a bit when she could as the supervisors were so busy overseeing the newer operators, they never noticed whether she flipped the correct switch when a call was connected. She was careful not to breathe, but with the chaos she heard on most of the calls, even her gasp was not noted.

Following the chatter along the line from the operators, she learned there was a mob confrontation at the Green Mill Lounge and the police were using that as an excuse to raid. She overheard names like Torrio and Capone, Bugs Moran and Dean O'Banion. Not knowing if they were all in the Chicago Outfit or from rival gangs, she tucked the names in her memory bank to share with Henry. She never heard him on a call, which didn't mean someone else hadn't picked up on it, but knew she would no doubt see a headline story with his byline in the morning paper. If she had learned nothing else about Henry Duglas, he was determined and dedicated, to anything he pursued.

Chapter 7

Henry caught the EL to the north side, impatiently tapping his foot as the train sped forward. A quick peek at the police blotter had confirmed what he already knew; deliveries were expected at the Green Mill tonight, a perfect time for a raid to catch bootleggers in action. He wondered if the raid was legitimate, or one of those times the coppers acted like they were enforcing prohibition laws but actually looked the other way. Checking his wristwatch, he hoped he could get there in time to find out.

The moment the doors opened he was out and running for the stairs down to the street. He was two blocks away and the unassuming neighborhood was quiet; almost too quiet, as though everyone with any sense was behind closed doors. A block later, just as he turned onto Broadway, gunfire erupted in the distance and he ducked behind a building. He might want to be in the middle of the action for a story, but he wasn't about to get shot for his job. The quick spurts of gunfire indicated the use of machine guns, the mob's weapon of choice, but it didn't last long. He held his breath to the count of ten. When no more shots were fired, he sprinted around the corner and hurried to where a crowd already gathered in front of the Green Mill Lounge.

Flappers and their dandy gentlemen were milling around to one side, apparently having spilled out of the Lounge but too fascinated to have the common sense to leave. Coppers were trying to contain the crowd. He wasn't interested in them and moved passed to the alley which had been blocked at both ends by police cars. The cops had several men lined up against the brick wall opposite the back door of the lounge. Others were breaking the bottles of booze in the two crates close to the door. So it had been legitimate, he thought as he edged his way closer to Captain Prescott. Before he could question the Captain, another policeman came out the back door of the lounge.

"No Capone, Captain," he said.

"You check the trap door exit?" Prescott queried.

"Yes sir. Had an undercover inside before the shakedown and he never saw nobody near the door."

"Of course not," Henry answered for the Captain. "Everyone knows Capone plays cards at the Congress every Friday." The derision in his voice had Prescott spinning sharply in his direction.

"You accusing me of being in cahoots with the man?" he growled at Henry. "Raiding this joint when I know he's not here just to look good?"

Henry knew he had to tread carefully. It wouldn't do to alienate anyone on the police force, especially Captain Prescott, apparently in charge of this particular event. Although from a neighboring precinct, Henry had heard of the man and most reports had him on the up and up.

"I'm not saying anything. Just stating facts."

The captain looked across the alley to where several men had been handcuffed. He scowled and Henry turned to see what had him scowling. He didn't recognize any of the apprehended men. "Who are they?" he asked and was surprised when Prescott actually gave him an answer.

"They're part of the North Side mob, not the Outfit."

"So?"

"So why would the North Side be delivering liquor to a known Outfit hangout?"

"Maybe they were here to steal it from the Outfit?" Henry suggested.

"Or maybe they hoped to see an Outfit establishment shut down so they could take control."

"Shutting down one lounge isn't going to stop either mob, just like raiding said lounge isn't going to stop the bootlegging." It was a never ending cycle.

"You do what you gotta do," the Captain said with a heavy sigh. "Wrap it up, boys. Get these thugs downtown."

The coppers started shoving several mob members towards the waiting wagon for transport. Henry edged closer and got a careful look at each of the four men being hauled away. O'Connor's face was forever etched on his brain, and none of the four resembled the man he sought. In fact, their baby-faced glances of fear broke Henry's heart. Every year, more and more young men started running with one of over a thousand mobs in the City trying to make names for themselves. They were given the dirtiest of jobs to "prove themselves" and too many of them ended up in the east river or a dark alley.

He made his way back toward the train station, grabbed the first one that stopped, then ended up having to switch twice before getting off at the *Daily Journal* building. He might as well take his story directly to the newsroom. It was well after midnight and he knew Jordan was still working. As he climbed the stairs to the newsroom, he wondered exactly what he had been thinking to kiss her like he had?

Actually he did know what he was thinking, although there had been no time for further exploration of the feelings she evoked. She caused his insides to feel like a dozen critters did the *Charleston* in his gut. He knew he hadn't been wrong about her returning his feelings, yet it bugged him because something felt off just the slightest bit and it was that small bit he couldn't put his finger on. He was so intent on his reporting job, and on tracking down his brother's killer, that everything else slipped past in the fog. He needed to be a little better tuned into her if he were to discover her secrets. And he was sure she had some.

He put in a call to Prescott's precinct to get names of the captured mob members. He pounded away on the typewriter, but pulled paper after paper out of the roller, each time not liking the direction the story took. It was always the same; one told by every newspaper in the city day after day. Police conduct raid; bootleggers captured; booze destroyed. Within a day, the mob would bail out their members, the incident forgotten only to happen at another speakeasy on another night in another area of the city. Would it ever end?

* * *

Jordan gave a sigh and relaxed in her chair at the switchboard. Even with hours left on her shift, she felt the worst was over and the calls had slowed to a trickle. She wondered how Henry fared. She certainly couldn't connect with him here, even if she knew where he might be. *Ah, for the love of a cell phone,* she idly thought with a giggle. There were definitely things she missed about her life; things she really hadn't thought much about because lately, Henry consumed her thoughts.

She knew she could survive without the technology of her time; she had proven that by adapting to her surroundings, although living in an upper class home did much to alleviate her anxiety. If she had not somehow been connected to the Barristers and had ended up on the streets, totally alone, things would have been much different. She missed her gramps and her friends, but had all the most "modern" conveniences. So, could she be happy if she never returned to the twenty-first century?

The thought plagued her and by the end of her shift she felt exhausted. There was a note in her slot as she clocked out and she wondered what her supervisor was docking her for this time. That seemed to be the way they let you know you had done something wrong – a slip in with your timecard. No discussion, and certainly no human resources department.

She tucked her bag under her arm and started to unfold the note as she exited the building.

"Good morning," a voice at her ear had her turning with a squawk, her fist flashing out to connect with a hard jaw.

"Holy sh--" She slapped her hand across her mouth. "I thought I was about to be accosted!"

He ducked quickly sideways. "I deserved that," he said, as he rubbed his jaw.

"You most certainly did," she replied. "And more for about giving me a heart attack. What are you doing here?" She looked quickly around, not sure why she worried about what others thought. "Is everything alright?"

He shrugged. "It wasn't much for being newsworthy," he said as he took her arm and they began to walk down the sidewalk.

"Was Capone or," she hesitated bringing up O'Connor's name.

He shook his head before she could finish. "No one of consequence happened to be there, which I believe was not coincidence, but by design."

"What do you mean?"

"You heard Tommy O'Connor's name, which means he's still in the city and probably up to no good. Captain Prescott thinks it's either the North Side mob or the Chicago Outfit trying to instigate trouble for the other. I think instead, it's O'Connor trying to instigate the trouble. He was part of the North Side, and if he can get the Outfit to kill off enough members of the North Side, he can step in and take over."

"Did you tell your Captain Prescott that?"

"Of course not. Very little can be said, even to a copper who's straight like Prescott, without it being spread across the city. That would just send O'Connor underground again, like he's been for the past five years. I need to find a way to ferret him out."

"You seem very adapt at investigating," she said. "Have you ever thought about being a detective instead of a newsman?"

"What's wrong with combining the two?" He stopped her in front of Gabby's. "Would you like breakfast?"

Jordan was so tired she hadn't even been aware of where they walked. "I'm so exhausted, all I long for is my bed, before I have to return to work again." That thought reminded her of the note she had tucked into her purse. She dug it out to read and was pleasantly surprised by the contents. "Well what do you know."

"How's that?" Henry asked and she handed him the note, which he read out loud.

"Due to your exemplary work, you are accorded two days off to recuperate and acclimate before returning to your regular day shift. –The Illinois Bell Exchange. Post Script – this is without pay, of course."

"Of course," she muttered, but still smiled at the extra time off.

"Wow. That probably doesn't happen often," he commented as they continued down the walk. "We should celebrate."

She thought it great that he wanted to see her again. The feelings were definitely mutual, but she was dragging. "Perhaps I use today to *recoup and acclimate*, then we can do something?"

"That would be swell. There's a new motion picture at the Chopin."

They were at her place and it was all she could do to climb the steps. "Good night, Henry." She gave him a quick kiss on the jaw. "I'm sorry I hit you."

"It's morning," he replied with a gentle smile, taking her key and opening the door for her. "but I understand. I'll call you later."

She closed the door quietly behind her, not wanting to disturb the rest of the household, although she figured Cook was already in the kitchen. Even the rich aroma of coffee couldn't keep her from bed, and within minutes her clothes, shoes and purse were helter-skelter on the floor, and even the sun peeking through the slit in the curtains couldn't keep her from her dreams.

* * *

"Miss." The noise buzzed like a pesky fly close to Jordan's ear and she swatted a hand aimlessly before turning over and burrowing into her pillow.

"Miss." There it was again. With a groan, she rolled over and stared blurry eyed up at Maddie.

"I'm sorry, Miss. I know you worked all night, but it is five in the evening and Cook's wanting to know if you'll be down to supper before you have to work again." The household staff was more considerate of her schedule than her aunt, and Jordan should have let them know that last night was her last time working over night.

"I should have let you know I'm done with the night shift," she said now. "I'm sorry."

Maddie stepped back in surprise. "There's no need to be apologizing, Miss. It's our duty to see to you, regardless of your schedule."

"Not when you don't know my schedule." She slid around to sit on the edge of the bed, picking up the tea cup Maddie had thoughtfully brought, even at five in the evening. Maddie didn't argue with her; of course she didn't. Jordan realized employee-employer relations were one thing that had been very slow evolving. That made her recall her dreams; the endless litany of past experiences and conversations that had swirled in her subconscious as she slept. She watched as Maddie straightened the room, picking up her discarded clothes.

"You don't need to do that."

Maddie looked over her shoulder with a smile. "I know things are different where you come from, but here it is my job, so I'd best get to it."

Her off-hand comment had Jordan's mouth gapping. How could the girl possibly know where she came from? The minute the door closed behind the maid, Jordan knelt beside the bed, reaching in to pull out the beaded clutch she had when she came through time. There was a pinched slip of paper between the clasp that let her know the clutch hadn't been tampered with since she had hidden it beneath the mattress that first night. With a sigh, she realized Maddie had meant the Iowa countryside, not the large city.

She hadn't touched the clutch since that first night, and now her hands shook as she slowly opened it, holding her breath. Would something in the bag send her back to her own time? Why hadn't she thought of that before? After all, touching a penny had catapulted Christopher Reeves back to his present in *Somewhere in Time*. She dumped the clutch upside down onto the floor in front of where she knelt. She spread the items out, touching each one but nothing happened. Her credit card, cell phone, housekey--even her driver's license with a hologram sealed beneath the plastic--nothing caused even a shimmer in the air around her.

She tapped the screen of the phone but the battery had long since died. She picked up the small leather-bound notebook that went everywhere with her, her thumb absently rubbing the indentations along the back side. Glancing down, she rubbed across the imprint again. She didn't remember the back being embossed. Looking closer, she turned it this way and that, trying to decipher what it was because it looked somewhat familiar. She flipped it over where a "J" embossed the front—her initial--which was the reason she had bought the small notebook in the first place. There hadn't been anything on the back, she was sure of that.

The embossing on the back looked different from the front, almost as if it had been burned into the leather instead of being stamped as was the front. Why was it so familiar? She looked at the other items, seeing nothing resembling the imprint and then she recalled the one other thing she had tossed in the clutch at the last minute.

The lock from the fencing. Grabbing the clutch, she opened it but there was no lock stuck to the lining. That didn't make sense. Everything in the clutch lay before her. Everything had come through time with her. Things that hadn't been invented in 1926 were scattered across the floor. Yet a simple lock had disappeared, leaving a clear imprint on the leather. What did it mean? Was it a clue to why she came to be in this time? Was it the link she needed to return to her present?

Her brain pounded from all the ramifications. She had no Google to do any research and couldn't even begin to think of a plan of action. How in the world did anyone find something out in this day and age? The worst thing was not having anyone to discuss things with to try and figure out the answer. She had always relied on her gramps to help her, for he had wisdom that only comes with age and there hadn't been a time when she couldn't ask his advice. She didn't think that applied to Grandfather Barrister, given her circumstances. If not gramps, she and her best friend, Caro, had always been able to talk things out. Again, not an option.

The only name that came to mind was Henry. He knew people and places in town and seemed very good at investigating and making deductions. From the beginning, she had felt safe with him. Perhaps if he saw the imprint, he could find out what made it. Well, she thought she *knew* what made it, but the how and why were mysteries, as well as figuring out where the lock had gone. She felt sure it had to be a clue to her predicament.

There was only one small problem with getting Henry involved. How could she ask him to help her without having to explain everything else, including how she came to be here?

Chapter 8

Henry found himself distracted at work to the point where he finally left his desk, telling the receptionist he was out on a story and didn't know when he'd be back. Grabbing a hamburger at the corner luncheonette, he meandered over to the park and sat on a bench, staring off into space. Even his favorite food didn't satisfy the cravings he had. Only one thing – one person – could do that.

Ever since the raid on the Green Mill, the disquiet had been gnawing at him. Chicago had grown more violent with so many mobs wandering the streets it was impossible to keep track. A person only ever heard of the largest, the Chicago Outfit, but numerous others were trying to make names for themselves with bootleg trafficking, drugs and even prostitution. He worried constantly about youngsters like Eddie, whose only choice to help take care of their families was to roam the streets, plying papers or flowers or day old bread from the bakeries.

Then in the midst of turmoil, Jordan had fallen into his arms one dark night. Now, she held a constant place in his mind. There was a naivety about her that called to his gentlemanly soul. But she also had a strength and determination that would put her on equal footing with many men he knew. She didn't appear afraid of hard work, and even though he didn't know her background entirely, he did know coming to live with an aunt such as Beatrice had most likely not been her choice. Yet here she was, and making the most of it.

Sometimes he would catch her staring off into space and he wondered at her thoughts. When he asked, she would give him a dazzling smile and spout some silly thing, but her dark brown gaze held secrets he could only wonder at for she held her own council. He felt that as they became closer, perhaps she would share those secrets with him, but it was not his nature to pry.

Neither was patience in his nature, and the kisses they had shared now fueled his disquiet. He realized he wanted more from Jordan than a peck on the cheek. He was tired of being alone, for not only had he lost his only brother, but his mum had passed two years ago. While he had plenty of friends and colleagues, that was not the same as having someone to share your most intimate thoughts and feelings. Yet because of the lies and betrayal he sometimes saw when investigating a story, he knew they would have no future until she shared her secrets with him. Honesty, too, was part of his nature.

The best way to make that happen, at least in his opinion, was to spend more time together. She would find him steadfast and an extremely good listener, as well as being adapt at ferreting out solutions to problems or keys to puzzles. He knew he could help, regardless of the secrets she carried. All he had to do was get her to trust him.

To that avail, he called to ask her about going to a Sox game.

"Baseball is a sport now,? she asked.

"What?" he must have misheard over the static on the line.

"I mean, they're playing now?"

"Sunday afternoon."

"I would be delighted," she said," if you agree to come back here for Sunday dinner."

"I would never pass up a home cooked meal," he said with a laugh.

When he picked her up and they walked to the EL, she seemed preoccupied at first, several times indicating there was something on her mind but when he asked for details, she shook her head. "Now's not the time. Tell me who's pitching today. My gramps...grandfather and I used to go to games all the time."

"All the time?" he smiled at the exaggeration, for she'd only been in Chicago a few months. Her comment was so like a female yet she appeared extremely agitated when he questioned her. He changed the subject and discussed today's line-up.

The game ended with a White Sox win but only in extra innings so they were a bit late to dinner. Beatrice huffed, worried that the pot roast would be dry, but Jordan's grandfather chuckled and instead asked about the game. While Henry could get the same meal of roast, potatoes, carrots and brown gravy at any of the restaurants in town, there was something special about sharing such a meal with people he enjoyed. After coffee with lemon cake for dessert, Jordan excused herself for a minute or two, leaving him to converse with the others.

"Do you have other aspirations than just being a reporter?" Beatrice asked.

He shrugged. "I like being a reporter."

"True reporting," said August Barrister, "is a gift. People want the truth but a good reporter can do so in a way that is both informative and entertaining." He nodded at Henry. "I read the *Daily Journal* and you have a good sense of story and turn of phrase."

"Thank you, sir."

"But it is the same; day after day of dreary news about the violence, or fear of aggression over in Europe," Beatrice continued her rant.

"I understand what you're saying," Henry said, fervently wishing Jordan would come back and save him. Beatrice acted as though he were personally responsible for the bad news. Hell, all he did was report it. "Once in a while, I get to do something upbeat, like reviewing a theatrical production or the newest vaudeville show.”

“Vaudeville?” Beatrice’s voice squeaked and she visually paled. She grabbed a glass of water and quickly swallowed.

“Now, Beatrice,” her father said calmly, “there’s nothing wrong with vaudeville. A bit risqué, perhaps, but we’re in what they’re calling the ‘roaring twenties’ and it seems that anything is acceptable.”

Beatrice pinched her lips together. Henry didn’t know what to say, but thankfully Jordan returned at that moment.

“Would you like to walk outside?” she asked and Henry couldn’t excuse himself fast enough. She lifted her jacket off the hall tree and he held it for her, then grabbed his hat and opened the door, stepping into the cool evening air.

“Fall is in the air,” she said as they stood at the bottom of the steps. “The mums are blooming in the back garden. Would you like to see?” She took his hand and led him around the corner of the house where a gate at the street opened into a small back yard. Having the end home on a group of row homes, it was the only one with back access from the street. Henry inhaled deeply, smelling that particular scent of decaying leaves and musty earth that only came with the crisp, cooler air of autumn.

The area wasn’t large but Barrister had installed four gas lanterns, much like street lights, so it wasn’t totally dark. Still holding his hand, she led him along a brick path lined with yellow and gold and burgundy flowers. The path led to a small group of wrought iron chairs with a table in the center. He unnecessarily held a chair for her and she murmured a thank you. She was entirely too quiet and it took all Henry's patience not to ask questions. He worried that she had grown tired of his company and thought to end their relationship, but why would she have brought him to this rather romantic location? He took the chair next to her rather than across the table.

"I have something that requires your help," she began.

His posture relaxed. "I had a hunch."

"How could you possible know what I was to say?"

He smiled. "You are very easy to read. Although I do not know the nature of your problem, I knew something was bothering you. How can I help?"

She took a small notebook from her pocket and slid it in front of him. There was enough light for Henry to see it was made of fine leather and well-stitched down the binding. As he picked it up he could feel distinctive markings and tilted it so it caught the light. A block letter – J – had been stamped on the front, the edge of the stamping very smooth, although worn down by handling or by design he didn't know. The back was also stamped, or so he thought until he looked more closely. A rather intricate design was engraved on this side with swirls and cutouts and loops entwined with each other. But this side looked as if it had been burned into the leather.

"They're not the same," he said as he continued to rub his hand over the back design. Edges of the cut were rough and tiny bits of leather brushed loose onto the table when he rubbed over the surface.

"That's what I thought," Jordan said, rather excited. "What does it mean?"

He glanced at her. "What does it mean?" he repeated. "Why would it mean anything?"

"Because there are two very distinctive imprints but completely different in make and design."

"This is the problem you need help solving? It's not even conceivably a fashion problem."

She looked rather crestfallen. He had no idea why such a thing was important, but if it made her look more favorably at him, he was game for about anything.

"This imprint has the look of a lock," he began, making it up as he went. "The outer edges are intricate, but the center appears to have been made with something more solid. And in the very center," he pointed with a pencil he had withdrawn from his coat pocket, "there appears what could be the keyhole."

"A lock. As I thought."

He looked at her. "If you knew that, why ask me?"

"Confirmation of a hypothesis," she said with a grin. "Now what would it have been used for and who did it belong to?"

"You certainly can't tell that from a simple imprint, which in all probability was an industrial production problem."

"How could that be?" she asked.

"Somewhere in the process of producing the notebook, the wrong stamps were used, or perhaps a lock from a piece of equipment fell onto the leather and was crushed beneath the rollers. Instead of tossing it as being imperfect, because that would cost the company money, it probably got tucked into a case of other notebooks and wholesaled."

"That doesn't help me know about the lock."

"Look, I can tell you what it's not. Given the intricate design, it's not a warehouse lock or that for a trailer or automobile."

With a sigh, she picked up the notebook. "I guess it's expecting too much."

He took it from her. "Why is this so important, Jordan? It's just a simple notebook with a unique imprint."

She gave him a sad look. "It's a mystery after all. Maybe something interesting to think about."

He got out a notepad of his own and tore out a sheet. Carefully, he positioned it over the back etching and using the side of his pencil, made a rubbing. Because it had been etched, or burned, so deeply into the leather, his rubbing was quite clear. He had no idea why this was so important to Jordan, but as he had come to understand days ago, she had secrets and if he were to find out what, he had to be willing to dig deeper.

He noticed her shiver as he handed the book back and tucked the rubbing into his pocket. "The breeze off the lake is cooler than normal," he said as he rose. "I'd best get you back inside before you catch a chill."

* * *

"Oh, God, he thinks I'm crazy," Jordan groaned when she closed the door behind Henry. He had given her only a light kiss on the forehead when he said good-bye with no promise as to when he'd see her again. Which meant he would most likely *not* see her again.

She made her way up to her room and fell across the bed in tears. She had thought she could find out more about the missing lock without telling him the whole story. Instead, she had mumbled and stumbled around the truth. She didn't even know if the lock had anything to do with her being in this century, but it was the only thing out of all the items in her clutch that had gone missing. That had to mean something.

She should have known that Henry, being the honest and forthright person he was, would question her explanation. He deserved the truth, but she had no idea how to do that. All she knew was that if she told him where she came from, he really would think she was crazy.

As she suspected, she didn't hear from him all that week. She looked for him in the crowds along the streets after work and on the train as she took it home. She sat on the front steps one afternoon enjoying one of the warmer days on her one day off that week, hoping he would stop by.

September had arrived with a sweep of wind and rain across Lake Michigan and the cooler weather had caused the leaves to begin their change. Bright oranges and red dotted the neighborhood and the small park across the street from the house no longer filled with mothers pushing strollers and youngsters running around in the grass. In her mind, she envisioned the same park across from the stores and loft she and her gramps shared. The trees were much taller then and a wrought iron fence had been built between the sidewalk and the grass of the park to protect youngsters from running out into the street. Otherwise, it was the same neighborhood she had lived in. Yet it was a lifetime away from everything and everyone she knew.

"Hello, JF, what's cooking?"

The sight of Eddie instantly cheered her. She hadn't seen him in a week; specifically last Thursday, and the Thursday before that. At his question, it dawned on her that he wasn't exactly here to see her, or to look after her for Henry.

"Did you come all this way to see me?" she teased.

"Well, yeah," he scoffed a shoe against the first step. At her look, he retracted, "Not exactly, but sorta?"

"Hmm." She would have teased him further but he seemed a bit anxious which was unusual for this particular street urchin. "What's up, EB?"

"I got a couple things on my mind, but first I gotta give you these." He held out a small stack of neatly folded white clothes, which Jordan recognized were napkins. "My mum washed and starched them right nice and made me promise not to get them dirty on the way here." He handed them off quickly. "You know how hard it is to keep a white thing white?"

Three white napkins, for three Thursdays he had shown up at just the right time for Cook's freshly baked cookies, which she always made sure were plentiful enough to send some home. That made today's visit no big surprise, although he said there was more on his mind.

"Please tell your mother thank you very much for laundering these. She needn't have." She stood. "Come around to the back with me and we'll see what Cook has in store for today. I was just about to have a snack myself." She knew Eddie's tender self-esteem wouldn't handle her just giving him cookies. It had to be a normal thing between them.

"Cook," she said as they came in the back door into the kitchen. "Look how lovely Eddie's mother returned our napkins." She placed them on the counter.

"Just in time to fill them up again," Cook said with a smile. She slid a plate of sugar cookies toward Eddie and he didn't have to be asked twice.

While Eddie devoured cookies, Jordan rummaged through the pantry and came up with a basket. "If this old basket isn't in use, perhaps we could just put some cookies in there and his mother wouldn't have to do laundry."

"That would work fine, I think," Cook replied. "And if Eddie doesn't think she would mind, I baked too many loaves of bread this morning so I'll tuck one in the basket with the cookies." Cook gave her a wink.

Eddie mumbled his thanks around a mouthful of cookie. With his mind on cookies and fresh bread, he had turned to leave before he spun back around.

"You and HD having a row?" he asked out of the blue. His hair was shaggy and in his eyes but Jordan was sure his forehead creased in wrinkles from a scowl.

She felt her cheeks heat and noticed Cook pretended not to overhear.

"I don't think so," she said cautiously because she really didn't know after their last date and frankly it wasn't anyone's business.

"Well, something's got him in a twist 'cause when I asked why he's so grumpy he told me to mind my potatoes." He hung his head. "He don't usually talk like that to me."

Jordan had no idea what that meant but figured it couldn't be good. "Should I write him a note?" She couldn't believe she was asking an eight year old for advice.

"Gore, no," he said with conviction. "You can't tell him I said nothing." He switched the basket to his other hand, then dug in his pocket. "'Sides, I almost forgot; he sent you a note."

He handed her the wadded up piece of paper which she smoothed out on the counter. "Did you read this?" She narrowed her gaze at him, wondering if that was why he thought they'd had an argument.

"No, I ain't nosy. 'Sides, I can't read that scribbly writing. I can just read books." He put his cap on. "I gotta go. Thank you, Mrs. Cook for the bread. It'll go super great with the soup my mum is fixing, I'm sure."

"Wait." Jordan quickly read the short note. "Tell him I'd be delighted."

He narrowed his gaze. "Does that mean yes?"

She laughed. "It means yes."

"Why didn't you just say so?" He was out the door, leaving it open for a rather cool breeze to waft into the warm kitchen.

Jordan barely noticed as she read Henry's dark, scrawl again, just to make sure she had read correctly.

Sorry for the absence, but people are out and my workload doubled. I have a reprieve tomorrow night and would like to take you to the Chopin. — HD

Certainly not the most romantic love note, but at least he didn't think she was crazy.

Chapter 9

Henry was frustrated that Jordan wouldn't tell him her real reason for wanting information about the imprint on her notepad. Although minor in the scheme of things, he felt if she wouldn't tell him that, there may be other things she hadn't told him. And yet something about her meant he couldn't stay away from her and it wasn't just her secrets.

She was dressed to the nines when he stopped to fetch her. He didn't know if there was a name for the drop-waist, filmy dresses of the day, but he loved the fact they were shorter and showed a bit of leg. Material was gathered near her hip on one side, creating what looked like a flower and causing that side of the dress to be ruched up even higher so he thought he saw her knee. The beaded neckline glittered in the evening light and caused a glow to surround her. Or perhaps it was her face that glowed as she met him with a ruby lipped smile that made him immediately think of missing the opening of the motion picture.

Although he hated to cover her figure, he dutifully helped her with her coat when she handed it to him. With a perky cloche on her head, she took his arm and they were off.

"Are we good?" she asked along the way.

"What do you mean?"

"Are we okay; you and me?"

He glanced down at her and saw her bite her lower lip. He realized that by not seeing her for several days, she had come to the conclusion that he didn't *want* to see her. Regardless of his unanswered questions, nothing could be further from the truth. He cupped his hand over the one she had tucked at his elbow.

"We're very good," he replied. "I apologize for not staying in touch but the newsroom was in chaos. There's talk about selling the paper and everyone's scrambling to keep their jobs."

"Are you worried?" She sounded worried on his behalf.

"Naw. I've been in the trade long enough I can get another job. Or maybe I'll quit the news and write books about the mob instead."

She stumbled on the walk and if not for her holding his arm, would have fallen. He felt a shiver go through her and he stopped, turning to pull her close. She tucked her head beneath his chin, her hands flat against his chest. He wondered if she could feel the rapid beat of his heart.

After a moment, she cleared her throat and lightly pushed against him. He reluctantly loosened his grip, not letting go completely. When she looked up, her gaze full of starlight, he bent to kiss her; a kiss that went well beyond propriety for standing in the middle of the sidewalk.

With a gruff "sorry", he unhanded her and turned to continue their walk. He licked his lips, still tasting the fresh peppermint of her lips.

"Don't be," she whispered softly, returning her hand to his arm.

The motion picture at the Chopin was a comedy, if such farcical, over the top antics could be called such, but Jordan couldn't contain her laughter throughout and that made him enjoy it all the more. She giggled at the slightest trip or stumble and seemed in awe of the actors' performances.

"I have never laughed so much in my life," she said later as they stood on the platform waiting for the train. "All the exaggerated actions and facial expressions; and the music!" She giggled yet again. "Thank you so much for taking me." She squeezed his arm.

"Don't they have motion pictures in Iowa?"

"I don't know; I've never been to I...I have never been to one in Iowa," she stammered.

There it was again, those little trips, as though she was talking around the actual truth. What was she hiding, and why? "Why did you tell me your name is Jordan when I've heard your aunt and your colleagues at the exchange call you Jodelle?"

"I don't care for that name. Is that so bad?" She turned and tugged him closer by the lapels of his jacket. "Are you looking for a story, Mr. Newsman?" If she thought to distract him with her ruby lips brushing his in a kiss, she did a damned fine job of it, at least for the moment.

"I could really go for a glass of wine," she said, then abruptly added, "or a cup of coffee."

He laughed. "So you're not a teetotaler, hmm?" When she looked at him in a panic, he added, "It's not like you'd be the only person in this town to drink, even if it's not legal. I know a place..." He stopped talking, tilting his head to the side to listen. Off in the distance he could hear numerous whistles; too many to be random, which could mean only one thing.

"Or maybe not tonight. It sounds like there might be another raid in the neighborhood." He scowled as he shook his head. "Whoever thought prohibition was a good thing?"

"Well, at least it will be over before long," Jordan remarked.

"How can you possibly know that?" Here she went again with her random remarks that made no sense.

She gave an elegant shrug, looking off in the distance before bringing her gaze back to his. "Surely the government will see the sense in making it legal with a hefty tax rather than not realizing any money from it the way it is being handled now."

"That makes sense so why hasn't the government figured that out in the past six years?"

She laughed. "Do you have any idea how the government actually works?"

"True. Locally, they probably make more money under the table in payoffs." The police whistles had stopped but he knew taking her to a speakeasy would be better left to another day.

He tucked his hand in his pocket and felt the paper he had left there from the other night, reminding him of what he had meant to tell Jordan earlier.

"By the way, about that embossed image on your notebook." He pulled out the rubbing he had made.

"Don't worry about it. It's just a silly thing." She seemed embarrassed that he had brought it up.

"No, it's intriguing and I'm sorry if I didn't take your interest seriously. It is a rather odd design, and it has given me something to think about other than the sale of the newspaper or the mobsters taking over the city streets."

"Fine, but it's no big deal." As intent as she had been the other night, now she didn't appear the least interested. Yet another mystery he would have to dig into further.

"So, your *not a big deal* is most likely a lock, which we knew," he added quickly when she opened her mouth to interrupt. "I showed the rubbing to a couple of locksmiths I know and they both agreed that it had most likely been made to be more decorative than functional. Because of the amount of filigree around the edges, it wouldn't hold up to a lot of banging around. There is really no way of knowing how it might have been used when it is only the front that was imprinted on the leather. One locksmith said good lock makers will have a maker's mark on the back side, just as watchmakers do, but again we can't trace it that way."

"So there's no way of finding out who owns the lock because we can't find out who made it?" Yet another change in her voice as now she sounded disappointed.

"Jordan, it would help if you told me everything."

She looked at him in surprise. "I have," she sputtered but she accurately read the disbelief on his face and pursed her lips. "I'm sorry. You are right and I owe you an explanation. Just not here."

At that moment, their train arrived and between the noise and the crowds, any attempt at conversation was useless. They rode in silence but he had positioned himself so he could study her in the near dark interior. She fiddled her fingers and nibbled on her lower lip, but it was her eyes that fascinated him the most. He would have sworn that she tried very hard not to blink, for if she did, he felt sure a tear would fall.

* * *

Jordan barely made it into the house and up to her room before the tears fell. She kicked off her shoes and crawled across the bed to hug a pillow. Everything was such a mess!

She liked Henry way too much, given her circumstances. He was so kind and understanding and even after she tripped over her tongue time and time again, he still took her on dates and kissed her senseless. But tonight he wanted the truth; a truth he had every right to if they were to continue their relationship. And yet if she told him the whole truth, he would probably run away as fast as he could. She had no idea how she would cope without him in her life.

On the flip side, what if they fell in love and she just disappeared one day? She didn't know what had brought her here, so had no idea how to avoid getting sent back.

She gasped. Did she want to go back? She missed her gramps and her friends, but truth be told, she had adapted to life here and every day felt normal to her now. Especially because of Henry.

Which brought her back to their relationship. She thought it was already too

143

late for "what if" when it came to her feelings for the man. Every time she saw him, her heart tripped just a little faster, and she wished she were bold enough to take their kisses to the next step. Did women in this era push the boundaries and instigate love making? Would that send him scurrying faster than telling him she was from the future?

"Augh!" she screamed into her pillow, then grabbed it and threw it across the room, barely missing the standing lamp that glowed softly in the corner. Scrambling off the bed, she knelt and slid a hand beneath the mattress, retrieving her clutch. Once again, she dumped the contents out on the floor, scattering cards and keys and cell phone. Where was the notepad? She dug back under the mattress, her fingers touching the rough leather, apparently having not put it back in the purse after showing it to Henry. She studied all the things from the purse. Everything she had tucked in there before she and Caro left for the Chamber meeting was from her life in 2022. Everything was still there, except the lock. That had to be the key to this whole thing. She idly rubbed her thumb across the imprint on the leather. She could think of only one thing to do even if it meant risking everything.

It was time to lay her cards on the table with Henry. All her cards. Would he believe what she had to say? Would he help her?

Jordan knew her plan was underhanded, but felt it was the only way. He was a man, after all, and she hoped the use of all her feminine wiles could soften the blow of what she had to say. So she had made sure both August and Beatrice were out of the house then enlisted Maddie's help, albeit under protest.

"Miss, surely you can't think this is proper," the maid said after reading what Jordan had written for her to say.

"No, it's not, but I have my reasons for doing it and you promised not only to help me but not to breathe a word to Aunt Beatrice and grandfather. Just tell them you heard me getting called into work."

"I know, but..."

"I wouldn't ask you, but my voice might be recognized at the telephone exchange, so you have to make the call." She clasped the maid's hands. "Please, Maddie. This is really important."

"And risqué," added the maid but Jordan was sure she heard a little envy in her voice.

"And romantic?"

With a sigh, the maid nodded. "Let's get it done before the missy comes home." She lifted the receiver then clicked the cradle to connect with the operator.

"*Daily Journal* offices, please." She tilted the receiver away from her ear so Jordan could hear the other end of the conversation. They were quickly connected.

"*Daily Journal*, how may I direct your call?"

"Mister Henry Douglas, um, in the newsroom." Jordan watched her squeeze her eyes tight. She gave her a light pat on the back in reassurance.

"Just read what I wrote," she whispered a moment before she heard Henry's voice. Thank goodness he was at his desk this morning.

"This is Douglas."

Maddie coughed, then said, "I have a message for you. Please meet JF at CPH for dinner this evening."

"What? Who is this?" Jordan could almost see Henry's forehead wrinkle in question.

In a single breath, Maddie rattled off the details, "JF, CPH, dinner," then slammed the receiver back onto the cradle to disconnect the call. "Oh my. Oh, dear." She grabbed the corners of her apron and began fanning herself.

"Breathe, Maddie, breathe."

"I am!" And indeed she was, but too fast, Jordan realized.

"Okay, slow down then. You were wonderful; you did great. You didn't say your name and you gave him all the information." She impulsively hugged her. "Thank you."

"Well, I never before heard of a lady asking a gentleman on a date for dinner. I don't think you'd even catch me doing such a thing." Shaking her head in disbelief, Maddie hurried out of the study to resume her daily chores.

Little did she know Jordan had much more than dinner planned.

* * *

Henry scowled at the telephone receiver before placing it back in the cradle. "What the hell?" he muttered looking down at the letters he had scribbled so he wouldn't forget. It wasn't Eddie who called, although the voice was young and high pitched. Eddie would have hunted him down to deliver a message. And few people knew the code that same young *spy* insisted on using.

He underlined the letters JF. That he knew was Jordan, although it hadn't been her voice on the telephone. The caller hadn't mentioned a time, but dinner was usually served around seven, so he put a number 7 above the word "dinner." It was the CPH that had him stumped but only for a minute. The Congress Plaza Hotel had an excellent restaurant although he didn't eat there often because it was a might on the rich side.

So there he had it. Jordan wanted him to meet her at the Congress Plaza for dinner at seven. Wow. That made him smile. A lady asking him out on a date. And not just any lady. She was the one he both wanted to see and hesitated, because she stirred conflicting emotions in him. They hadn't spoken since they had gone to the Chopin. Perhaps she needed that time to fabricate another deception, because no matter what she said, she was hiding something from him. To give her the benefit of the doubt, she had said she would tell him, when the time was right. Perhaps tonight was that time. He looked at his wristwatch. How could he manage until seven tonight?

He had no sooner thought that but what his editor yelled at him from his office. "Douglas, they're brawling down at the docks again. Get your ass down there and see what's up!"

He grabbed his hat and hurried to the stairs, happy to have a story to wile away the time. In the end, it took a whole lot longer than he would have liked. By the time he found out what had happened – a cargo ship not wanting to pay dockworkers to unload but instead insisted on their own men; the scuffle between said two groups of men and the aftermath of broken crates of dishes from who knows where – Henry had just enough time to race back to the office, type up a short but concise report and get back home for a quick bath and shave.

He hoped he hadn't missed Jordan as he entered the lobby of the Congress. As always, the elaborate design and elegant chandeliers, along with the posh furnishings, made him pause in appreciation. Light glimmered off gold foil wallpaper and brass light sconces. People milled about talking while others sat in deeply cushioned chairs sipping what he assumed were non-alcoholic beverages, but one never knew. The congress was rumored to be the headquarters of Al Capone, and where that mobster was, the booze followed. He walked toward the restaurant and peeked inside but didn't see Jordan anywhere. Besides, he didn't think she would request to be seated by herself.

After several minutes, he finally approached the front desk. "Excuse me, I'm looking for a woman."

"Aren't we all," the cheeky desk clerk chuckled until Henry glared.

"This particular lady," he emphasized the word, "would be about this high," he gestured, "with blondish-brown bob cut hair, brown eyes and red lips."

The desk clerk narrowed his gaze. "Are you HD?"

Horsefeathers! Did everyone know? He'd have to talk to Eddie. "Yes."

The clerk turned and reached into a pigeonhole, extracting an envelope. "The lady asked me to give you this." He held it up, but didn't immediately hand it over. Henry pulled out a coin and slapped it on the counter.

"Have a good evening, sir," the clerk chuckled as Henry turned and walked away. He didn't open the envelope until well away from the front desk, although he figured the clerk knew what was inside.

The key fell out into his hand. The attached metal tag had 222 stamped on it and Henry headed rapidly toward the elevators.

* * *

The Congress rooms were quite eloquent with a separate sitting room from the bedroom and bath. Jordan had changed from her work clothes into her best dress, storing her bag in the clothespress and now paced nervously around the small table the room service waiter had set up. The candles flickered, the crystal water glasses and china glistened in the soft light. All she needed was Henry and he was late. What she wouldn't do for a very large glass of wine at that moment!

She heard the key rattle in the lock and held her breath. Henry closed the door behind him and removed his hat, but didn't venture further into the room. Only his eyes moved; his gaze following the curve of her hip, up to her breasts and then he stared directly into her eyes. She thought how handsome he was and how he made her heart race just looking at him. Then she thought about how kind and thoughtful and generous he was and how he fought for justice and truth. She suddenly realized she couldn't go through with her plan; at least not in the original way she had planned.

"What have we here?" he questioned as he strolled across the room to where she stood.

"You're late and dinner is getting cold." Her emotions were in turmoil and her voice sounded snarky. She could feel a tear well.

He stopped and cocked a brow. "Did we somehow marry and I didn't know?"

She started flapping her hands and sputtering. "Of course not. I'm sorry; I just wanted everything to be perfect."

He grabbed a flailing limb and pulled her close enough she could smell his aftershave. "It is perfect. You are perfect."

And he kissed her, long and deep, to the point Jordan thought of going back to her original plan of seduction. Reluctantly, she pushed against him. He deserved better than that.

"Dinner will be cold."

"Who gives a damn?"

Yes, he was indeed all man, she thought, but gave him a smile and backed away. "It's lamb chops. They are horrible when the sauce congeals." He still didn't release her so she offered him something better than a lambchop. "While we eat, I have a story to tell you. A story that couldn't be told over a cup of coffee at Gabby's."

He held the chair for her, poured water into the crystal glasses and removed the dome from the entree, dishing up the chops and various roasted vegetables. As he sat, she noticed him glancing around the eloquent sitting room.

"I know what you're thinking," she said. "How can a telephone operator afford something like this? Is the secret I'm withholding a side hustle, like bootlegging?"

He actually looked shocked. "I would never impugn your integrity in such a manner. Besides, if you were bootlegging, we wouldn't be drinking water." He tipped his glass to her. "What is a side-hustle?"

"It's a job that makes you money, sometimes more than your real job." He looked thoughtful and when he opened his mouth to speak, probably to ask more questions, she waved him off. "It's not a side-hustle, but when I first got here, my aunt insisted I help pay expenses for my keep. So when I started working, I would give her some money when I got paid. But my grandfather had started giving me an allowance before I found a job, and he continued to give me an allowance after I started working. An allowance larger than what I gave Beatrice for expenses."

He chewed thoughtfully before starting his investigation. She could almost see the wheels in his brain turning. "So if you aren't a bootlegger and you have an excess of money, are you an heiress but do not want your aunt stealing your gold, or silver mines?"

She laughed. "No such luck. I'm simply frugal and decided to splurge a little. The story I have to tell isn't about money at all. It's about the lock that is imprinted on that notepad." She paused, sucked in a breath, and added, "And about my life."

He carefully put his utensils across his plate and leaned back in his chair. If he thought to look impartial, he missed badly because Jordan could see the interest spark in his eyes and his shoulders tightened ever so slightly.

She wasn't sure where to start. "A very long time ago, a poem was written about a couple who were madly in love and would meet secretly by a bridge but then the man was called to war and while gone, he found a new love. His first love died of heartbreak and out of superstition, local women started hanging love locks on that bridge in an attempt to safeguard their love."

"I believe I read that piece," he mused, "although I cannot recall the title or poet. I do know it was not a 'very long time ago'."

His lips quirked and Jordan figured he didn't think much of her storytelling. Just wait until she got to the punch line.

"That's inconsequential," she said. "The popularity of love locking took off and an Italian movie was made, inspired by the same named novel, *Ho Voglia di Te*, which means I want you."

She could see more questions forming so she hurried on. "Paris has always been known as the city of love, and soon people were putting locks on the *Passerelle des*

Arts, a pedestrian bridge. Over the years, thousands and thousands of locks were added to the point where the structural integrity of the bridge was compromised, so the mayor of Paris made it illegal to put locks there. The ones that were on it were removed."

"What does any of this have to do with the imprint of a lock you have?" He leaned forward, elbows on the table, gaze intent.

"To help defray costs of rebuilding the bridge in Paris, the Mayor auctioned off grids of locks. My gramps and I went to Paris and bought a section, and I believe the imprint is of a lock I had taken off the grid and put in my purse the night I...bumped into you." She knew she was leaving out the most crucial part, the scariest part.

"Usually something of this magnitude and interest gets picked up by foreign reporters and sold to American newspapers. I read widely, not just the *Journal*, and I have never heard about any of this love locking nonsense except the poem. When did all of this happen?"

"The book and movie were produced around...oh-six or oh-seven. The Paris grids were removed in...fourteen." She gritted her teeth.

"That doesn't make sense. This is 1926. I would have heard something about all this. And I don't understand what you said about having the lock in your purse. Where is it then?"

Jordan was panicking. She could feel her heart pound. She spoke in a rush. "The book was published in 2006, the Paris locks were removed in 2014 and I bumped into you when I was attending a meeting at the Kirkland in 2022."

Silence filled the room. He slowly put his hands palms down on the table, fingers spread wide. He didn't look at her; and then he did and her heart sank.

"2006, 2014, two...thousand...and...twenty-two? You are telling me you know all these things that *haven't happened* yet because you are *from the future*?"

"Yes," she whispered because she feared the worse--he didn't believe her. "I can prove it."

"Ha!" He shoved back from the table so hard he knocked his chair over. "First you suckered me in with your innocence and smiles. Then you lure me here to tell me some cockamamy tale so I would...what, write your story and turn it into a sensation novel so you could trot around the countryside like a carnival act making yourself rich?"

"No!" He had it all wrong. "I asked you here to seduce you but realized you had a right to the truth first."

"Lady you wouldn't know the truth if it hit you broadside." He stormed toward the door. "You've got bats in your belfry and I want no part of it!"

Chapter 10

Henry stormed out of the hotel lobby, ignoring the cabbies waiting for passengers and walked rapidly down the sidewalk. He rubbed a hand through his hair, realizing he had forgotten his hat but no way in hell would he go back for it.

He headed for the waterfront; the place he always went to think. The water usually brought him solace but tonight the crashing waves, which meant a storm was approaching, only fueled his anger.

He had begun to think he might be in love with Jordan. She was smart and capable and they conversed on any number of topics. Her happy laughter, her enjoyment of the most ordinary things, had been endearing. Now he saw it for what it was. The preposterous lies she had told him only made him madder at himself to think he was that gullible or that hungry for female companionship. Hell, her name wasn't even Jordan, but Jodelle, and he had fallen for that lie too.

He kicked at everything in his path — rocks, a stray piece of driftwood, even the sand. Finally his anger exhausted itself and he sat on the sand, arms propped on bent knees. And he thought; revisiting every conversation, dissecting every word much as he did when proofing his stories. He looked for holes, suppositions instead of fact, theory instead of evidence.

Maybe we'll send a man to the moon one day, she had said when he talked about the Wright Brothers. *Prohibition will be over soon,* she had commented when he mentioned the stupidity of the laws.

A thought niggled at the back of his brain and he closed his eyes to recall the very first time he had seen her. He had been talked into attending an event at the Kirklands because his editor wanted a story on the great Houdini and the Kirklands were hosting the magician. He had paced at the bottom of the steps leading up to the mansion, waiting until the very last minute to enter because he didn't believe in the nonsense Houdini fed the crowds in his performances and wondered how he would write an impartial article.

Out of nowhere, Jordan had fallen into his arms. *Out of nowhere.* One minute he paced, the next he held a partially conscious, beautiful woman in his arms. She had been confused and disoriented, calling him by another's name and telling him he shouldn't be here; that she shouldn't be here. He thought at the time she might have bumped her head. But what if she hadn't?

It hadn't been that many years ago when transportation had been slow and hazardous. Now trains went faster than one could imagine, and he had no doubt that the Wright Brothers aeroplane would soon revolutionize transportation. But fly a man to the moon? That seemed inconceivable, and yet in just his lifetime, he had seen the invention of telephones, electric lights and air conditioning; elevators and skyscrapers, automobiles.

There seemed to be no end to man's inventiveness, but was it possible to invent a way to travel through time? He could not envision how that could be done. If it had to do with speed, he knew of nothing in this world that could travel fast enough otherwise everyone and his brother would be zipping from one century to another.

What if it wasn't an invention, but rather an accident? She said she shouldn't be here, which implied she had not gotten here intentionally. He had found her, confused and helpless, and they had formed a friendship in which she felt comfortable around him, he was sure of that. Now he had left her once again helpless and perhaps fearful of what lay ahead. The last glance he had of her before he slammed out the door was one of anguish. What kind of cad was he?

He sat stewing on the shore of the lake until the sun had just begun to peek above the horizon. With it came resolution. He didn't know if he believed her, but he did know he had strong feelings for Jordan and couldn't leave things as he had. He needed to hear her out. Besides, he just recalled the last words she had said to him.

He hurried back to the hotel, hoping Jordan hadn't checked out and gone home. The elevator moved at a snail's pace, even though it was only up a single floor. Hurrying down the corridor, he inserted the key and quietly opened the door.

"Oh!" She gasped as she turned toward him from where she stood by the window. The early morning light cast a halo about her face, and even from this distance he could see her eyes were red and puffy; a glitter of tears still swimming in her gaze. Whatever she wore floated around her as she turned, her slender figure visible through the filmy folds.

"What was the last thing you said to me?" His voice came out gruff and demanding.

She took a step back and her brow furrowed slightly. "That you deserved to know the truth?"

He cleared his throat as he rapidly shook his head. "Not that. I can't deal with that at the moment."

The tiniest of smiles lifted the corners of her mouth. She stood a little straighter. "I asked you here to seduce you."

"That," he said emphatically. "Regardless of everything else you said, is that the truth?"

"Yes," she whispered, her eyes growing wide as he strolled across the room, lifted her into his arms and carried her into the bedroom.

* * *

He came back, Jordan mused silently as she woke to the warmth of a hard body against her bare back. They hadn't talked when he returned, at least not verbally, but how her body had sung for him and he had answered in kind. She knew the talk was coming, but whatever the future held, she had this moment and thought to take advantage of that.

Rolling over, she found his deep green eyes open, capturing her gaze. A lazy smile caught her attention, recalling the way those lips had felt on her skin; how they had taken her on a ride to the heavens and beyond. She felt it only right to return the favor.

She started at his chin, nibbling gently then licking a path down his throat.

"Are all women from...your time so forward?" he whispered then groaned as her hands roamed his body.

"Sh," she breathed against his skin.

"What you said about going to the moon; or what about..." He sucked in a sharp breath when she tweaked a particularly sensitive part of his anatomy. Rising on her elbow, she squinted at him.

"You want to ask questions at this particular time?" She slid her tongue seductively across her lips.

He chuckled, grabbed her tight and rolled over. "No, ma'am." And she had a reprieve for just awhile longer.

* * *

When Jordan finally crawled out of bed, she realized in a panic that it was very late in the morning. In fact, it was probably midafternoon. She flew around the room grabbing clothes and throwing them on helter-skelter. She raced out of the bathroom and straight into Henry, a cup and saucer of coffee sent flying across the carpet.

"Whoa." He grabbed her arms to steady her. When his gaze slid over her body and came back to rest on hers, she knew he misunderstood.

"I am not trying to sneak out," she said before he could say anything.

"It wouldn't do you any good," he replied with a smile. "I know where you live."

She didn't understand his good mood. "We can't be found together in a hotel room. I don't know, but it has to be well past check out time and heaven only knows how many times the maid has already knocked on the door."

He took the bag from her hand and led her into the sitting room, where a rolling cart held coffee, a dish of fruit and another of tiny muffins. "All is well," he said as he poured her another cup of coffee. "I called the front desk and requested the room for another day, called for room service and told the lovely maid I didn't need fresh towels."

Her mouth dropped open. "Do you do this often?" He appeared far too knowledgeable about clandestine rendezvous in uptown hotels.

He laughed out loud. "Absolutely not, although I believe I wouldn't mind at all."

The intense look he gave her had her blushing to her hairline.

"My question to you." He held up a finger when she mumbled *here it comes*. "My question is are you on duty at the telephone company today?"

Oh," she relaxed, even though she knew there were questions to follow. "Actually, I have today off, because if last night had gone according to plan, I wouldn't have wanted to go to work this morning."

"According to plan?" His remark was so naive, and he looked so innocent, she wrapped her arms around him, stood on tiptoe and kissed him soundly.

"My seduction plan."

"I almost ruined that," he said with a frown. "But I'm not so sure you did the seducing."

He pulled her hips to his and she felt herself falling under his spell again. She forced herself back.

"I only have today off and should probably show up for supper or Beatrice will no doubt kick me out of the house." She went over to her bag, opened the clasp and took out her clutch. "While I would much rather walk right back into the bedroom and try to forget what I said last night, things have changed," she paused, "really changed, and I want nothing but the truth between us."

"In that case, you can tell me that everything you said last night was just a huge joke."

"I wish." She took his hand and led him over to the sofa, where they sat close but not quite touching. "I know it's hard to believe, and I have no idea how it happened, but I have proof."

"First, is your name Jordan or Jodelle?"

"Jordan," she said without hesitating. "I came to be at the Barrister's and coincidently the niece, Jodelle, was supposed to come to Chicago but changed her plans. There was a letter in her trunk. It is just another very weird coincidence, but helped me so that my appearance wasn't such a surprise." She pulled out her driver's license and handed it to him. He studied it intently, reading all the fine print.

"You can drive a car?"

She had to laugh at his take-away from a piece of plastic with a color photograph on it and the date of when she was born and 2025, the date the license expires. She gave him her credit and debit cards and saw his eyes zero in on the expiration dates as his fingers slid over the raised print.

"These are used to purchase things; everything from a cup of coffee to an automobile. They're called credit and debit cards."

"You have no money?"

"Yes. I must have money in the bank in order to use the cards. I just don't have to carry cash around with me."

He shook his head. "I'm not sure I understand, but I can't deny it." He looked at her and his eyes glittered with a fervor that set her back just a bit. "I have so many questions."

"Let me start." She opened the clutch again. "Remember when you said how easy it would be if you had a telephone you could carry with you to report the news?" Again he nodded. "Welcome to the future." She handed him her cell phone.

He turned it over and over in his hands. Since it didn't turn on, it was harder to explain how it worked. "It has a battery, which is dead, so it won't turn on. But with this, you can call anywhere in the world, without using an operator."

"There are no wires."

"It's a cellular phone, so the sound waves bounce between towers without wire. I don't understand all of that, but in the future, much of our technology is wireless – telephones, radio, television, computers."

He still had a confused look on his face, so she grabbed a pencil and asked for the notepad she knew he always carried. She drew a picture of her phone, little squares indicating all her aps and contacts. "Each of these is an application you can use. This is a list of all the people I know and call often. This is a shopping link, and this is a link where I can look up just about everything. All you do is tap the ap and it opens to what you need. The telephone in the future is like a computer."

He shook his head and ran his fingers through his hair. "And a computer is…?"

And thus began an afternoon and evening of a million questions, punctuated only by an intensive round of lovemaking and a light dinner delivered by a discrete bellhop. While he set up the table, Jordan took a minute to ring the home number, hoping that Maddie would answer. She didn't even have to lie to the trustworthy maid.

"Oh, Miss, so glad you called. Your grandfather chose tonight to do inventory at his store and your aunt is out and about in that mysterious way she has adopted of late."

"So there is no need for me to come home anytime soon?"

"Hello? I'm sorry Miss, the connection is bad." Then the line went dead. Jordan hung up with a smile. There had been nothing wrong with the connection. Maddie didn't want to hear any excuse Jordan would have made so she wouldn't have to lie about it later. She didn't know what that said about her for corrupting the household staff.

"It's all so fascinating," Henry said as he held her chair for her and they sat to eat. "The technology, the advances in science; the money! I mean, we have millionaires like Astor and Carmichael and Kirkland, but billionaires?" He shook his head in disbelief.

"You have to remember while people earn more money, the cost of living is also extremely high comparatively."

"Speaking of money, I gave the bellhop the necessary to take care of the hotel room for last night and tonight."

"You didn't have to do that. I have money."

"Regardless of how free things might be in the twenty-first century, this is only 1926. And while women have the right to vote, it would still be unseemly for one to check in and out of a hotel, especially unescorted. Actually, even if they are escorted but not by a husband. Besides, I'm not without funds myself."

"Do newsmen make that much in salary?" She immediately added, "That was rude. Sorry."

"Don't be. I'm sure you have just as many questions about this century as I do about yours." He smiled. "Well, I suppose not quite as many as you have a written history of this time. But to answer your question, my job has given me access to many of the well to do in this town, and on their advice, I have invested in several companies that I feel will continue to grow. I live well enough on my reporter's salary so the stock dividends I receive are reinvested."

"You play the stock market?" Her heart pounded.

"I guess you could say that," he replied. "Is that important?"

In everything she had told him so far, she had tried to stay away from major world events, because if he knew and tried to change something, what else might be altered? But the Great Depression was only a few years away and he would be living through it; they would be living it if she couldn't find a way home. She couldn't let him lose what he worked so hard for.

"I'm going to tell you something that you have to swear never to breathe a word. You can not leak it to the press. You can not—"

"Stop." He reached across the table and grabbed her hand. "I understand why you can't say anything about being from the future. People would go to any length to get information from you; information to use to their advantage."

"What I need to tell you can be used to your advantage."

"Am I so untrustworthy?"

"Of course not, but we don't know so many things – how I got here; if or when I can go back; how or if anything we do will change something vital in the future."

"You've been here over four months and nothing out of the ordinary or unexplainable has happened that I know of."

"Except the very fact that I am here."

"There is that," he said with a smile. "You being here with me; that's two people's personal history and doesn't affect the grand scheme of things."

"You don't believe your being here makes a difference?" she asked.

"Only on the very smallest of scales," he said. "Now tell me what concerns you."

"Tell me first what stocks you have."

"Are you after my fortune now?" he quipped.

"Humor me."

"Hmm. ExxonMobil and General Motors because I have a feeling automobiles are here to stay. And according to what you have said, fuels like oil and gas will always be in demand."

"Okay, that's good," Jordan had never been involved with the stock market but knew some of the major stocks and those two were still viable in the future.

"Then there's the General Electric company," he continued, "again for obvious reasons. Just recently I had a friend who said Coca-Cola might be a worthwhile investment but I wonder if it's only doing well because people are substituting it for alcohol. I can't see where a fizzy drink will ever be widely distributed." He looked at Jordan and she couldn't keep the smile off her face. "Then again..."

"The stocks you have are all still public companies in my time, so they seem like good investments. The thing is in the not-too-distant future the economy goes into a depression and the stock market crashes. People lose their fortunes, their homes, their jobs. Some companies rebound, others do not."

He opened his mouth to question her, but she quickly put her fingers to his lips. "Please don't ask me how or when. I honestly don't know what triggered it because it was well before my time and so I only read about it in history class. And even that was a long time ago."

Thankfully he dropped the subject and asked her to explain more about the technology of television. That appeared to be more interesting to him than the sports leagues or fashion.

Sometime during her narrative, he had managed to undress her, scattering her dress, stockings and underthings across the sitting room. It had made it rather difficult to describe TV series and movies. She completely lost her train of thought when he began kissing her senseless, and sitcoms never made it into the discussion.

"So the motion pictures and this television thing have sound? People speak directly to you?"

She was cradled against his naked body, her head on his chest and his arm holding her close. She had no idea how he could even speak, much less pick up the thread of conversation they had been having quite some time ago.

"It's all pre-recorded and played on the television or at the theater, but it's only one way. It seems like the people are speaking directly to you but you can't talk back to them."

"And was there really a show called 'Mr. Ed' about a talking horse?"

She tilted back her head. "Did Eddie tell you that?"

He smiled. "All the comments you've made before actually make sense now. Perhaps except for one."

She couldn't think of anything that she hadn't told him. They'd talked all day and half the night.

"That very first night, you said you shouldn't be here."

"Well, that was certainly the truth."

"But you called me by another name – Harry Gallagher – and you said I shouldn't be here either."

She sat up in bed and stared at him. She hadn't thought about Harry Gallagher since she had been dropped into this century. Now, in the dim light of a lamp, she looked at Henry and saw Harry. They had the same color hair and eyes, the same chiseled chin and sharp nose. They even did the same job.

"You looked like someone I knew," she replied, "so I definitely was confused that night."

He couldn't be Harry. Harry was a bit of a snob and rather conceited. Henry was warm and funny and very likeable. Still, a shiver raced down her spine like a bad premonition and she curled closer against his side.

Chapter 11

Henry sat on the couch the next morning, staring at all the things from Jordan's clutch. Although he still had a hard time believing that she had actually come from the 21st century, in some ways he was jealous. He thought maybe it would be fun to participate in her world but knew that was impossible. The best he could do was try to get her back, although he now realized he very much did not want her to go back to her own time.

He rubbed his thumb idly across the imprint of the lock. He had asked so many questions about the future, they hadn't gotten around to discussing the lock.

Jordan came out of the bedroom fully dressed and with her small overnight bag in her hand. He knew they had to resume their lives but it was not going to be the same. He handed her the clutch and she tucked it inside the bag.

"With everything we've said and talked about, we never discussed how you might have appeared in this century," he said. "Why do you think the lock has something to do with it?"

"I was at the Kirkland's," she said. "It was raining and I tried to bring down my umbrella to go inside when it started thundering and lightning and there was a flash. That's all I remember until I woke up in your arms. I had the lock in my purse and now the lock is not in my purse. It has to be related to the how or the why I am here."

"Okay. That means we need to track down the lock. I'll check back with the locksmiths. One of them had a catalog and said he would go through it. Perhaps they can think of somewhere else we can look."

She lifted her coat from the hook, and he took it to help but paused. When she turned back to him, he cupped her shoulders and pulled her close. "I wish this didn't have to end; that we didn't have jobs to go to, or people to see. I wish..."

She interrupted him with a kiss. Starting slowly, peppering small kisses across his mouth, down his chin and back up. Then she clutched his lapel and slanted her lips and he thought he would drown in the delight of sensual prickles that went through him. When he knew one more second would cause him to do very ungentlemanly things, he set her aside with a sigh.

"I will leave first and you wait for the next elevator. You should not be seen coming out of the hotel with me. I will meet you down on the corner and walk you home."

"You don't need to do that," she protested.

"I insist," he replied. "What we have is not a one night stand, Jordan, and I don't want you to treat it as such. You have come to mean something to me and I want to see where this relationship goes. Don't you?"

"Yes," she replied although she sounded dejected, "but you have to understand I have no idea what the next day, or the day after, will bring. What if I just disa—"

He put a finger to her lips. "Don't say it. Let's take one day at a time. In the meantime, we'll try to track down the lock."

He gave her one more soft kiss and walked out the door, hoping she would wait as he had instructed. He wanted nothing to tarnish her reputation. He exited the hotel and realized at least he had left the anger from the first exit behind. He had no idea where he and Jordan were headed, but he had to take his own advice and look forward to one day at a time.

He casually leaned against the building at the corner, one foot flat against the brick behind him, hat low on his forehead. In under a minute, he saw Jordan hurrying to meet him. He reached for her bag and put the strap over his left shoulder, leaving his right side open for her to tuck her arm at his elbow.

"Do you feel like walking?" he asked.

"Definitely. I'm going to have to sit for hours when I start my shift, so I really do need the exercise now."

As they walked, he asked more questions about things in the next century. It seemed inconceivable that cars could go so fast, or that planes had basically replaced boats for transoceanic trips. "And you had an influenza epidemic as we did back in '18?" he questioned when she talked about the advances in medicine and polio and smallpox vaccinations.

"It was called Covid-19," she said, "and several million died, not just in the US but around the world. Travel was stopped. Businesses and restaurants closed. People worked from home and children were schooled remotely."

"How could that happen?"

"Remember I told you about computers? You can remotely connect with others, either to conduct business or to do school work. The thing is, after the pandemic was over, employers found they could continue to have their people work remotely, which meant lower overhead for them, not having to maintain large office buildings. People liked it too, so we've become rather a remote, non-associative society. Personally I missed interacting with people and visiting while I waited in line for coffee or food, or at the grocery store. I couldn't wait to reopen my store."

Henry had found from their conversations that Jordan was a very independent, educated businesswoman and realized he liked that. Unlike many men of his time, he wasn't threatened or worried that woman would take over. If they had the brains and wherewithal to do so, more power to them. All too soon they arrived at her house. He handed over her bag after she opened the door.

"I'll ring you if I hear from the locksmiths," he said. "Otherwise I don't know what more we can do."

"Thank you for your help," she replied, "and for believing in me." Her smile was shy.

"I could write a piece on what I learned, but it would probably cost me my job as no one would believe it! So, your secrets are safe with me." He kissed her on the nose and turned to go. "Think of me at work."

* * *

Instead of taking the EL to the newspaper office, Henry walked along the waterfront even though the wind cut through the light weight of his suit. The sun shone but fall meant colder days and more storms coming in across the lake. He pulled his hat lower on his forehead and flipped the collar up on his coat as he took time to digest everything he had learned in the past two days. Although totally improbable, he could almost envision the world Jordan came from. Every business he passed brought forth the question – "did that still exist in 2022?" As he entered the *Daily Journal* office, he could hear the presses running in the basement and felt somewhat sad to believe that there were few print newspapers in the future; everything was on the computer. So there were still reporting jobs, according to Jordan, but not the newsrooms and deadlines that led to the hustle and bustle that got his adrenaline pumping every day.

That seemed to be the case even today, he thought, as he looked at the assignment board. Since he was late to work, very little remained on the board and the best assignments had been taken, some even by the junior reporters. Normally that would have bothered him, but then normally he wouldn't have been late to work. His reasons caused a smile and he actually didn't give a damn that the only thing left was to do a review of the New Palace Theatre, the latest Vaudeville theater to open. Putting his initials in the blank, he stopped at his desk and grabbed a fresh pad and pencil.

Normally he couldn't get excited about society news and preferred crime and sports, but since his mind was on Jordan and all that encompassed, jotting notes about a new theater and musical wouldn't take much brain power. He could probably even get the manager to write the theater description and the producer to write the information about the vaudeville show. Not his normal MO, but he could get by with it for a day.

The New Palace Theatre had opened at the beginning of October; another in a vast parade of various entertainment venues, but in this case there seemed to be reason for praise, he thought as he entered the opulent foyer. Huge decorative mirrors, breche violette and white marble graced the interior, reminding him of photographs he had seen of the Palace of Versailles in France. The walls were adorned with gold leafing and wood decorations, as well as a series of complex arches and intricate brass ornamentation.

Henry took the stairs two at a time, opened the huge double doors into the vast auditorium. Whatever show currently in production was in the middle of rehearsals so he quietly walked down a side aisle to the third row from the front and took a seat. The director sat in the middle of the first row and the stage director stood to the right, yelling at the chorus line, which seem to be having a problem keeping straight across the stage. The piano came to a tinkling halt.

"One, two; three-four," shouted the director, clapping his hands to the correct tempo. "Not one...two...three...four. Again!" He waved a hand at the pianist, clapped his hands in cadence and watched with a critical eye as the chorus line began their routine, apparently in harmony this time as he didn't interrupt until the end of the number.

Henry glanced from one dancer to another, the girls of various heights but stocking clad legs kicking high in sequence. The costumes were as skimpy as ever, and more so than the last theatre production he had seen. It would be a wonder if the *Ladies of Decency* (the same women constantly protesting for continued prohibition) weren't in protest outside on opening night. His gaze slid past the last girl and back along the line when suddenly he jerked upright in his seat.

"Beatrice?" His gaze jerked back to the last one in line. What was Jordan's aunt doing in a chorus line at a vaudeville show? Sure enough, the minute he said her name out loud, she stumbled, glanced his way before covering her face with her hands and hurrying off stage.

"Stop, stop," yelled the stage manager, waving his hands in the air as he stormed across the stage in Henry's direction. The director stood from the front row and turned, also heading his way.

Henry stood his ground, but did quickly apologize. "Excuse me, gentlemen. So sorry for the interruption, but as long as I have your attention, can I ask you a few questions for the *Daily Journal?*"

That's all it took for both men's frowns to turn to smiles, for anyone in the entertainment business would never turn down the opportunity for free advertising. Within minutes, he had enough information for his article, thanked both men and turned to leave. While they were gathering the dancers back for the rest of rehearsal, they didn't notice as he worked his way backstage, searching for Beatrice. After poking his head into several dressing rooms, he gave up and left the theatre by the back door. He definitely thought it curious that someone as stern as Beatrice Barrister was secretly in a vaudeville chorus line; an activity he felt certain wasn't within a lady's repertoire. It would seem he and Jordan weren't the only ones with secrets.

Later that day he called to ask her on a date, only to have Maddie tell him that she had been called to work the night shift again, training new employees. While he admired her work ethic, he was disappointed that events prevented him from seeing her. Then he became just as busy as the police and federal crime agencies launched a massive night raid on dozens of speakeasies and area clubs. Hustling from one precinct to another, trying to get a handle on the main mobsters who disappeared from custody as fast as they were brought in, he was disappointed not to find Tommy O'Connor among them. Regardless of rumors about his disappearance, Henry felt sure the man was still alive and living under an assumed identity.

Jordan called the next week to invite him to dinner. "It seems forever since we've had a chance to...talk," she spoke quietly.

"I haven't been any more available than you," he replied. "Are you done with night shift now?"

"Yes, and this time, they have given me three days off. I'm thinking about taking a train trip."

"Seriously? You're leaving town? There are things we need to--"

"We'll visit tonight," she interrupted, then quickly said good-bye and hung up. Henry stared at the telephone. Why had she been so abrupt? Did she regret their time at the hotel? He doubted she would have called him if that were the case. Since she hadn't completely blown him off, he called on his patience to wait out the hours until dinner.

He had almost forgotten about his encounter with Beatrice at the theatre until Maddie opened the front door for him and he was immediately shown into the study. She quickly closed the door behind him and he turned to face Beatrice, who paced back and forth in front of the unlit fireplace. He grabbed the hat off his head and started to greet her but she frowned, slashing her hand in a downward movement. He snapped his mouth shut, not understanding why she might be mad but knowing silence was better for the moment.

"Mr. Douglas, you must understand...that is, I'm not usually...um..." Even from a distance, he could see the blush rise on her throat and infuse her cheeks.

Henry suddenly realized that she wasn't mad but rather embarrassed. Any thoughts he had about using his knowledge against her faded away.

"Beatrice, you apparently have some talent to make the—"

She interrupted him with a discreet cough.

"—ah, to do what you do, but you can't expect not to be recognized by your friends."

"We wear masks in the actual production," she stated in a huff.

He shrugged. "Well, it's none of my business at any rate."

"But your article?"

"While I named the architect and the producer in my write-up, the cast were not named at this point. My publisher was more interested in the fact that another theatre had opened. I'm sure after opening night, there will be more reviews." He hoped a mask would protect her secret, but that was not his problem. For now, he sought to reassure her.

"Believe me, we all have secrets," he said as the study door opened and Jordan walked in, dressed to the nines in a black sparkly dropped waist dress with several strings of beads around her neck and a feather fluttering from a band around her forehead. Speaking of, here stood the larger than life, most beautiful secret he had ever beheld, and he knew he would give his life to make sure no one found out.

* * *

Jordan felt a moment of panic when she entered the study and heard Henry's words. She glanced quickly between him and her aunt. Surely he hadn't told her about them; or worse yet about her own background?

"Eh, your aunt was asking me about the new theater in town," he stammered, " and I told her my review was secret until the paper printed it." He grinned, though she didn't think it looked quite genuine.

Beatrice hurried across the room, anxious to leave. "Dinner will be in fifteen minutes. Don't be late." She paused at the door and gave Jordan another glance. "You look quite ducky, Jodelle. I hope the two of you have a pleasant evening out."

Jordan's mouth dropped open with the compliment, and when the door closed behind her, she turned to Henry with a giggle. "She has never complimented me in her life. At least I think that was a compliment. What did you say to her?"

Instead of answering, Henry grabbed her hands and pulled her into an embrace. His lips were firm and hot against hers and she quickly forgot everything except the kiss. He backed her against the door and the heat from his body had her near melting into a puddle.

"Tell me you're not leaving town for three whole days," he groaned between kisses.

"I only said that so I could get away and not have to show up for dinner every night," she whispered, then peppered his neck with kisses. Instead of his usual suit, he wore an open-necked sweater of the softest wool, the dark green complimenting his eyes. She could feel his flat stomach as she slid her hands downward, but he captured her wrists before she got far.

"That will never do if you expect me to stay for dinner." He grinned at her. "Tell me your plan."

"Is the Blue Spruce Resort still open at Lake Como?"

He frowned for a moment then smiled. "It just *recently* opened," he corrected her.

"We used to go there when I was a kid. It's not so far away, but it would be out of the city where it's too easy to run into someone I know."

"You want bears and wild creatures from the forest?"

"I want quiet and anonymity."

"Any company?" He kissed her nose.

"Perhaps a handsome newspaper reporter, if he promises not to print my exploits."

He arched back to look at her with a wide, not so innocent gaze. "Exploits? As in more than one?"

A knock sounded at the door. "Dinner's ready, Miss," Maddie spoke softly.

Jordan flashed Henry a teasing grin over her shoulder as she opened the door. "Numerous." She glided out of the room to a very frustrated male groan.

After dinner, they bundled up and caught the EL to the Sunset Café. Jordan was happy that Henry now knew her secret, because she wanted to experience so much of Chicago in the 1920's that no longer existed in the twenty-first century. Although she knew he wouldn't take her anywhere dangerous, such as the Green Mill, Capone's hangout, there were other speakeasies just as well known.

The Sunset Café was a jazz club and they were soon immersed in the bluesy, smoky atmosphere. Jazz was in its infancy but making a real impact in places such as New Orleans, Kansas City and Chicago. She loved the rhythms and soulful sounds; music she and her gramps had listened to frequently.

"This place is a safe haven for black American performers," Henry told her as he held out her chair, "but it is also one of the few places where any ethnicity is welcome."

She grabbed his hand when the trumpet player stood, belting out a familiar tune though she couldn't think of the name. "That is Louis Armstrong!"

"You've heard of him?"

"You forget where I'm from. He's an icon. He's considered the ambassador of jazz." Overwhelmed, she felt a tear slip down her cheek. She was living history, which was hard to explain. The bluesy sounds made her recall how she and Gramps would play old records on the equally old record player in his shop. The thought of him made her heart ached. He wouldn't know what had happened to her and that made her sad. She needed to find a way home to him.

Henry handed her his handkerchief even as he kept his gaze on the stage and pretended she wasn't crying. She studied his profile and wondered when she had fallen in love with him? He was such a gentle soul, even if he thought otherwise, and it made her dilemma all the worse. How was she to leave him, if they did find a way? Even worse, what if she left abruptly in the same manner as she had come into his life? While they knew that could happen, they didn't speak of it and so it didn't exist. Was it better to stay wrapped in their safe cocoon and ignore the possibilities?

It was one more reason she wanted him to come with her to the resort. Not knowing how much time they had made each moment precious, and she wanted to spend them with him.

"Come with me to Lake Como," she whispered in his ear.

He turned and her lips grazed his. "You couldn't keep me away."

Chapter 12

Jordan had agreed to meet Henry at the train station as she didn't want Beatrice asking questions or making snide insinuations. She was pleasantly surprised when she wished her a happy trip and to enjoy her time off.

The train trip itself was uneventful, but she did enjoy watching the scenery go by. The trees were bursting red, orange and yellow; interspersed with evergreens. Whenever she glanced across the seat to Henry, who of course had a newspaper in his lap, butterflies would alight in her stomach. It wasn't that she didn't know what would happen at the resort. She had been the one to invite him. There was something about him that touched her deep within where no one had ever been. Every day was a gift which both beguiled and terrified her.

"Henry, what if I just disappear one day?" she blurted out, then looked quickly around. The early morning schedule meant the train was almost full, but it appeared no one was interested in their conversation. And her comment didn't seem to surprise Henry in the least.

"Five years ago, when Sullivan was killed, I came to the understanding that I could not control everything, no matter how hard I wanted." The paper rustled as he set it aside and leaned forward, taking her hands to stop their nervus twitching. "All we can do is enjoy one day at a time while we try to find the cause of this...event."

She chewed her lip, unsure of telling him what was really on her mind. "Don't you see? That's the problem. What if we find out how I came to be here, which opens a portal or whatever to allow me to go home, but maybe; maybe I don't want to go home." She held her breath.

His eyes narrowed and darkened; his hands tightened on hers. "How can you not want your life back? How could you not want to go back to a world of such fantastic advances and marvels that I can't even begin to imagine?" He pitched his voice low to prevent anyone overhearing, yet she could hear in his tone that he thought her world was amazing.

His words made her realize he might not feel the same way about her as she did with him. He was the one reason she might hesitate to return to her own time but perhaps he wasn't ready to hear that. "Never mind. I think I'm confused over the whole idea and want to talk myself out of being disappointed if I can't return home. I guess we keep trying to find the key."

"Not for a few days," he said as the train squealed into the station. He stood and retrieved their bags from the overhead bin. "For the next two days, we are going to forget the world – both yours and mine – exists. There is just you and me." He bent to kiss her forehead before motioning her ahead of him to the train exit.

They took a short taxi ride which soon brought them down a tree-shrouded road to the resort and Jordan gasped. Late morning fog drifted across the lake and mingled among the tall trees that curved around the back of the house. "It's so romantic," she said as henry helped her from the taxi.

"It's rather spooky," he replied.

"Nonsense. It is everything I remember."

They were met by the owner, who introduced himself as Austin Mugridge and immediately said, "Our resort is encompassed by blue spruces, maples and other trees and bushes. A brook runs close by. It's peaceful, the air is fragrant, and birds will wake you in the morning with their songs."

"It sounds lovely," Jordan said as Henry signed the register. He turned the register back to the owner, who pursued the signature and reached in a keyhole behind him for a key.

"This way, Mrs. Douglas." He started down the hall.

Jordan felt her cheeks warm and looked at Henry, who simply gave her a wink and nodded for her to follow the manager. Their room was on the first floor at the end of the corridor. A small fire had been lit in the hearth of an elegantly styled sitting room.

"Every room has a private bath," Mr. Mugridge said, opening a side door and then another which contained a large bed. Jordan's blush continued to spread until she felt extremely warm all over, and it wasn't from the fire. "We serve meals family style, but we do offer room service if you prefer."

Henry dropped their bags and dug in his pocket for a tip, which the owner refused. "Your enjoyment of our small property is pleasure enough." With that he closed the door, leaving Jordan standing in the middle of the room, feeling as though she were on the precipice of a grand adventure. She watched Henry remove his outer coat and hang it near the door, followed by his suite coat and tie. He was so handsome, so caring and so...so everything. And he chose to spend his time with her.

"Why do you look so panicky?" he said as he crossed the room to where she stood by the fire. "Are you sorry we came?"

She was shaking her head before he even finished. "Of course not. I am wondering how I got so lucky as to fall into your arms that fateful day?"

"I would say I'm the lucky one," he replied just before he scooped her into his arms and turned toward the bedroom. "You are everything that is good in my life, Jordan."

She had no reply for that other than to wrap her arms around his neck and kiss him, which caused them to bump into the door then walls like a billiard ball before they finally fell laughing onto the bed.

"I thought it would be enjoyable to take a walk around the property," she said as he kissed a heated path down her neck.

"Later," he mumbled, his fingers going to the buttons on her silk blouse.

"Or perhaps you might like to try fishing," she wiggled beneath him and he groaned in return. "I hear trout are a challenge to catch." She teased him with another wiggle.

"There is only one challenge I am up to at the moment," he braced his arms on either side of her and captured her gaze. His green eyes flashed intently.

"I can be more difficult to land than a fish," she murmured.

He pressed her down onto the mattress. "Not if I have the right lure."

She burst into laughter, knowing that whatever tomorrow might bring, she was exactly where she needed to be today.

* * *

Their time at the resort was idyllic. They did manage to take a walk in the forest and enjoyed dinner with other lodgers one evening, but for the most part they kept to themselves in the cozy room and in each other's arms.

Of course, their lovemaking was interspersed with a million questions as Henry couldn't stop asking about things in her world.

Jordan began to think she could live this way if indeed there was no way to return home. As Henry cuddled her close on the sofa in front of the fire, she thought that perhaps she didn't even want to return to the twenty-first century. "It's not so very different," she finally said. "You have electricity and indoor plumbing and cars."

"How can you say that? The technology alone is so far advanced of anything we have now. Not to mention space travel and fast food restaurants."

She poked him with her elbow. "Sometimes technology is not always a good thing. There has been criminal activity due to the internet like banking fraud and stock market scams."

"In other words, mobsters and criminals continue to exist, just as they have from the beginning of time."

"And there are still men such as yourself who try to uncover evil and bring people to justice." She turned to him. "Which brings up the question as to how you managed to get time off to come with me."

"I happen to be on very good terms with the publisher, in addition to making his newspaper one of the world's best by writing some of his most impressive exposés. He also knows about my brother and that I will do anything, go anywhere to find his killer." He shrugged. "So if I happen to disappear for a few days, he doesn't worry."

She hugged him tightly. "If we could google him, we could find out what happened."

"See, I told you there were advantages in the future," he said, not missing a beat at her mention of *google*. He pulled her closer. "But since we don't have the internet, what can we possibly do instead?"

* * *

Jordan was enjoying a hot, steamy bath the next morning when Henry walked in reading the newspaper. Seeing as he was already dressed, she assumed he had been down to the front desk. He didn't seem aware of her presence.

"Did you bring breakfast back with you when you got your newspaper?" She teased as she knew the paper came first on his list of things to do each morning. The newspaper slowly lowered and his gaze slid from her head to her toes. He didn't say a word; just consumed her with a hungry gaze as though they hadn't spent most of the last two days in bed.

A knock sounded at the door.

"They wouldn't let me bring it back but assured me it would be delivered promptly." With a deadpan expression, he added, "Now, I wish I had told them to wait an hour."

She kicked water at him then reached for the towel he held out. "Get the door. I'm starving." He didn't move when she stood. "Henry. Go let him in or I'll throw your newspaper in the bathwater." He hurried out of the room, closing the door behind him so she had privacy to finish. When she emerged minutes later, wrapped in one of the resort's fluffy white robes, he was already at the small table where breakfast had been laid out. Jordan inhaled the sharp aroma of coffee and the tangy scent of sausage and her stomach growled. Henry was already buried behind his newspaper, although she noticed it wasn't the *Daily Journal*.

"And have aliens taken over yet?" she asked as she poured herself a cup of coffee.

"If they have, no one's reporting on it," he replied in a perfectly serious voice.

She laughed out loud. "I love y..." she caught herself before adding, "...your sense of humor." Still, she could feel her cheeks heat.

He folded the paper and dropped it to the floor beside him. As much as he had his rituals about the newspaper, he gave her his complete attention when she was in his vicinity. Yet not always with the intensity he did now. "And I love..." he paused as she had done, "...your laughter." His eyes glittered and his lips quirked into a smile. He stood to hold her chair, the awkwardness quickly dispelled.

"There was an article about Harry Houdini," he said as he cut into his slice of ham and began eating. "Apparently he is returning to Chicago for several performances at the New Palace Theater. He's making a name for himself and can now garner a much larger audience than when the Kirklands held their private events for him in the past."

"He is one of the greatest magicians of our time," Jordan said. When Henry raised a brow, she amended, "He will be considered so."

"He's an escapist; an illusionist. You can't tell me he doesn't have keys and picks hidden on his person, or other ways of escaping."

"The power of magic is in the audience, not the performer. You have to believe," she teased.

"Regardless, it got me thinking. Besides a locksmith, who else would have an abundance of knowledge about locks?"

Jordan wanted to believe she could return to her own time. Yet as she looked across the table, her heart hurt with the idea of leaving Henry. What they had was so special; so unique, she realized, not for the first time, that she would happily give up the world she had known for the world in which there was Henry Douglas, and love.

* * *

The clanking of the train wheels should have lulled Henry to sleep, for they hadn't spent much of their time at the resort in bed. Well, they had, but not in the pursuit of sleep. Now, he watched Jordan as she perused the passing scenery. He wouldn't have misspoken at breakfast if the words he had almost said – I love you – had indeed come out of his mouth. His gaze caressed her features although he already had them memorized. She was beautiful but that beauty came from within. For all that had happened to her, she managed to live in a world foreign to her except for what she knew of history. She had adapted readily and he wondered if he would be as resilient if it happened to him.

He knew he had fallen in love with her before he had known she was from the future. That only added to her uniqueness. She was a kind and gentle woman, even respectful of Beatrice, who did not treat her well. Part of it had to be her attitude toward Eddie, who praised her endlessly. Children inherently know if adults are good or evil and he had the feeling Eddie would choose Jordan over him, even for the short time he had known her.

He was jarred from his thoughts as the train swung sharply around a curve and began to slow. They would be at the station soon, and so many thoughts still rattled around in his brain, the foremost being what was he to do about Jordan?

Their search was to find her a way back to her own time, but their entire past days together had led him to a singular conclusion. He did not want her to return to 2022. He loved her and he wanted her in his life. He needed her there. If he told her how he felt, would she give up her quest and stay here with him? Did he have the right to ask that of her? And even if she did want the same thing, would fate allow them to stay together?

Chapter 13

Henry was quiet on the trip back to the city, but Jordan had her own confused thoughts and couldn't summon the energy to engage in conversation. They took a taxi to the house, where he carried her bag up the steps and followed her in when she unlocked the door.

Beatrice met them in the foyer, dressed to go out. "You're back," she said with surprise and Jordan detected a nervous warble in her voice.

"I told you I'd return this evening. Where are you off to?"

"I've been invited to the New Palace Theater."

Henry coughed and when she glanced his way, he covered his mouth with a hand, but his eyes twinkled. "Really?" he managed to squeak out.

Beatrice tilted her head at a haughty angle. "Certainly. I have decided I enjoy being in *the audience* at the theater, even if the performance is somewhat colorful. Besides, Mr. Farintino, the producer, was kind enough to invite me."

"Really," Henry squeaked again. Jordan looked from one to the other. Something was going on. She wouldn't get anything out of Beatrice, but Henry on the other hand...

Before she could question him, he grabbed Beatrice's coat from the hook and held it out for her. "Have an enjoyable evening," he said and actually winked at her. "Take the taxi I have waiting. I'll find a way home."

"Thank you. You're very kind."

The minute the door closed behind her, Jordan turned on Henry. "Who *was* that woman?"

Henry burst out laughing and couldn't or wouldn't stop until Jordan stepped close and cupped his head with both hands. "What secret do you hold that would cause Beatrice to be...nice?"

He gave her a quick kiss. "I suppose it is no secret now, since she appears to be dating the producer rather than taking instruction from him as part of the chorus line."

"Are you serious? Beatrice has been disappearing because she was dancing in the chorus line of a vaudeville show?" Every word rose in pitch until she was practically squealing. Her eyes narrowed. "And you knew?" She slapped his chest. "That's why she's been so nice to you. Why didn't you tell me?"

"Honestly, it just happened recently and I had many, many other things on my mind and more important secrets to keep."

"Well, if it makes her nice to be around, I'll bake Mr. Farintino a cake so he continues to take her out."

He pulled her close and his face grew serious. "Beatrice can handle him. We have other things to do. But first, thank you for sharing the weekend with me."

"You don't need—" she began, but he put a finger to her lips.

"And thank you for believing in me enough to share your secrets with me. I will do whatever it takes to help you find the answers you seek."

She heard the words, but his tone of voice was less than convincing. She wondered if he was having second thoughts, just as she was. Dread sat heavy in the pit of her stomach and she didn't dare ask, for fear she wouldn't like the answer. Instead, she wrapped her arms around his neck and kissed him like there was no tomorrow. Because one day, that might well be the case.

"Pardon me, Miss," Maddie interrupted their interlude as she hustled by. "I was about to start the fire in your room for when you came home." She gave them an unrepentant grin and hurried up the stairs.

"At least *she* approves of me," Henry said.

"Oh, I'm sure you have Beatrice's favor, too. She's impressed with anyone who can 'one up' her."

He frowned at her clique. "You know what I mean."

"I didn't deliberately go out of my way to discover her secrets."

"Still, it's great to be in the plus category."

"And will I be in your 'plus' side if I can get tickets for the Houdini performance?"

"Absolutely. Let me know when." Regardless of any ulterior motives, she wanted to meet the famous magician.

* * *

She didn't hear from Henry for several days and wondered if he forgot about getting performance tickets, but from what the girls on the telephone exchange night shift said, there had been constant nightly raids across the city as the police force tried to capture bootleggers, shut down illegal speakeasies and stills operating in the city. They hoped the constant pressure would topple the liquor industry, but Jordan knew it would only become more secretive.

She knew Henry would be in the thick of it, rushing from precinct to precinct, collecting names and other information to get his newspaper the top stories in addition to hunting for the illusive man who shot his brother. Working most nights and doing follow-up the next day would have left him little time for entertainment, so she was surprised when he met her outside of work three days later.

"I managed tickets for Houdini's last performance tonight. I know it's late notice, but things have been non-stop."

"I've heard that from the night shift," she replied with a smile. "I'd be delighted to go."

Her delight began to turn to displeasure as they sat awaiting the beginning of the performance. Henry had been complaining ever since picking her up and she'd had about enough.

"If you don't like Houdini and don't believe in magic, why did you come?"

"It's not magic. He's an illusionist and escapist."

"When you don't know how something is done, I consider that magic."

"Alright, I'll give you that. But the man wants everyone to believe in *his* magic and yet he takes it upon himself to discredit those who believe in other types of illusions."

"What are you talking about?"

"He makes it a point to debunk mediums and spiritualists, saying there is no such thing as contact with the departed."

"Well, I don't think those two views are mutually exclusive."

"Granted, but it's mildly contradictory for him to say he doesn't believe when he and his wife, Bess, have a pact that when one of them dies, they will try to contact each other through seances."

"How would you know that?" she asked in disbelief.

"Society's matrons are notorious gossips," he whispered just as the small orchestra that had been playing hit a crescendo and the curtains rose. "I was at the Kirkland's for his performance, don't you remember?"

She did recall that night, what seemed a lifetime ago. She had gone to the Kirkland building as it was the chamber offices, not a private residence. Now, knowing that Houdini had been there in 1926, at the same moment but ninety-six years earlier than her, made her think the man might be more important to her story than she originally thought.

From the moment the illusionist walked onto the stage, Jordan was captivated. He was rather small in stature but had the confidence and stage presence of a giant. From the simplest of handcuff escapes to his more daring act of popping out of a trunk in which he had been shackled and locked inside, she marveled at his skill. His wife, Bess, acted as his assistant, prancing across the stage with chains, then padlocks, showing the audience how strong they were. During one escape attempt, she even had an audience member come onto the stage to put the last lock in place on the vertical glass box Houdini had stepped into.

The curtain around the glass was closed and Bess held up an oversized clock with large hands that indicated only minutes. She set it to zero and pushed a button and the second hand began to move to the sound of the orchestra playing a mysteriously eerie tick-tock beat.

"How many minutes?" she called out to the audience.

"One!" Everyone shouted back.

The eerie tick-tock of the orchestra matched Jordan's heartbeat. The entire audience appeared to be holding their collective breaths.

"How many minutes?" Bess called out again.

"Two!" Louder this time. There was nothing better than audience participation.

The tick-tock sped up before the entire orchestra burst into a crescendo and then stopped in silence.

"Bess, my love, how many minutes?" This time, a loud male voice asked the question from the back of the theater. Everyone turned as Houdini marched down the aisle toward the stage. The curtain around the box opened to reveal an empty glass container. Thunderous applause erupted.

Jordan turned to Henry with a grin. "Don't tell me you can't believe in that."

"He is quite the showman." That seemed to be the best she would get from Henry, the doubter.

Houdini and Bess bowed and walked off stage, but the audience didn't want the show to end. The applause continued until they reappeared. This time, Bess helped the magician into a straitjacket, carefully buckling all the straps, pulling each to make sure the audience could see that he was secure. When she stepped back, Houdini stood perfectly still. Then, in a matter of seconds, with what appeared to be only a few twists and turns, he was standing there holding the straight jacket out in one hand before dropping it to the stage floor.

Although the audience wanted more, the two performers didn't return after taking several bows. Gradually people began filing out of their seats. Henry stood, holding out a hand to Jordan.

"As long as we're here, I might as well get a few comments from the man for an article."

Always in search of a story, she cautioned him. "Please don't get into a discussion of his beliefs. I'd hate to find you padlocked in a trunk somewhere." At his look of mock chagrin, she waved him away. "Go on, I'll see if I can have a look at his locks."

She watched Henry weave through the crowd, swimming upstream as it were, until he disappeared through a door at the side of the stage. She stepped into the aisle, now fairly empty, and walked down to the other side of the stage and up the stairs. Men were already taking the stage props such as the glass container and securing his trunk on a roller bed for transport.

"Excuse me, may I have a look at his locks?" She stepped closer to where one of the men was laying several items into the top section of the steamer trunk.

"I'm sorry, ma'am, but nobody is allowed to see the magician's things."

"Only for a minute, please." She had caught a glimpse of a silver and gold lock on the tray and needed a closer look. "It's rather important."

The man waved to one of the crew waiting for instructions and he moved forward. Jordan thought he was going to move the trunk and she desperately wanted to see the lock. She took a step forward before suddenly being grabbed from behind and bodily lifted off her feet.

"Wait. Let me go!" She kicked out as he turned her away from the trunk. Her connection to his shins didn't faze him

"Sorry, ma'am. Boss said you don't belong up here, so off you go." His arms loosened and for a moment Jordan thought he meant to throw her off the stage. Instead, he sat her roughly down and gave her a healthy nudge in the back. She stumbled, grabbed the curtains to catch her balance, then hurried down the stairs as she saw Henry come back from the dressing room.

"They won't let me look at his locks," she explained when she caught up with him. "We have to go ask Mr. Houdini."

"Not a good idea," he replied as he guided her up the aisle toward the exit instead of backstage.

"Why not?" She tried to pull to a stop but his hand on her back kept propelling her forward.

He grimaced. "Because I didn't exactly follow your advice, so my conversation with the man was...longer than 'no', but the rest is unprintable."

She sighed. "At least he didn't ship you off in a trunk. We'll have to find another way because I really think I saw the lock in his trunk."

That stopped his hurried pace. "Are you sure?"

Now she shrugged. "Maybe? They wouldn't let me close, but at least one had both silver and gold. That matches the metals on the lock I had. What are the chances of it being the same lock?"

"The idea was that we might speak to Houdini to see if he recognized the maker of the lock you had from the etching as he's undoubtedly an expert on such devices. I'd say the chances of them *being the same lock* are zero to none. Unless you can speak with Mrs. Houdini, woman to woman, we'll never know."

"All right. I can do that," Jordan said, hoping to convince herself as well as Henry. They had seemed so close, and she wasn't about to let Henry's stubbornness get in the way.

* * *

Jordan never had the opportunity to visit with Bess Houdini. The morning society pages held a message from Mrs. Kirkland, who appeared to be the magician's champion. "I am truly saddened that Houdini's visit to the city has come to an end. It is unfortunate for those Chicagoans who did not take the time to attend his performances that the magician is on a tight schedule and has left on the morning train for destinations east. If Chicago is ever to become the center for society and the arts, we must all take the time and embrace the opportunities that are so generously offered."

Jordan had never met Mrs. Kirkland, and her comments seemed rather rude. Apparently she was the self-proclaimed matron of Chicago society and as such felt it her right to admonish others. Jordan left for work, sincerely happy not to be part of the Kirkland circle.

Her good mood lasted through the morning, but shortly after her short lunch break, her supervisor tapped her on the shoulder. Jordan removed her headset but before she could question the woman, she scowled.

"Follow me," she said curtly and turned away. Since Jordan couldn't recall any mishaps on her shift, she couldn't imagine why she was being summoned. Until they walked into the front foyer and she saw Henry standing there, hat in hand.

"This man insists on speaking with you, though he has no authority and we prohibit such encounters during working hours. He refuses to go away." There was no mistaking the animosity in her voice.

"I didn't ask him here," she tried to defend herself.

"That is beside the point. He is here, insisting. So speak to him and be done with it. I will mark your timecard accordingly and put the required reprimand in your file. Another mishap and you will lose your position here. We can't have it."

The entire time she spoke, Jordan's cheeks grew more heated. Henry looked uncomfortable as well. The minute she left the foyer, Jordan turned to Henry.

"What the hell?" The curse slipped out and his eyes widened. What did he expect? It was mild by the standards of her time. "I have been listening for names on every shift," she hissed the reminder of his request to keep her ears open while on her headset. "There is nothing so important about your precious mobsters to cost me my job!" She could think of no other reason for him to barge into her work.

He stepped toward her, pulling an envelope out of his breast pocket. "You won't believe what I got in the mail this morning." His excitement only fueled her anger, but he didn't notice.

"Unless it's a ticket home; to my home—"

"Just read it." He held the envelope out
and Jordan could see a fancy designed
return address. She looked closer –
Masterlock, Milwaukee, Wisconsin.

"What?" She cleared her throat.

"I told you John Appleton said he would
write another locksmith he knew about the
design. Apparently, Harry Soref, a locksmith
in Wisconsin, knows."

She quickly opened the envelope and
withdrew the letter.

"My friend,

*"I was most curious to receive your
letter with the enclosed sketch. I had not
seen that design since it was given to me to
commission a padlock by Harry Houdini.
As you know, Harry is himself a master
locksmith but wanted me to use my newest
laminated steel materials for this particular
padlock.*

*"The lock mechanism is masterful even
though the intricate gold and silver façade
is just so – for theatrical looks only and of
no other use. It is a one-of-a-kind creation,
so it is odd that you have a rubbing of said
lock.*

*"I hope this is useful information for
you. I look forward to hearing more about
this etching and the reason for your inquiry.*

"My regards, Harry Soref."

"Good lord, is everyone in this century
named Harry?" Jordan looked up from her
reading.

"That's your take-away?" Henry's brows lifted in disbelief.

She looked at the letter again. "Harry Houdini commissioned Harry Serof to make him a lock…" Her voice trailed off. "Oh, God. It *is* Houdini's lock!"

"The reason for my urgency in getting here to see you. We need to get to the hotel and request that lock."

Jordan's excitement faded. "Damn it! They left on the morning train."

Henry burst out laughing. When Jordan speared him with a glare, he held up both hands in defense. "I didn't know you had such a mouth on you," he said with a grin.

"You have no idea what I might say if I get really mad." She deliberately slowed her breathing as she folded the letter and inserted it into the envelope. "We were so, so close." Her eyes began to water and she turned away.

Henry's hands were warm on her shoulders as he pulled her close. "We'll catch up with him. I'll go to the news office and see if I can find the schedule for where he would be heading next. Then we catch the first train to follow him."

"Henry, I can't just take off again. You heard Miss Grant. I'll lose my job."

"If the padlock is the same as the one that imprinted your notebook, that means you *brought Houdini's padlock with you to a time when Houdini was performing*. If you get your hands on that lock again, do you honestly think you will be coming back *here* to your job?" His voice was deathly quiet.

She pitched forward, lightheaded, and Henry managed to catch her before she hit the floor. He half carried her to a bench by the wall and she sank with a plop onto the hard wood.

"What are we going to do?" she whispered.

He turned his head away, staring at the wall. She watched his Adam's apple bob convulsively. When he returned his gaze to hers, his face was the saddest she had ever seen. He took her hands though his were shaking ever so slightly.

"We have to see this through," he said but his voice quivered.

She took a deep breath and slowly nodded.

"Go back to the switchboard. I'll get a message to you when I find out where he went."

He pulled her to her feet and when she felt steady enough, he released her hands.

"I..." She wanted to tell him how she felt, but now was certainly not the time for declarations.

He seemed to sense her thoughts. He kissed her softly on the forehead before putting on his hat and turning to leave without another word. There were no words, for neither of them knew what the next hours, or days, would hold.

Jordan managed to get through her shift and take the EL home before collapsing onto her bed, emotionally exhausted by the events of the day. There was hope, so why did she feel so hopeless?

She fell into a fitful sleep until Madde knocked on her door to say she had a telephone call. She hurried downstairs in her stocking feet. Beatrice looked up from the magazine she read, opened her mouth, probably to reprimand, but upon seeing Jordan's disheveled appearance, snapped it shut again. Jordan ignored her, turning into the study and grabbing the telephone receiver.

"Hello?"

"Jordan, it's Henry. I couldn't find Houdini's schedule in any newspaper, so I called Madelyne Kirkland who said they're set to perform in Detroit in two days' time. There aren't any trains leaving tonight, but we can catch the early morning dispatch. I'll be by to pick you up at six."

"Six?" Jordan groaned.

"You all right?"

"Hmm? Yes, fine. I'll be ready." Jordan tried to sound positive even as her stomach flipped and her chest squeezed so tight she could barely breathe. The minute she hung up, she hurried back up to her room, closing the door behind her, only to find Maddie setting the fire in the hearth.

"Was that your man?" she asked with a grin.

"My man?" she repeated, then realized that even if Henry hadn't given his name when he rang, Maddie knew everything that went on in the residence. She thought about trusting the maid with her secret, but decided instead to simply say thanks.

"I suppose he is that. In fact, we must go away early in the morning, and I'm not sure when we'll return." *Or if,* she thought silently. "I want to thank you for befriending me when I first arrived."

"Nonsense," replied the maid, "It's easy to be nice to nice people." She turned at the door, a serious expression on her usually cheerful face. "Will you be all right, Miss?"

Jordan had absolutely no idea what tomorrow would bring. "I hope so." She managed a brief smile.

After Maddie left, Jordan looked around the room and in the clothes cabinet, trying to decide what to pack. She finally gave up, deciding that if things went well, she wouldn't need any of the clothes she had here in 1926. And if nothing happened, they would return to Chicago on the next train with nobody the wiser.

Sleep illuded her although she laid down and tried to rest after taking a bath. She had missed dinner and sneaked downstairs for some cold cuts she knew Cook had in the icebox. Although her stomach protested, she ate a sandwich and drank a cup of tea, carefully washing her dishes when done.

She was dressed and waiting by five-thirty and when she could stand it no longer, tiptoed downstairs, carrying her shoes in one hand and her clutch in the other. Cook would already be in the kitchen, but Jordan hoped any noise she made would be covered by Cook's pot banging and cupboard door slamming. The instant the grandfather clock began to strike the hour, she slipped on her shoes, grabbed her coat and quietly slipped out the door. Henry was just getting out of the taxi.

"Good," he said as she rushed toward him. "I didn't want to ring the bell at this hour."

She slid onto the cold leather seat, and Henry climbed in behind her. As the taxi started, she grabbed his hand.

"You're cold," he said, rubbing the top of her hand with his warm one.

"Nerves," she managed to say.

"Tell me about it." They both seemed to be thinking the same thing, and yet neither could put those thoughts into words.

"Here you are," the cab driver said.

Henry paid the man and opened the door, reaching back in for his briefcase after Jordan exited. Early morning fog made it almost impossible to see the train station, and Jordan grabbed Henry's arm to keep from stumbling on the rough ground. Inside the depot was not much warmer than outside and Jordan shivered in her coat.

Henry purchased their tickets, which included a train switch in Indianapolis and explained the schedule, but Jordan paid little attention. She was trying very hard not to get sick.

A whistle blew and Henry nudged her out the door onto the train platform where they were immediately enveloped in the fog again. It was difficult to tell the train engine steam from the fog, as both created an eerie scene reminiscent of all the Halloween movies she had watched as a kid. She almost giggled at the thought when she realized today was actually Halloween.

Henry guided her along the track until they were about midway. "We can board here and walk inside to our seats," he said as a conductor set down a small stepstool.

She stopped, unable to take another step. "Maybe this isn't a good idea," she whispered.

Henry stepped in front of her, his back to the train. "What do you mean?" He tilted her chin so she had to look directly at him.

"Maybe we shouldn't go after the lock." Her stomach churned even more.

"Are you saying you don't want to try to go back to your own time?" He sounded as confused as she felt.

"Do you want me to go back?"

"This isn't about me. *Do you want to go back?*" He emphasized each word, getting louder even over the hissing of the steam.

"Yes. No. I don't know," she cried. "I love you." Silence met her declaration and when she looked up, she found Henry staring over her shoulder, a deep frown marring his features. She turned to see a man several yards away, leaning against the depot wall, a fedora pulled low over his forehead. Even so, Jordan realized he was staring right at them.

"Get on the train," Henry barked, trying to turn her toward the small steps.

"Who is that man?"

"Tommy O'Connor," he hissed.

She grabbed his arm to catch his attention, the name panicking her.

He refused to look at her. "Jordan, do as I say. *Get on the train.*" When she didn't move, he circled her waist and bodily lifted her past the stepstool onto the train carriage.

She turned in outrage, only to have him push his briefcase into her arms. "Take this and get inside. I'll be right behind you." Even as he spoke, he stepped away from the train.

"Henry, don't." She reached for him, but he was beyond her grasp, walking parallel to the train but toward the man in the fog.

She hurried through the door and down the aisle to an empty bench. She jerked open the window, then grabbed the frame when the train lurched to a start, whistle blowing and steam rising.

"Come back!" she yelled, barely able to see his dark silhouette.

She watched as the fog created a slow-motion drama. A second dark shape moved toward Henry. A bright flash, followed by the sharp crack of a pistol shot, split the air for a brief second before Henry disappeared from sight.

"Henry!" she cried, but her screams were swallowed by the fog.

Chapter 14
Chicago, 2022

Henry woke with a gasp and bolted upright, immediately falling back, the pain in his side so intense he thought he'd pass out. Instead, deafening noise and a jumble of voices jarred him to awareness. He tried to move but felt tied down. He groaned past the mask covering his face.

"Hold tight, Mr. Gallagher, I've got to stop the bleeding." The disembodied voice sounded very concerned and Henry wondered if he were dead, or at least close to it from the amount of pain. "We're less than five from the hospital. Just hold on." The last of the words were lost as Henry faded into a whirlpool of color.

He came to when they transferred him to a different hard surface. The pain had ebbed but when he tried to open his eyes, the bright light had them slamming shut again. He mumbled beneath the mask.

"Hang in there, man." A hand to his shoulder accompanied the voice. "Shot in the right side," the voice went on. "Not sure if it hit anything vital but we had a hard time controlling the bleeding." Someone poked along his side, the pain slowly ebbing as a prick in his arm indicated morphine had been administered.

Were they talking about him? He concentrated on what he remembered; anything to take his mind off the pain. He and Jordan had just reached the train platform to board for Detroit. They were in pursuit of Houdini who had something she wanted. But he had seen Tommy OConnor, the gangster who had been standing on the train platform; the man who had killed his brother He couldn't go with Jordan until he had confronted the bastard.

Oh, God. Jordan. He fought the drowsiness, managing to reach the mask covering his face and ripping it off. "Jordan?" He lashed out at the man beside him, grabbing his shirt with what little strength he had. "Where?"

Someone from the other side replaced the mask. Henry squinted past the bright lights, trying to speak but all that came out were muffled words. "Where is Jordan?" Had she been shot too?

"You were alone," the man he had by the shirtfront said. "A homeless man sleeping in an old railcar found you in-between some tracks. There was no one else around."

Not on a train platform? His arm dropped weakly to his side as his vision blurred. At least Jordan was safe. His last coherent thought was that he hadn't told her how he felt about her. That oversight would be corrected as soon as he woke up.

* * *

Waking up didn't occur for over twenty-four hours, though Henry didn't realize it and even when he finally came to, he had no idea where he was and how he got there. The minute he opened his eyes, the room was flooded with men in white jackets; doctors he assumed, and women with bright colored smocks and trousers. They tapped and probed and took his temperature and listened to his heart and told him how lucky he was that the bullet hadn't hit any vital organs and he'd be up and back to normal in no time.

From the pain in his side, Henry wondered how long "no time" converted to actual time. Once the doctors filed out, two men in suits replaced them, flashing badges too quickly for him to read but identifying themselves as detectives. He should have realized something was wrong when they insisted he was found in the middle of 95th Street near Illinois Ave. He told them he had been ready to board a train and they told him he was mistaken.

"How does one mistake what one is doing, when only that person has knowledge of their action?" he asked as politely as he could manage.

The taller of the two looked blank for a minute, then broke into a rusty laugh. "Good one, Gallagher. Always twisting the words around like a puzzle. My wife, she likes your wandering columns but for me, you should stick to the historical gangster stuff."

Henry tilted his head and looked from one man to the other. He vaguely recalled the ambulance person calling him Gallagher but had been in too much pain at the time to think about it. He used his first and middle names – Henty Douglas – in both his columns for the post and his personal life. How did they know his real name? And he had done very few columns on gangsters as his editor tended to frown on him calling attention to the mobs that secretly ran Chicago. But that wasn't important at the moment.

"Did you find Jordan; the lady with me?"

Short man scratched his head. "No one was with you; no one was seen in the area where you were found – 95th and Illinois." He repeated as if Henry hadn't just denied being on the street. "Why were you at the old train depot anyway?"

"Catching a train," Henry replied. "They run every day."

This brought another laugh from the two men. "Not since the sixties. And not at the old depot since the forties."

The men were giving him a headache and their story was confusing. Jordan was with him; they were boarding a train.

"You got shot."

"Well, at least we agree on that," Henry mocked.

"But who shot you? I'm sure you've made some enemies over the years with some of the stuff you write." This was the short guy, who apparently wasn't a fan.

"Tommy O'Connor," Henry said.

"Never hear of him," the man replied.

"He considers himself a big time mobster, but he's a minor player in the runner business. I wasn't intentionally looking for him but he knows I've been gathering information on him and Danny Walsh; both gangsters and neither of whom have been seen in years. Now, they're suddenly back in Chicago?"

"It's no wonder you got shot, you trying to get something on those guys." He lowered his voice, "Just a word of advice, leave the numbers runners alone. You'll get nothing but trouble and we don't have time to clean up your mess."

It shouldn't surprise Henry that the police wanted him to stay out of it. Word was always circulating about corruption within the police force, although he knew it didn't apply to all policemen. Still, running a little rum and shooting a man tended to require different attention, if you asked him.

He reached for the button the nurse had said could be used to call her. The minute she came in the room, he dismissed the two police officers. "Find Jordan Foster. If not to corroborate my story than to at least make sure she's alright. I'll heal without any more of your attention, thank you."

"We'll be in touch," the tall one said.

"Will you?" he replied with an arch of brow. They no more wanted to investigate a shooting by a gangster than to quit taking kickbacks from the illegal liquor trade.

"I may have to limit your visitors, Mr. Gallagher," the nurse said after the door closed behind the two.

"Why is everyone calling me that?" He let his gaze roam over the petite form of the nurse, strangely attired though she was. Where were the long skirts and starched aprons and those cute little hats they always wore to cover their hair?

"You had no identification on you when they brought you in; only a small pad of paper in your jacket pocket, but the ambulance driver recognized you from your column, and maybe a book cover or something?" She shrugged off any concern about his identity, but an uneasy feeling had settled in the pit of his stomach. He rubbed it gently, careful not to tamper with the white bandage on his side.

"Are you hungry?" she asked, noticing his action. "The doctor didn't put any dietary restrictions on your chart, so I can get you a late lunch, if you like."

"One of those hamburgers everybody's raving about and some French fries."

"I don't think anybody's raving about our burgers," she replied with a laugh. "They tend to be dry and they refuse to salt the French fries. How about some spaghetti and a nice salad?"

He wasn't much of a salad guy but at the moment he was hungry enough not to argue with the cute nurse. He had a more critical issue to attend to as soon as she left the room. Gingerly, with his hand holding his side, he slid out of bed to find a toilet. Leveraging himself up, he grabbed the bar at the side of the bed when the room began to spin. Sudden loud noise filled the room and he frantically looked around for the source. Braced on the wall in one corner, a large screen flashed with a man shouting at him to buy laundry detergent.

Henry fell back onto the bed and searched the buttons on the side rail. Finding an arrow, he pushed it until the voice on the box lowered to a reasonable tone. All he could do was stare. Every conversation he had had with Jordan flashed through his mind. He hadn't believed her at first when she explained where she was from – almost a hundred years in the future. But he had to be looking at what she called a television.

His gaze rapidly took in the rest of the room. The monitor with its quiet beeps and wiggly lines was no doubt standard in hospitals, but the small screen next to it with the keyboard in front was not; at least not to his knowledge. He picked up a small cylindrical device from a base and turned it over, recognizing a keypad for a telephone although the shape was entirely different and there was no cord connecting it to the base. He pushed the zero and held it up to his ear.

"Hello, may I help you?" the voice said and Henry grinned. Amazing.

"Connect me to Miss Jordan Foster," he replied. Finding her would be easier than he thought.

"Is she a patient?" the voice asked.

"No, she's..." Henry's heart pounded and he set the phone down as gently as if it might explode. In the sudden understanding and excitement – yes, excitement – of knowing what must have happened when he was shot, it now came to him that while he might have come to the future, he had no idea whether Jordan had also returned to her time. And he still wasn't sure exactly what that time period was.

Was it even possible? He continued surveying the room, looking for anything that would call his bluff and remind him he had been shot and perhaps the trauma was inducing hallucinations of some sort. Given the time he had spent with Jordan and the stories she had told, there was little doubt he would dream about the future, if indeed he were dreaming. He closed his eyes tightly, hoping to clear his vision yet when he opened them, everything remained as it had been, including the large screen where now a half-naked woman was washing her hair. Any illusions he may have had about brain trauma were shattered when a man walked through the door and threw a newspaper at him.

"God damnit, you disappear for months on a story only to let us get scooped by the Times and the story is about you!" A balding man in a rumpled suit, almost as wide as he was tall, stormed into the room. He looked vaguely familiar but at this point, Henry wasn't making any assumptions.

He groaned as the paper hit his side. He had never heard of the Sun Times, but directly beneath their flag, headlines in bold black shouted at him, "Reporter shot in broad daylight."

"I told you to leave that story alone. Now you not only got scooped, you're laid up for who knows how long." The man barely paused before continuing, "Could be good for some column inches, though. Your fingers still work, don't they?"

This had to be his editor, though damned if Henry could remember his name. Actually, he wouldn't even know his name if his understanding of the situation was correct. That might take more time, and he didn't want to get fired in the meantime. From everything Jordan had told him, money was a very necessary commodity.

"Sorry they didn't give me a pad and pencil in the ambulance," he grumbled, testing the man's attitude. "I could have written a nice first-person point of view. Maybe even taken a photo of the hole in my side."

The man's jaw dropped, then snapped shut and he looked a bit chagrined. Then he barked a laugh and slapped his thigh. "I knew there was a reason I kept you around. Remind me of myself back in the day. I'll have Penny drop off your laptop. I'm not paying you to lie around."

The nurse came back in with a lunch tray. "You'll have to leave. Mr. Gallagher has had enough visitors today." She turned to him. "And you, why are you trying to get out of bed?"

"I need to get out of here," Henry said, the sudden stress of the entire situation causing a pain in his chest. The monitor clicked faster.

"Not today," she retorted, setting his tray on the table and helping him back into the bed. She pointed to his editor with one hand while she listened to his heart. "You; out." She looked down at him. "You; relax. You'll be here a while."

But Henry didn't relax. As soon as the nurse shut the door, he grabbed the newspaper his editor had left, his gaze landing on the tags under the newspaper banner. "Holy mother of God," he whispered in awe. The date of October 31, 2022, jumped out at him. At the moment he couldn't recall whether Jordan had said what year she was from, or just "the future." But they had been on the train platform on October 31. His brain grappled to comprehend the fact that instead of dying when Tommy O'Connor shot him, he had gone through time to almost one hundred years in the future.

Was this better than one hundred years into the past, where he knew what had happened? He wondered if he should be more upset; hysterical even, over having been thrown into the future against his wishes. He no doubt would be if not for Jordan. He suddenly understood why she had been so confused and why she had kept her origins a secret for so long. For all that Jordan had told him and what he had seen already, this could prove an exciting time. He just needed the knowledge to navigate through it. With that in mind, he devoured the newspaper from front to back.

"Holy catfish! Thirty-five thousand dollars for a car? I won't make that in a lifetime." He whistled under his breath. But when he read some of the ads for jobs, he was equally surprised at the salaries and thought perhaps one could afford almost anything in this day and age. He found the column this guy Gallagher wrote, although the date was from several months ago with a small caveat stating the writer was on hiatus. He squinted at the grainy photograph, only an inch or so square. He supposed it looked like him, or he looked like it. No wonder people mistook him for the writer. People tended to jump to conclusions and in this case, it was easy to do. He had the same name and looks. He even did the same type of job.

He closed his eyes and tried to recall every detail of his time just prior and after getting shot, although the after part was rather more hazy. Yet the instant he thought of Jordan and how he had ignored her in favor of facing off with O'Connor, his brain crashed. He had to find her; to know that she was okay.

How did one find out if another person existed? The telephone operator hadn't been that helpful but perhaps she only handled the switchboard for the hospital. This time when he picked up the telephone and the woman asked how she could help, he asked for an outside line. "Dial nine," she said and hung up.

So he did, then dialed zero when the tone came on. This person wasn't any more helpful when he asked to connect to Jordan Foster. In fact, it didn't sound like a real voice at all, if that were possible. "There are three hundred sixty-two Fosters in the greater Chicago area. For more information, visit your provider on line with an appropriate address."

Henry's head throbbed. If not for the understanding nurse, he might think he was in a foreign country because he didn't understand half of what he heard, on the telephone or the television. He went back to reading the newspaper; at least that was in English. He was amazed at the format changes over the years. The print was larger and more uniform and the ink didn't smudge. The news was similar and yet different – stock markets, shootings and robberies; local, national and international news. From what he could decipher, the world hadn't learned its lesson from the Great War, and politics were as corrupt as city affairs had been back in the day.

He laid the paper aside and turned his head toward the window although he could only see blue sky and a few puffy clouds. How was he to cope in this world? He had been amazed and at first doubtful when Jordan had tried to explain all the inventions and changes in her time. After all, she had no proof and couldn't produce any evidence that things such as remote control existed. Now, perhaps it was he who was losing his mind or only imagining things. Perhaps the trauma of being shot and falling had injured more than his side. It might be natural for him to hallucinate about things Jordan had told him. Perhaps...

"Hello. May I come in?"

He turned toward the charming voice to see a redhaired pixie standing in the doorframe. Her lilting accent reminded him of his mother and instant homesickness swept over him.

"Has a fairy come to take me home?" A bit of the brogue crept into his voice;

something he tried very hard to erase on a daily basis. Her look of confusion told him his imitation needed work. He waved a hand in dismissal and she took it for permission to enter. She promptly put a slim metallic object on the table in front of him and a sack beside it from which the most amazing aroma arose. He wasn't one for alliteration, but in this case it was true.

He snatched open the bag and pulled out a wrapped package, warm to the touch. Opening it, he discovered a hamburger, one of the newest foods sweeping the restaurants in Chicago. It was a good-sized meal on a bun that a person could eat while going about their business instead of sitting at a table with plate and silverware. He ate them almost daily as it saved an incredible amount of time and he hated to cook for himself.

Without thought he bit into it and closed his eyes in ecstasy. It wasn't how he remembered, but still tasted divine. "You are an angel. How'd you know?" he mumbled between bites.

"Because you eat them every day?" she asked with a raised eyebrow.

He still hadn't come to terms with who he was or why he was here, but apparently some things didn't change through time. "How do you know that? In fact, who are you?"

He was laid up in bed with tubes and wires attached all over and yet she backed away from him as if he might leap on her person. He popped the last of the hamburger into his mouth and wiped his hands on the closest thing, the bed sheet.

"Wait; wait," He waved a hand as she slowly backed toward the door. "Look. I've been shot. I don't remember much. Help a guy out, would you?"

"You were shot in the side, not the head."

Whoever she was, this gal wasn't taking crap off him. "I fell and hit my head when I was shot." A weak excuse, for sure, but possible. She appeared to think it over.

"You don't remember me?"

"Sweetheart, I don't remember my own name." Stick to the truth as much as possible, he told himself. It's easier to remember than a pack of lies. Yet his comment had her scowling again. "What?"

"I'll give you a pass this once, but don't be calling me sweetheart."

"What do I call you?" Hard to believe any woman not wanting to be called by an endearment. But one never knew anymore. Ever since women gained the vote just a few years ago, everything changed. We, as in all the beleaguered men he knew, were having a hell of a time figuring out what was proper anymore, and apparently that was still the case one hundred years later.

"My name is Penny O'Neil and just so you don't have to ask, I'm your assistant at the *Tribune* and Mr. Harris asked me to come by with your laptop so you could work." She pointed to the shiny object beside the crumbled hamburger sack.

He worked for the *Tribune*? He grinned as he slid his thumb along the seam of the object and it popped open. He was liking this condition more and more – until he watched a screen turn colors, flash and a picture of mountains filled the space, along with a small box with the word "password" beneath it. He had seen typewriters at the Chicago Daily Journal where he worked, but he rarely used one and nothing he'd seen looked like this. He preferred his pad and pencil.

"Password?" he said blankly.

"Nothing," Penny replied, grabbing his lunch bag, which was regrettably empty, and throwing it into a metal receptacle across the room.

"It states I need a password," he repeated.

She gave him a long look and he wondered if she saw through him. He could hardly say he didn't know the password because he wasn't this Gallagher fellow. Where would that leave him? His best bet was to play along until he could at least get out of here.

She turned the keyboard toward her and rapidly typed, enunciating slowly, "N..o..t..h..i..n..g."

"That's a dumb password," he said without thinking.

She grinned. "That's what I said when you told me, but you said 'there's nothing on this anyone would want to steal. It's not like I keep government secrets on this laptop'."

"I keep government secrets?"

"Get real, Gallagher. You don't remember much of anything, do you?"

"My name is Henry Douglas."

She sighed, put her hands on her hips as she studied him intently. "I'm sorry about your accident and that you're having trouble remembering things, but if you want to continue getting paid, it's Harry Gallagher."

She had a point and after all, that was his name. Just a moniker he hadn't used since he was thirteen. He turned back to the screen which fascinated him because after she had entered his password, it changed to a bedazzling array of little files, each labeled differently, and he longed to read all of them. But the most mesmerizing was a flashing symbol above the word search. He didn't want to ask her what this meant for she already thought he had a screw loose. He recalled what Jordan had said about searching for things on a computer and he realized that this one small blinking symbol held the power of the universe for him.

He glanced back at Penny, who didn't seem to know what to do now that she had followed through with his editor's orders and brought him food. "Thank you for the hamburger, and this," he gestured toward the typing machine.

"I could have told Mr. Harris you don't usually use your laptop, but he was in a mood." She gave a shrug.

"Yes, he appeared to be when he stopped by." He glanced around the room. "Do you know what they did with my clothes?"

"You can't leave," she started.

"Look in that little cupboard," he said, pointing. When she opened the door, his suit hung on some hooks. "There should be a pad and pencil or two in the jacket pocket."

She dug through all the pockets and came up with the requested items, along with a single key.

"That's it. How do guys get by with only a couple pockets?" she murmured. "I need a backpack and then some." She hoisted the so-named item and slung a strap over her shoulder.

"Come back tomorrow, Penny," he said, hoping his voice didn't sound as pleading to her as it did to his ears. While as unfamiliar as the rest of this world, she at least didn't judge him and she tolerated his questions.

She gave him a smile, a small wave, and closed the door behind her.

He quickly flipped his notepad open to a blank page, but his pencil paused over the paper. How could he even begin writing down the things he needed to know? For once, he pushed the pad aside and stared at the tiny blinking symbol. Sucking in a breath, he typed in his full name and hit the enter button.

Hours later he laid back, exhausted by all he had read. An aide had brought him dinner which he ate without tasting, the bright screen captivating all his attention. There really was a Harry Gallagher who wrote columns for the Tribune and books on historic gangsters, especially those who had lived in Chicago. There were so many parallels in their lives and it seemed everyone thought he was that same Harry Gallagher. He wondered what happened to that man.

When Jordan had come through to his time, she had been mistaken for Beatrice's niece, Jodelle Foster. They didn't know what had happened to Jodelle except for the letter in her trunk indicating she wouldn't be coming to Chicago. In his case, did he have to worry about the "other" Gallagher showing up? Harris had said he was undercover. Would that last long enough for Henry to find a way back to his time?

He looked again at the man in the pictures with short spikey hair and a scruff of a beard. He rubbed his chin, feeling the prickly hairs where he was always smooth shaven. He supposed there was some resemblance. It was no wonder people were mistaking them.

When the aide came back for his dinner tray, he casually asked her if there were other things on the television that he could watch. He had assumed, and correctly it seemed, that she wouldn't question his lack of knowledge as she casually pushed a button on the railing panel and the large screen blinked and another picture popped up.

"Just keep pushing that button until you find what you want," she said. "I like NCIS on Monday nights." She turned and left before he could ask what the initials meant.

A few hours later, Henry was done with the television. He watched a police program only to find out it was total fiction. He switched channels to find a comedy, if the laughter coming from the screen was an indication, but he didn't find it humorous. The people on the screen made reference to things he had no knowledge of so while there might be a slight learning curve about modern culture, it was lost in translation.

He found that if he were careful, he could get out of bed and to the toilet without alerting the nurse. The tube they had inserted in his arm hung from below a bag of fluid, which was hooked to a pole above his head. When he unplugged it from the wall and no alarms went off, he felt he had accomplished quite the feat. Gingerly, he put on his trousers as he had come to realize his back side was on full display otherwise. His feet were encased in a ridiculous pair of socks, but he felt they were good enough for him to venture forth.

No one stopped him as he walked down the quiet hall. The nurse at the central station didn't even look up and Henry wondered how far he could get before they reigned him back in. He turned to look behind him and his side cramped painfully, causing him to suck in a breath. Maybe he didn't want to sneak out after all. He managed to shuffle back to his room and climb into bed, feeling exhausted after such a small exertion. He was used to walking all over Chicago and realized his recovery would take a little longer than he thought.

Chapter 15

After another two days in the hospital, reading every newspaper he could find and spending hours on the search mechanism of the laptop, along with bugging every nurse as to when he could go home, the doctor finally signed his release papers. Penny had left him the newspaper number, because obviously he didn't remember it, and she had agreed to stop by his apartment for fresh clothes before picking him up. He used all that as an excuse because he didn't know where he lived, even after all the searching he had done on the other Harry Gallagher. It would take some time for him to assimilate himself not only into this century, but into the life of another man, even if he found he had much in common with that man.

Now, later that morning, he felt at odds when Penny opened the door to an apartment complex for him. After all, he was a gentleman and that was his job, but his side ached enough that it took all his determination to walk upright. Not that he would admit the nurse might have been right when she told him not to leave the hospital.

As weak as he was, he refused to lie around. He desperately needed to get out of the sterile room and do something, although exactly what that something was had not yet completely gelled in his mind.

An older man scurried around a desk in the center of the foyer and practically skipped to meet them, his hands clapped in front of him. "We are so happy you are back, Mr. Gallagher." He spread his arms wide to encompass the entire building, though there was no one else in the lobby.

"Thank you, hmm...Jack," Henry looked past him to the name plate on his desk. "Good to be...home."

The man handed Penny a small plastic card. "I had a new card made so if his original is in the apartment, destroy it. It won't work anymore."

"Thank you for your help," she politely replied, taking care of things he felt he probably should, if only he knew what they were.

"No problem. We change the door codes periodically for security anyway." He reached across the desk and gathered a stack of letters and newspapers. "I pulled your mail from the delivery, Mr. Gallagher, but I'll toss these newspapers. They're a week or more old anyway."

"No." He reached out and grabbed the rolled up papers. "I'll take them." As much as things had changed, the *Tribune* was still a link to his life; well, the life he had known until a week ago. At the moment, they were also a learning tool as he tried to restructure his life in what might as well be a foreign country.

Jack jerked back in surprise but Penny just shook her head as he clutched the papers to his chest and followed her to the elevators. Just as he had noted the address of the apartment building, he continued to watch closely at everything she did, knowing he would have to repeat the process in days to come. There was no gate and inside door to be secured by an assistant in the compact space of the elevator. Penny inserted the card Jack had given her into a slot then pushed a button marked '35'. The doors slid quietly shut and if not for the row of blinking numbers above the door, Henry wouldn't have known they were moving for there was no clanking or jerky movement; no whirling gears that you hoped wouldn't fail as they lifted you into the upper reaches of the newest skyscrapers.

His glimpses of the skyline of Chicago had amazed him as they had barreled along the freeway at what had seemed the speed of light. Of course there were skyscrapers in his time, but most consisted of no more than twenty floors. According to the button Penny had pushed, he lived on the 35th floor, and there were more above him.

The doors opened and he peeked out before stepping across the slight opening between elevator and hallway. He looked left and right, then left again. He clutched the newspapers tighter. Nothing was familiar; of course it wasn't, and when he looked at Penny, he knew that she knew he had no idea where he was. Again, she shook her head and turned to the right, walking halfway down the length of the hall before stopping. He reached into his pocket for his key before realizing it wouldn't work. Her lips pursed in a frown, then she inserted that plastic card into a slot, turned the handle and pushed open the door. It would seem that little piece of plastic was of paramount importance. He idlily wondered if he could pay for food with it; if perhaps in this future the world did not run on currency at all but some kind of plastic credit.

He had no time to exclaim over the immense size of the room they entered before she started in on him.

"Look, Mr. Gallagher—"

"Henry," he interrupted, "or Harry if you prefer."

She paused. "Harry. I've only worked for you a year, and I can't say I know much about you. I had to coerce HR to even give me your address. But in the time I have been at the *Tribune*, I have gotten a sense of things and something is off. Really, really off."

He turned to where she stood, back against the door, as though ready to bolt at any moment. He couldn't blame her because she was right and he felt just as ready to bolt. If only he could.

"I was shot, Miss O'Neil," he needlessly reminded her.

"That doesn't explain why you remember nothing about your life prior to last Thursday," she stated.

"I hit my head when I fell?" he added. Even to him, that excuse had begun to wear thin.

With a sigh, she laid the plastic card on the side table by the door. Her hand hovered above a slim black device which she picked up and tapped once, then again.

"It's no wonder no one could contact you." She held out the device. "Your phone's dead. Would you please charge it and keep it on you, even if you're investigating something undercover. Next time you get shot, you might not be so lucky as to have a good Samaritan nearby."

He took the device. "I have great hopes there won't be a next time." He said distractedly, already mesmerized by yet another electronic device – a telephone no larger than his palm?

"You probably have nothing to eat in the fridge," she said. Henry looked up to see her frown once again, her voice full of resignation. Poor Miss O'Neil had the misfortune of working for, and at the moment looking after, a man who she apparently felt belonged in a home for the simple minded.

"I can manage," he said, hoping to convince himself as well. "I recall a small grocery not very far away."

"You cook?" The amazement was evident in her voice.

That was one thing he knew he could do. He might have been the youngest in the family, but his mother had seen to it that he and his brother had learned not only to cook, but how to sew at least a button and a seam.

"I'm sorry," she immediately apologized. "It's just that you seem to live on greasy hamburgers and pizza."

That made him grin. "You have to admit the invention of the hamburger beats just about anything in recent history."

"Hardly," she replied with a laugh and it seemed to break the tension between them. Henry hoped so as he really needed a friend; perhaps a confidante, if he was to survive here.

"Bear with me, will you, Penny?" he asked to make certain.

"Of course," she said with no hesitation and Henry could only hope she wouldn't bail when she found out – if he needed to tell her – exactly who he was and where he came from.

She reached for the door handle but turned back. "By the way, Mr. Harris said to remind you a column is due tomorrow."

"He knows I was cut loose from the hospital?"

She nodded. "He had to sign the insurance papers since you had no identification on you." She pointed toward the wallet on the table. "Remember that next time, too. You can email me your article for proofing if you want."

He glanced at the laptop she had brought up with her; the one from the hospital; the one he supposedly used like it was another appendage.

"It'll be easier if I write it long hand," he said, rubbing his side. Another excuse but he needed more time to learn about this century. He mentally laughed. As if a lifetime would catch him up on all the inventions, regardless of how fascinating he found them.

"I'll come by after work tomorrow and pick it up," she said.

"Harris said it was due tomorrow."

"He always says that," she said with a shrug and then she was gone. He heard the distant ding of the elevator as his gaze swept the room; his room; his apartment.

He slowly turned to survey the space more closely. He had never required much and had lived in a boarding house most of his adult life, so this singular dwelling was larger than an entire house. A huge sofa of soft brown leather faced a fireplace, braced on each side with bookcases which held not only books, but a variety of art and glass figurines. Books had been a luxury growing up and he possessed only a few. While anxious to peruse these, he was more interested in what else the apartment contained.

On the opposite side of the room, a counter with a few stools in front divided the space between the living room and kitchen, which contained a stove, refrigerator, coffeepot and a contraption over the stove he would have to investigate later.

His attention was captured by the floor to ceiling windows that took up most of the far wall. The view of the city was unlike anything he could imagine, the skyline extending much farther along the lake than it had so many years ago. Although he had toured the Wrigley Building when it opened, it rose only thirty floors in the air. He wondered briefly if this was what it felt like looking out of an airplane window. Did airplanes even have windows?

Hours later, his stomach growled, reminding him he hadn't eaten and Penny wouldn't be back until tomorrow. He pulled his attention from the computer screen, gingerly stretching his arms above his head. He considered himself a smart man, having grown up on the streets and learning things the hard way. But it had taken him hours to figure out the small telephone. Locating a cord to charge it, as Penny had said, he couldn't get it to turn on. Finding photographs of such devices on the small computer was all well and good, except there were hundreds of different types of phones. Using one illustration, he held the device up to inspect the screen and it magically blinked and opened with little squares like the screen on the computer. He pushed the button on the side that he knew turned it off, then back on and held it up to his face. Again, it turned on.

"Okay, one problem solved," he muttered, setting it aside to continue his cram session. Who would have thought it would be so hard to simply exist. Since he had no cash or access to his bank account with which to buy anything to eat, a bigger priority with each passing hour, he had examined the wallet on the table only to find more of the plastic cards that opened his door and the elevator. It took some time, but he discovered the difference between a credit and debit card, and between Uber and Uber Eats.

Satisfied with his progress for the day, in that he understood how to go about getting himself fed, he wandered down a short hall into a massive bedroom, the bed taking up most of the space. Everything seemed overly large in this century, but the moment he sat on the edge of the bed, he fell back in ecstasy as the mattress felt like he floated on a cloud. Unwilling to waste time sleeping at the moment, he sat back up, groaning as his stitches pulled. With all the space and modern appliances, he wondered if this apartment had its own bathroom, or if he would continue to share with the other residents down the hall.

What he found through the door off the bedroom had him stripping in an instant and stepping into a large, tiled space with several water jets spraying at different angles, hitting his body with water as though standing in the rain, except this water was hot. There were bottles labeled as shampoo and body wash and even after he thoroughly washed and rinsed, the water continued to beat down on him in a heavenly hot stream. He decided at that moment that as long as this dream continued, if that was what it was, he would enjoy every aspect of life in the twenty-first century.

He found a closet full of clothes and although the trousers were a bit large, a belt fixed the problem. The chest of drawers contained everything from underwear to sweaters and he pulled on a soft green, long sleeved shirt that was heavier than an undershirt but not as bulky as a sweater. The small logo on the breast wasn't one he had seen before, but that would continue to be the case for most everything he encountered.

Finding an outer coat in a closet near the front door, he reached for the plastic key card Penny had left there. His hand paused above the wallet, for a moment feeling guilty at the thought of using another man's money, but realizing he had no choice, he tucked it in his pocket and left for his next adventure, if it could be called that when he only wanted something to eat.

The late afternoon sun did nothing to warm the crisp breeze blowing in off the lake. No matter where one lived in downtown Chicago, the wind found a way to weave through the streets and catch people unaware. Today, the air didn't smell as clean as Henry recalled, and when he looked up between the buildings, haze hung thick enough to obscure the tops of the skyscrapers. Apparently modern inventions and technology came with a cost.

He walked slowly, the pain in his side a dull throb but it still felt good to be up and about. As he remembered, a small grocery store stood on the corner a few blocks from his apartment complex and he grabbed a cart before walking the aisles. Only when he remembered he had walked and would have to carry groceries back did he curb the amount of items he put in the push cart. He could always return another time, he thought, as he went to the cashier. He watched carefully as the person in front of him finished his shopping as he chatted with the saleslady. When it was his turn, he held his breath as he mimicked what he had seen, sliding one of the plastic cards along the small machine.

The clerk gave him a paper receipt. "Thank you for shopping with us. Have a nice day."

Feeling as if he were getting away with something illegal, Henry kept looking over his shoulder as he walked out of the store. It was both exciting and anxiety-producing to live in a world where one did not know all the nuances needed to survive.

Jack hurried to open the front door when Henry approached. "Good evening, Mr. Gallagher. You sure you should have gone out?" It seemed Jack wasn't a doorman like those available at the better hotels, but he maintained a desk opposite the elevators and kept track of the comings and goings. As now, when he handed Henry the mail and newspaper. "You usually have your groceries delivered."

"I needed a little fresh air," Henry replied as he dug in his pocket for the elevator key.

"Getting brisk out there," Jack nodded. "They say we're in for an early, and colder winter this year."

Henry agreed and turned toward the elevator.

"Have a good evening, Mr. Gallagher."

For all that had happened and with everything he had to learn about the present, Henry hoped for more than one good evening. As he opened the door to the apartment, he thought that as long as people kept calling him Mr. Gallagher, he should be in the clear.

Henry grilled the steak he had purchased and devoured it as he read the latest newspaper. From what he could decipher, Chicago had just finished celebrating most of the year 2022 as a centennial of sorts in honor of what was historically known as the R*oaring Twenties.* He found it disconcerting that the time *in which he lived* was now relegated to historic archives.

After he finished eating and washing his single plate and glass, he sat down to jot off the article he had told Penney he would write, using the newspaper information for reference to recall those times from his own point of view. He wrote how roughly only thirty percent of households had electricity and yet innovative new inventions such as washing machines, refrigerators, radios and televisions were being created to make life easier. He added how the telephone, an apparent inseparable link between people and their world, had at one time needed a very helpful telephone exchange operator instead of the disembodied robotic voice of this day. He reminisced about the invention of the hamburger, of course, and how mechanical marvels such as automobiles and airplanes were only beginning to come into prominence.

"The *Twenties* were certainly roaring into the new century as people were changing, becoming bolder and with a more rebellious attitude," he wrote in conclusion. "Women, especially, once given the right to vote, were taking it upon themselves to toss modest 'Victorian' fashion out the window. Yet while mellow new music called 'jazz' was a great hit at speakeasies and clubs alike, organized crime was at an all-time high, fueled by prohibition. Even so, people had begun to discover the variety to be found in city life, and fewer lived in rural areas and farms. The economy was booming and there was money to be made."

He pushed the yellow pad with his column aside and picked up his small note pad, flipping it open to one particular page. His finger traced the rectangular drawing and each small square inside it, recalling the day he had learned Jordan's secret and she had drawn this picture, trying to explain what a cell phone looked like. It was the only thing he had that allowed him to acknowledge what he had shared with her had been real; that she was real.

Now, every line he wrote took him back to the months he had shared with Jordan. Every word made him ache for her and he couldn't begin to imagine where she was or what had become of her.

Chapter 16

The sun broke the horizon as Henry drank his coffee, staring out the windows from his seat on the couch, which he had turned, with difficulty, to face the spectacular view. Who would want to face the fireplace when he could view a wall to wall painting that fluidly changed like the scenery of a silent film. Though he had slept soundly for being in a foreign place, he had still awakened before the sun.

The news on the television had a weather forecaster who said it would be an unseasonably fifty degrees today, and though weathermen were notoriously wrong, Henry had decided to take the man at his word and venture forth. He wanted to begin looking for Jordan, and felt the best places to look were in the city itself, not on an internet search. Besides, he had done that last night and it yielded nothing helpful.

He made an egg sandwich for breakfast, wishing he had remembered bacon, and after cleaning up, went to pull clothes out of the closet. "The man has taste," he muttered as he slid a camel colored cashmere sweater over his head. Reminding himself he was just borrowing the man's wardrobe, he finished his morning routine. Making a face in the mirror, he thought perhaps the first stop he needed to make was at a barber, for his hair had begun to wave and droop over his ears.

He carefully collected the necessary items for venturing forth, wallet in a back pocket, door key card in front pocket. Although he knew no one to call, he still unplugged the small phone and tucked it into a pocket of his jacket. Since he recognized that his apartment building lay near the inner loop of the EL, he found it easy to get around even though several streets either no longer existed or had name changes. Many stores on Michigan Avenue were the same and he gazed in awe at the fashions of the day displayed in the windows.

He was saddened to find that Gabby's, a favorite hamburger joint of his, had closed during the pandemic and never reopened, although the building remained. Jordan had briefly talked about COVID-19, just as deadly as the Influenza of 1918, so he understood how devastating it had been even though other places appeared to be thriving.

He grabbed the EL uptown, getting off at Broadway where many of the speakeasies and jazz clubs had existed. There was an eerie sameness to the storefronts and yet establishment names were different; the buildings showing the wear and tear of one hundred or more years. He found the Green Mill Cocktail Lounge, but the bartender who served him a soda told him this wasn't the same place as the Green Mill Gardens where Al Capone had purportedly visited.

"Do the tunnels still run beneath the streets?" Henry asked, recalling the escape routes bootleggers had often used.

The man gave him a speculative look. "Not many people know about those."

Henry gave him a weak smile. "I used to be quite interested in..." He stopped as the barkeep shook his head.

"Best keep your interests to yourself," he said, his gaze following a tall man in a dark suit who walked past and disappeared behind a door at the back of the room.

Until that moment, Henry had been under the assumption that the mobsters had disappeared when prohibition had ended. What a ridiculous premise. His editor, Harris, had railed at him for pursuing gangsters. It would seem that Henry had more research to do if he were to keep himself out of trouble.

He stopped at a barber, opting for a totally different look with the back and sides short and the top spikey. He even had his beard trimmed although he didn't quite understand paying for a shave that didn't take all the whiskers off, but it seemed there was some skill required to shave one's face and make it look like one hadn't shaved at all.

When he walked outside later, long afternoon shadows shaded the street as hordes of people scurried by, heads down looking at their phones, no one interacting or even apologizing when shoulders bumped in passing. This was his town; he had lived here all his life, and yet he suddenly felt incredibly lonely as though he were a stranger in a foreign land. There was only one person who could fix that, and while he thought to head for home, he had one more stop to make. Fear had kept him wandering everywhere in the city today except for the one place he should have gone first. The longer he postponed it, the more nervous he became about going.

He caught the EL and got off near the park at the waterfront. By memory, he turned down the street, walked two blocks and turned again. His heart sank. Even though the street names had changed, the park on the right looked familiar, though trees were taller and a black wrought iron fence paralleled the sidewalk. Yet instead of neat, family row homes, a series of eclectic small businesses ran the block where Jordan had lived. He stood in the twilight, watching as the antique store at the corner turned off its business lights for the night. In a moment or two, lights came on in an upstairs window but it couldn't displace the shadows that swallowed him.

Penny jumped up from the bench in the lobby when he entered.

"Where have you been? I told you I would be back. Why didn't you answer your phone?"

Henry pulled the device from his pocket, pushed the button and held it up. When the display flashed, it said a missed call from Penny. So that had been the noise he heard at the barber shop.

"Sorry. Why didn't you go up? My column is on the kitchen table." Still depressed from his outing, he walked past her to the elevators.

She hurried after him. "I can't go waltzing into a guy's apartment."

"You were in there yesterday." Her logic confused him.

"Yesterday I was helping you. Today, I'm..." She seemed as much at a loss for words as he was.

She followed him into the elevator and although she didn't say anything more, he could feel her staring at him. He opened the apartment door, this time holding it for her to enter, then dropping the key on the side table. He took off his jacket and hung it on a hook. When he held out a hand for hers, she shook her head.

"I won't be staying. I just came for your article."

He handed her the notepad and she quickly perused it, her frown deepening as she silently read. She looked up at him, her gaze intent.

"What?" he questioned.

"This isn't your handwriting." She waved the pad at him.

"It most certainly is. Remember, I was—"

"Don't give me the *I was shot* crap," she interrupted. "It doesn't explain this. What's going on?"

"I'm...ambidextrous. My hand cramped so I used the other one." *Lies, lies. How often would he have to lie to live in this time?*

She continued to stare at him and he wondered if she could read his mind. Finally, she sighed. "Well, at least getting a haircut makes you look more like you, even if you are acting very strange." She flipped through the pad. "Where's the second column? You always write two at a time so you're ahead of deadline."

Having decided his priorities, he shook his head. "Not this time. Harris said he needed column inches but I need time off. Can I do such a thing?"

She looked at him funny, but said, "I don't have the authority to say, but you should be able to get time off, not only sick leave since you were shot, but you never take vacation time so I'm sure you've accumulated several weeks."

"Even when I was undercover?"

"Well, I guess. You were still employed, so you would still get paid."

"How do I find out?"

She looked at him, concerned now "You might want to see a trauma doctor or a brain specialist. You didn't get shot in the head, but you are apparently having difficulty remembering your entire life and how it works."

"That's rather sarcastic, don't you think?"

"I'm sorry, but you don't seem the same person at all."

If she only knew, Henry thought. He gave her a woeful look.

She sighed. "Call HR and ask about your PTO."

"Can you do that for me?"

"Of course not. That's private information and they won't tell me anything."

"Fine. You get one more column."

She turned to open the door but paused when he called her name.

"Thank you...for everything," he said, *but mostly for not questioning me too deeply,* he silently added.

"Get well, Harry." The door snicked shut behind her, leaving him alone with his thoughts.

Since it was evening, Henry couldn't call the newspaper office until the next day. Already rather bored with the television offerings, after dinner he ran a hand over a shelf of books by the fireplace, realizing they were all written by one Harry Gallagher. Pulling one out, he discovered his picture on the back cover; or rather a picture of the man he was impersonating.

"How strange," he murmured, reading the inside flap bio. Although they lived almost one hundred years apart, there were uncanny similarities not only in looks but in their lives. He was one of two children, had been an investigative reporter before he started writing his columns, and had an insatiable interest in gangsters of the early twentieth century. Turning the book over, Henry saw it was about bootlegging in the 1920's. Other titles on the shelf were about various mobsters, including an entire volume on Al Capone.

Henry wondered in the intervening years since he had lived, if anyone had discovered what had happened to people like Tommy O'Connor, who had purportedly disappeared in the 1920's. Because of his own situation, was it possible that instead of disappearing, which the newspapers sometimes used as a euphemism for being dead, other people had somehow traveled through time by accident, as happened to him and Jordan. Deciding the volume he held would make good reading, he took it with him to bed. Instead of getting very far into the era of prohibition and bootlegging, he fell asleep dreaming of Jordan.

"This is Henry Douglas…Gallagher," he stammered, holding the small telephone up to his ear.

"Yes, sir. This is Maggie in Human Resources." A perky female voice came through with no static or disruption. Henry grinned.

"I was shot as you may know."

"Of course, it's all over the newspaper offices."

Of course it was, he thought. Some things, like gossip, never changed. Remembering the term Penny had used, and having looked it up before he called, he asked, "How much PTO do I have? I need to recuperate."

After a pause, she came back on the line. "You have three weeks of sick leave and another three weeks PTO."

"Fine, put me down for all of it."

"I don't think I can. It has to be cleared with Mr. Harris."

"Do whatever you need to, Miss, but I won't be back for some time." Perhaps never, he thought, if he could find a way out of his current dilemma. All he could think about was Jordan. What had happened to her after he disappeared? She would think he was dead and that made him want to rail at the universe for the cruel joke that had been played on them. He had to find a way back to her and that meant focusing all his time and energy in a singular direction.

Chapter 17
Train to Detroit, 1926

Jordan couldn't stop crying, and she didn't give a damn if the other passengers on the train stared at her strangely. She dabbed her eyes with the already soaked tissue she had pulled from her clutch. The station and Henry had long since been lost in the fog, the train having pulled away from the platform before she had a chance to get off, though she had begged the conductor to stop.

What was she to do? She didn't know if he had been shot, if that was the flash and sound she had heard. Had he survived? She continually tapped her feet on the floor, as though trying to hurry the train along to the next station where she could get off and return to Chicago.

"When will the train stop?" she asked the conductor when he asked for her ticket.

"Not before Indianapolis,' he replied.

"No, no. I have to get off before then."

"Miss, your ticket is Chicago to Detroit with a train change in Indianapolis. If you'd wanted not to go as far, you should have bought a different ticket." He handed her back the piece of paper and continued down the aisle.

More tears flowed as Jordan turned to face the window. The morning sun burned off the fog and turned the countryside golden, but she couldn't appreciate the beauty until she knew where Henry was. As the train barreled eastward, she whispered a prayer that he could somehow catch up with her.

After the longest hours of her life, Jordan was up and moving down the aisle before the train came to a complete stop in the station. She clutched Henry's briefcase to her chest, her only lifeline to him at this point. The moment the conductor stepped onto the platform, she hurried down the few steps and rapidly walked into the station.

"Do you have a pay phone?" she asked the clerk behind the cage. He didn't even look up but pointed off to the right. Jordan hadn't honestly thought there were such things yet but hurried to the cubicle. Digging in her clutch, she pulled out a little coin purse and dumped it on the small counter.

"Chicago exchange, please," she said when the operator came on the line. At least she knew how this process worked. After several clicks and transfers, then depositing the proper coins and going through the newspaper switchboard, she finally had a voice on the other end of the line.

"I need to speak to Henry Douglas immediately. It's an emergency," she said.

"He hasn't checked in today," the woman on the other end replied. "I'm not sure when to expect him."

Jordan's heart was pounding. "I don't mean to sound alarms, but he was at the train station this morning and there was an altercation with another man and I'm afraid he was shot."

"What?" the woman shouted. "Who is this?"

"Please, ask around. Has anyone seen him?" She listened as the woman shouted across the newsroom in question.

"No one here has seen him. Who is this and how do you know he might be hurt?" She sounded as though she were ready to blame Jordan for whatever had befallen Henry.

"We were traveling to Detroit," Jordan said, "so I'm now in Indianapolis waiting for the next train. If you find him, please have him send a telegram for Jordan Foster to the Detroit station so I know he's all right."

"Ah," the woman said with a sigh, "you're *that* woman. There has been much speculation about you here.'

Jordan heard a distant whistle and a call for the next train, so she didn't have time for gossip. "Please, someone has to know where he is."

"He doesn't always check in if he's on a story." The hesitation was clear in her voice. "You're sure he was intending to go with you?"

"I'm not some hysterical woman afraid of being dumped," she shouted angrily. "He could be hurt. You need to find him." Another train whistle, much closer this time and Jordan knew she was out of time; and almost out of coins, she realized when the operator asked for another five cents.

The train pulling into the station was not the one she needed to board and according to the station master, her train was running late because of livestock on the tracks somewhere west of here. She paced the station, weaving around other travelers who seemed intent on being happy as they set about their travels. She was fast becoming a basket case, and she finally stopped in a corner and gave herself a stern lecture, unmindful of anyone who thought she had a screw loose for talking to herself.

"Should I go back to Chicago? If he's hurt, he might need me." Then she answered herself with, "But if he's not hurt and is catching the next train to Detroit, you'll miss him. You need to stick to the original plan. Where the hell's a cell phone when you need it?"

She felt she really didn't have much choice but to continue her journey. Starting to pace once again, the aroma of cooked meat hit her, making her stomach growl. She hadn't eaten all day and looked around, spying a restaurant at the far end of the depot. Bless whoever Harvey was, she thought, as she hurried to get in line at the Harvey House.

Even after a meal of roast and mashed potatoes and gravy, Jordan's stomach didn't want to settle and she knew it was a lost cause until she knew if Henry was all right. Eventually the train arrived, she boarded but knew she wouldn't get to Detroit until very late in the evening.

As soon as she deboarded, she hurried to the clerk's window but he said no telegrams had come in; there were no telephone messages to be had, and there would be no other trains from Chicago that night. She tried to get through to the newsroom again, but apparently even if the presses were running for the early morning edition, the switchboard was silent.

She sat on one of the wooden benches off to the side, not at all sure what to do. The last of the many travelers had long since left and the large, empty space echoed the click-click of her heels as she nervously tapped them on the wood floors.

"Miss, you should be going," the clerk exited his booth and locked a door behind him. "There's nothing but freight passing through the rest of the night, and most of that doesn't even stop until it gets to the stockyards." He shuffled toward her. "Were you meeting someone? Have a place to stay?" His brow furrowed as he spoke.

She tried to smile. "Thank you for your concern," she said. "It's a mess and I'm sure you'd rather be home with your family than listen to me babble."

"When I get home, I'll be listening to my wife 'babble'," he said with a chuckle. "You're a mite younger than her, so I don't mind, though don't you be saying that if you should ever meet."

His gentle humor made her laugh, which in turn lifted her spirits. She had been surviving 1926 for several months now. She could survive a night in Detroit on her own. She stood, shook out her skirts and grabbed Henry's briefcase. "If you could point me to the nearest hotel, I'll get a room and start anew tomorrow."

"Do better than that. I'll walk you there myself, seeing as it's on the way." He crooked his elbow and Jordan happily tucked her arm in his, glad to have an escort in the strange town.

As it happened, the hotel was right around the corner and in minutes, the doorman stepped up to hold the door.

"Miss got in a fuddle when her train ran late, Thomas. Can you see she gets a room?"

"Not a problem, George," the doorman replied. "You'd think they'd have those trains figured out by now," he added, "it's not like they're some new-fangled invention. Why, just the other day I read about people being able to get where they're going by flying in an aeroplane. Can you imagine that?"

"You wouldn't catch me up in the air," George replied.

Jordan could tell the two men were good friends and no doubt passed the time nightly with the latest news and gossip, but she was bone weary and just wanted a bed. Besides, in her current state, she might just tell them a thing or two about transportation which would fuel their conversations for days.

"Excuse me?" she interjected politely.

"Sorry, Miss," Thomas said, holding the door open.

"Good luck to you," George added as she walked inside, out of the chilly night.

The desk clerk regarded her with suspicion, most likely because she was a female traveling alone but also she had no baggage. Thomas vouched for her and she had soon signed the register and headed for the elevator. The room wasn't quite as eloquent as the hotels in Chicago, but all she wanted was a place to lie down. Since she had no other clothes, she carefully laid her skirt and blouse over a chair, washed her stockings in the small sink and draped them over a towel to dry. After scrubbing the grime from her face and arms, she laid down on the bed.

Instead of sleeping, her mind kept going over the events of the morning but no matter how many times she replayed the scene, it made no more sense than when it had originally happened. Henry had said the man's name was Tommy O'Connor and she knew from previous conversations that he was the man whom Henry believed had shot his brother. Everything that happened after she boarded the train was a blur and because of the train's movement and the fog, she didn't know for sure that Henry had been shot. She kept telling herself he was fine and would find her; that they would finish this quest together.

* * *

Jordan felt she hadn't slept at all when she crawled out of bed as the sun peaked through the curtains. Her eyes were gritty and she would pay a ransom for a toothbrush. It was unfortunate the hotels of this era had not discover the courtesy of amenities for their guests, for she had only a small bar of soap and a thin washcloth and towel.

There was also no telephone in the room so as soon as she dressed, she rushed downstairs, positive she would speak to Henry today. After getting her bills changed, she found the small booth and started the process, inserting the proper coins when instructed.

"Newsroom," the female voice was far too perky.

"Henry Douglas, please." Silence met her request. "Hello, are you there?"

"Are you the woman who called yesterday?"

"Yes," Jordan answered hesitantly, not liking the sound of the woman's voice.

270

"Thank goodness," she said, "I was hoping you would call again. We have had everyone looking for Henry in all the usual places and nobody's seen him. We even checked his boarding house and he did not sleep there last night."

"Oh, God," she gasped. "What about the train station?"

"We sent two reporters there, right after you called the first time. They found no signs of a mishap and no one remembers hearing anything sounding like gunfire. We also checked the hospital and," she hesitated, "and the morgue."

"People don't just disappear," Jordan snapped before realizing how absurd that statement was. Of course they did; she was a prime example. The tears began but she bit her lip to keep the sobs silent, trying to think. "What about that little newsboy who follows him around? Do you know him?"

"We all know Eddie. He came by yesterday and told us he thought something had happened to Henry, but we brushed him off. Until we later got your telephone call." She sounded as worried as Jordan. "It's unlike Henry even if he's on a story. Someone usually knows what he's about."

"Have you called the police?"

She gave a short laugh. "Journalists and coppers have a love-hate relationship here, although Henry seemed to get along with them better than most. The desk sergeant said he'd 'have someone look into it', but it will most likely get swept under the rug."

"Deposit five cents, please," a different female voice spoke up.

"I have to go," Jordan said. "I'll check in again when I get back to Chicago."

"I'm sorry I didn't have better news," the woman replied before hanging up.

Jordan slowly replaced the receiver then sat and stared off into space. She would not believe Henry was dead. If he had been shot, someone would have found him, taken him to the hospital and there would be a record. If he had not been shot, he would somehow have gotten in contact with her after missing the train. Having loved to watch all the detective shows with her gramps, it was all too easy to believe he was being held hostage somewhere; perhaps for ransom but more than likely for information he knew. Afterall, Chicago in the 1920s was rife with crime.

Even that last scenario made her feel a little better than the first presumptions. She wiped her eyes with a handkerchief. Now she needed to get to Houdini as quickly as possible so she could catch a train back to Chicago. Her vision blurred and she felt suddenly light-headed, putting a hand against the wall to steady herself. She fumbled to find a chair, falling into it and dropping her head into her hands.

What was she thinking?

They came to Detroit because Houdini had the lock that was most likely the conduit to her traveling through time. But if that were indeed the case, how could she possibly use the lock here to return to her own time without knowing what happened to Henry? And honestly, did she even want to go back; to leave Henry and the promise of a life with him here?

Knowing she was thinking too much, she hurried over to the front desk. She would take one thing at a time.

"Excuse me," she caught the clerk's attention from the newspaper he was reading. "Can you tell me the theatre where Harry Houdini is performing?"

His eyes widened. "Haven't you heard? The man died after his performance last night!"

Jordan's knees threatened to buckle. "What?"

"Right here," the clerk pointed to the front page of the paper. "Magic Won't Bring Back the Great Houdini" in bold black headlines jumped out at her.

Jordan had always believed if you were a good person, the universe would be good to you in return. Sort of like karma. Yet for some reason, the universe had conspired against her back in the spring, and didn't seem inclined to stop anytime soon.

"You okay?" the clerk asked as she swayed against the counter.

She gripped the edge to steady herself, closed her eyes briefly then nodded. Turning around, she slowly walked toward the doors and out into the sunshine. People chatted as they walked by; a car horn honked, and life went on even though hers had ended in too many ways to count. She glanced around but nothing was familiar. She turned toward the train station, knowing she had to return to Chicago if only because it was a little more familiar than Detroit although just as empty.

The clerk from last night looked up in surprise when she approached the ticket office. "Leaving so soon, Miss?"

It took all her energy to answer. "Ticket to Chicago, please."

After consulting a rate table, he said, "That'll be seven dollars and seventy-eight cents."

Jordan dug in her bag, pulling out some bills and dumping her coin purse on the counter. Could things get any worse? "I only have seven fifty." She blinked hard, but the tears escaped anyway.

"Things not going so well, huh?" His voice was sympathetic and it only made Jordan feel worse. She shook her head.

"Well, fares are based on miles traveled, but I can't just have you dropped off in the middle of nowhere, now can I?" He took the dollar bills, wrote out a ticket, stamped it and slipped it through the opening. She saw it was through to Chicago. "The train's on schedule, which gives you time for a cup of coffee and some toast before you board." He pushed her coins toward her.

"Thank you, George," she said, recalling his name from last night.

His face lit in a smile. "I hope things get better for you, Miss."

Jordan took his advice and felt slightly better after getting something in her stomach. Still, a heavy weight pressed down on her shoulders and it took all her energy to climb the few steps onto the train when it arrived. She slumped onto an empty bench seat and tossed Henry's briefcase on the seat across from her, hoping it would deter anyone from sitting close by. Staring blankly out the window, she let the tears flow. She had never been much of a crier, always more willing to fight whatever happened rather than giving in to the anguish. But today she was through with it all. While disappointed at not getting to Houdini, she was devastated by Henry's disappearance and could not seem to think about her next steps.

The train jerked into motion and she reached across to grab the briefcase before it slid to the floor. Instead of setting it beside her, she held it close to her chest. The worn leather was soft beneath her fingers, and when she sniffed lightly, she smelled Henry. Why had he brought his briefcase with them in the first place, she wondered idly. They had only planned to be gone for a day. What was so important that he needed it with him when they traveled? Her fingers slid across the clasp. The longer she thought about it, the more curious she became.

Although she felt a little guilty, she opened the clasp and flipped back the flap. She used the excuse, to herself, that she needed to see if there was identification inside so she would know where he lived and be able to return it to him when she got to Chicago. This was also to reaffirm her belief that he was not dead and would be waiting for her in the city.

She pulled out a paper tablet, full of his scrambling handwriting and almost set it aside, having little interest in any police article he might have been writing. Instead, she quickly became intrigued by what appeared to be a commentary about geese.

If you walk near the trees and shrubs in the park by the edge of the lake, you might happen upon a group of geese. This spring there were six – three pairs if their behavior was any indication. By the end of May they had hatched a gaggle of geese and pedestrians along the walkway could often be heard complaining about the refuse the feathered creatures left behind. One woman called the newspaper office every day for a week because a goose chased after her, as if the Daily Journal had anything to do with fowl of that nature. I had seen this particular woman on my daily walks, and I do believe if she would quit feeding them bread scraps, they would not be begging her for more. But what do I know; I'm not a goose.

I have, however, learned quite a lot from this group of feathered residents. They never get too far away from each other, especially after the goslings hatched. I can also tell exactly where the babies are, even hidden in the grass or beneath the shrubs, because there is always a guard on either side of the group, head held high and unwavering. I'm not familiar enough with geese to know which gender it is. It could be the patriarch, standing watch over his charges, but I like to think it is the mothers who are always the steadfast protectors. Either way, the guards do not move an inch if you approach and it is you who will step to the side, or ride your bicycle around them, even if you are much bigger and it is your city. During the spring, until the goslings are fully feathered and can fly, this particular area of the park belongs to them.

I have heard that geese mate for life and wonder if other studies have been done on them. They appear to have a great sense of commitment and family and are very protective. They also have the patience of Job. I watched one day as they ventured across the street – crossing guard at front and rear and other adults scattered amongst the young ones. Traffic did stop, but after fifteen minutes more than one horn honked to hurry things along. The geese were not in the least intimidated by the vehicles that could flatten them in a heartbeat.

Today there was a new occurrence and I stood for some time watching – from a safe distance, of course. This year's hatchings had lost their down and now had feathers and their heads were marked with the black and white of their tribe. The only way to tell them apart from their parents was their size for they were small in stature and not yet built for the long-distance migration which they would eventually undertake. Even as they picked through the grass for bugs (I believe geese eat bugs), fully capable now that they were grown, there remained a stalwart guard at either end of the group.

And off to the side, outside of the cluster of scrambling toddlers but close to one of the guards, was another gosling. This one was far behind the others in development. Its body still covered with down, it lay in the grass as if unwilling or unable to join in the lunch the others were enjoying. I took a step closer and the guard (it had to be mother) took two steps closer to the baby but her gaze was steady on me. This hatchling was a full three weeks or more behind the rest of the group. I had to wonder with nature in all its glory, how that had happened. It certainly put a wrench in things for the rest of the gaggle as they couldn't venture far or fly to new feeding grounds and leave an unprotected baby. You could tell by the way the adults acted that this baby, regardless of *how poorly it developed or how much care it required, would not be left behind.*

There is much to be learned from a goose.

Not surprised, Jordan felt tears slipping down her cheeks. Over the past months, she had read Henry's accounts of bootlegging raids, city government rulings and even the occasional theater review. But this article was different and it truly showed the man he was. His words evoked emotion and humor; a love of nature and the world around him; kindness and empathy. It was truly who he was, and her heart ached at the thought of losing him.

"You won't," she muttered to herself. She couldn't have been sent back to this century to fall in love only to have that love thwarted.

She set the notepad aside to see what else she could discover about Henry. She pulled out a ragged-edged black and white photograph of two young boys standing in front of a woman. Her hands rested on each of the boys' shoulders and while she had a serene smile on her lips, both boys were grinning impishly. Perhaps in their early teens, Jordan could see a resemblance between the boys, who were probably brothers. Upon looking closer, she tenderly touched the face of the shorter boy, the dark hair and smile had her guessing this was Henry, standing by his brother and mother.

She set the photo aside and reached in for more, pulling out a stack of what looked like stock certificates. He had told her about his investments, and from what she could see, he had quite the portfolio, including some shares in Coke-a-Cola, which were only recently purchased.

Further search uncovered a bank savings account with—wow—a several hundred-dollar balance and a brown envelope with almost one hundred dollars in cash inside. Given what she knew of the wages and living costs at this time, he was fairly well off, especially if one included his stock certificates.

She carefully put everything back into the briefcase even as questions arose. She didn't question how he had so much money or the money to invest in the stock market. Even in a city like Chicago where the crime rate was out of sight, Henry was an honest soul who did his best to make the city a better place. He certainly didn't work for the mob.

So why would he carry such things around with him? She listed what he had – stocks certificates, cash and a bank book, a picture of family – everything he owned that was valuable. Then she recalled that he had carried it on the train when they went away for the weekend. And he had brought it with him as they searched for Houdini and her way home. She gasped as understanding hit.

Henry had been planning to go with her if she found the key to returning to the twenty-first century.

Chapter 18

The train ride back to Chicago was interminable, even though it took the northern route and was hours less than what Jordan had experienced while getting to Detroit. She stared out the window without really seeing anything, the events of the past two days replaying in her mind. She kept going back to the items in Henry's briefcase, more convinced than ever that he had intended to try and accompany her if she managed to go back to her own time. Her heart ached that he would have given up everything he knew to be with her.

She reread the goose article and wondered if that, too, had been written, not really about geese, but about them. He had stuck with her when she told him her secrets. He had stayed by her as she tried to navigate a world unfamiliar to her. He had loved her enough to go with her. Of course, all that was moot now, and she didn't know what she would do without him.

The conductor called out the stations as they stopped along the way, but Jordan sat where she was until they finally arrived in

Chicago. With a heavy heart, she stepped onto the platform, a sharply cold wind sweeping across the open space. She tugged her thin coat more closely around her and hurried through the doors. The station building wasn't much warmer but at least the wind was blocked.

"JF!" A high-pitched voice screeched her name as her legs were tackled in a hug. She instinctively reached out, her hands encountering boney shoulders beneath a threadbare coat; a hat covered head no higher than her waist. Just when she thought she couldn't feel any worse, she looked down to find Eddie's gaze, full of sorrow and confusion. In the middle of the busy Chicago train station, all she could do was hold on to the youngster and cry along with him.

"I've been waiting and waiting for you. Where is HD?" he asked on a sob. "Where did he go?"

Of course Eddie would know of Henry's disappearance. Not only did he follow the man around like a puppy, but the news office woman had said they talked to the boy about Henry's whereabouts. She gently unwound his arms and guided him over to the side and out of the traffic pattern. They sat on a bench and for a moment she didn't know what to say.

"Honestly, Eddie, I don't know what happened." She said. "We were supposed to get on the train, then he saw a man he knew. The fog was thick and when I looked out the window, he was nowhere in sight. I couldn't get off the train, so I was hoping someone might know something when I finally came back."

He shook his head. "The lady at the newspaper office asked me. I've looked everywhere and can't find him." He ducked his head and she could see the color rise in his cheeks. "I even asked some of the...theater dancers but they all said he don't come around any more."

That was information Jordan could have done without, but then she supposed it was apropos for the times.

"He would let me know even if he went undercover, so he must be hurt."

Jordan took his hand and squeezed. He was much too young to be so world weary.

"We have to find him," Eddie continued. "People don't just disappear."

Keep telling yourself that. Jordan kept that thought to herself. "Right now, I'm too exhausted to think straight. You need to go home, out of this cold, as do I. Then tomorrow, we start looking."

The youngster seemed okay with that, even if it wasn't much of a plan. Together, they walked out of the train station and headed to the EL. Jordan gave him money to ride, not knowing exactly where he lived but wanting him to be safe. Besides, it was Henry's money and she was sure he would take care of the boy.

"Crickets! My ma will think I robbed a bank," he exclaimed when she handed him a ten dollar bill.

"I want you to buy a coat tomorrow before you see me." At his hesitant look, she added, "Your mom wouldn't want you to catch cold, would she?"

"No, but I'm thinking I should use this to get her a coat; and maybe some soup and bread."

Jordan dug in her pocket and gave him another ten. "Here, now you have enough for both. Just don't let anyone see you flashing it around."

His eyes widened. "Did *you* rob a bank?"

His innocent question made her smile; her first in many days. Hopefully tomorrow they would find answers.

The house was dark and quiet when she entered and she thought she'd made it upstairs undetected until Maddie knocked softly and let herself in. "I would have lit the fire if I'd known you'd be home tonight, miss." She hurried over and lit the fire, flames soon causing shadows to dance across the ceiling.

"Thank you, Maddie. If you can help it, please don't tell my aunt I am home. I'd like one night of sleep before her interrogation."

"You might not need to worry," the maid said. "Lately Miss Beatrice has been a bit more...soft?" she finished questioning.

Jordan could only hope as she didn't think she could handle anything more at the moment. She grabbed her robe and left for the bath, hoping for a long, hot soak to clear her mind.

* * *

The next morning Jordan came down the stairs to find Beatrice at breakfast. When she saw Jordan, she stood. "Do you have a minute?"

Perplexed at the gentle sound of her voice, Jordan nodded and sat down opposite her at the table. Maddie appeared with a cup and pot of coffee, and at Jordan's nod, returned to the kitchen for her breakfast.

"Your young friend was pounding on the kitchen door at the crack of dawn," she said with what Jordan felt was a hint of humor. This was not the Beatrice she knew. "He wanted Cook to wake you first thing."

'I'm so sorry," Jordan said. "I..." She didn't know what to say.

Beatrice reached across the table and covered her hand. The gesture so surprised Jordan that she felt tears prick her eyelids. She bit her lip to stop its trembling.

"I owe you an apology," Beatrice said and when Jordan immediately started to protest, she held up her hand. "I need to say this. When your mother became sick and I offered to look after you, I had forgotten that you weren't a little girl anymore. I thought I would have the opportunity to shape a young girl's mind; help her get along in this changing world. Then you showed up, all grown and full of your own ideas about your life, and after getting over my anger, I was full of jealousy."

"Of me? I had no idea what I was doing here or anything about this world." *Literally*.

"Yet you have adapted so well and, seem quite happy with your life. My jealousy stemmed from just that, until I decided to learn from you instead of the other way around. I began to dance," she said softly and her face went all dreamy, "and I fell in love."

All this confession and emotion was too much for Jordan, who had her napkin up to her eyes as the tears flowed. While she was happy for Beatrice, her own heart broke into little pieces again. Beatrice couldn't seem to stop the flow of her newfound self-awareness. "I have read about your Henry Douglas, and if there's anything I can do; any way in which I can help..."

"I don't know why he disappeared, but I won't stop looking until I find out what happened to him," she burst out. "I won't believe he's dead!"

"All right then. Father has many contacts both here in the city and across the state. I'm sure he will make some telephone calls. Speaking of which, Miss Grant has already called this morning. She stated you didn't show up for work yesterday and while that is subject to dismissal, she said you were too valuable an employee to lose, and she would give you a second chance today."

"To hell with Miss Grant," Jordan said under her breath, but Beatrice heard.

"I realize you are in distress, but no lady should spout profanities, regardless of the circumstances."

"Sorry." She cringed, for Beatrice didn't deserve her disregard. "I can't go to work. I have to look for Henry."

"Well then," Beatrice settled back in her chair in thought, "we will have to come up with a likely excuse to keep you from working for the next several days." She gave Jordan a stern look. "It will be up to you to make sure you're not seen gadding about town."

This time it was Jordan who reached for her aunt's hand, giving it a squeeze.

"Can we go now?" Eddie asked as he burst through the kitchen door followed closely by Maddie, who wasn't fast enough to catch him as he raced around the table to Jordan's side.

"Eddie, this is Miss Barrister and you need to apologize for interrupting."

He looked cross but at her stare, he muttered, "'cuse me, ma'am." To Jordan, he added, "Cook is trying to stuff me like a Sunday chicken and if we don't leave soon, I'll bust out of my pants."

Jordan tried to hide her smile.

"And do you know how a stuffed chicken looks?" Beatrice surprised Jordan by asking.

"No, ma'am, but I'm fixing to find out come this Sunday, thanks to Miss Jordan."

Jordan took a closer look at the youngster. "You were supposed to buy a coat with that money."

He blushed but didn't apologize and Jordan knew he worried about his mother. She stood up and pointed him to the front room. "So our first store is Woolworth's," she said, "for both of us." She recalled how cold she had been yesterday.

"Wear my wool," Beatrice called after her. "I'll telephone Marshall Field's and have one delivered later today. You can't run around town in this weather without being properly attired."

Jordan stopped and turned. "Thank you," she said softly.

Her aunt's lips trembled and she turned aside, waving a hand. "Go find your man."

Jordan was very happy she had put trousers on that morning, along with sturdy walking shoes and her hat with her aunt's coat because Eddie was shivering by the time they got off the EL and hurried into the warmth of the department store. The wind blew fiercely across the lake, making it even colder and Eddie said he thought he saw snowflakes, not that it would stop them from their search, he had added. She found him a warm coat and pair of mittens, but he refused to give up his news cap for a wool beanie, so she settled for a pair of earmuffs.

Once they were better attired, Eddie led the way to the boarding house where Henry lived. Mrs. Brown had not seen Henry for several days and informed them she would have to clear his room if he didn't show up by the end of the week to pay his rent. Jordan convinced the woman to let her take a look in the room, but they discovered nothing except a few suits and miscellaneous clothing items in the dresser. Not one single personal item could be found. As Jordan had suspected, everything he valued was in his briefcase.

From there they went to the *Daily Journal* offices and talked to anyone who would listen. Because he was one of their own, everyone had been on the lookout for Henry, but so far no one had seen or heard from him. The newsroom secretary said they had even sent out a ticker tape, which would go to news agencies across the country. Jordan assumed that was like a BOLO but even so, she intended to visit the police next.

They stood inside the front door of the newspaper, reluctant to go out into what looked to be a snowstorm.

"Told you it was going to snow," Eddie said.

"Yes, you did," she replied needlessly. Normally she loved snow, but not when she had to trudge around town in it, looking for clues that weren't materializing. Every stop depressed her further.

Having only nibbled at her breakfast, she was hungry and decided lunch would give the snow time to stop before their next destination. "How about a hamburger?" she asked Eddie.

His face lit in a grin, then he tilted his head to the side with a frown before straightening with the grin back in place.

"What was that about?"

"After everything Cook made me eat for breakfast, I had to check to see if I was hungry again."

"I take it you are?"

"I haven't ever had a hamburger before," he added. "Are they any good?"

"Henry says they're the best thing ever invented," she replied. "Do you want to see if he's right?"

This time he whooped, pushing the door open for her and out they went into the storm.

Even with Cook's huge breakfast hours earlier, Eddie downed a hamburger and French fries, then finished off her fries. The food cheered the youngster but Jordan was feeling desperate. Even so, she trudged along to the police precinct, hoping for answers to questions she was getting tired of asking.

As they approached the station, Eddie hung back, and when she opened the door to go in, he pulled her aside. "Look, you go in and ask the questions. I'll wait out here."

She bent down to look him in the eyes. "Are you in trouble with the police, Eddie?"

He vigorously shook his head. "No, it's just the coppers always look at us and think we gotta be pickpockets and thieves, if we don't have a pile of news sheets to hawk on the corners. So it'll be best if I stay out here."

But it's cold and still snowing," she argued.

He just grinned. "I got a warm coat."

"I'll hurry," she said, giving him a quick hug. If she wasn't careful, she could easily grow attached to that kid.

The desk sergeant saw her coming and even if he didn't know her, he must have suspected her intent because he stood and tried to scoot around the platform desk, thinking she didn't see him. Jordan quickened her pace and stepped right in front of him.

"Excuse me, I need to ask you some questions."

"You a reporter?"

"No," she said and watched him relax a little. "But I want to ask you about one – Henry Douglas."

He wagged his head back and forth and moaned. "Dang it all, that's all anyone's beating their gums about these days. Why's he so important? People go missing every day."

"Please, can you tell me what *everyone* is saying?"

"Because the newspaper ran an article about his disappearance, every Tom, Dick and Harry has been reporting seeing him, or hearing about what happened to him."

Jordan's stomach plummeted. "What happened to him?"

The sergeant shook his head. "That's the problem. We've gotten reports of him drowning in the lake, getting run down on Michigan Ave, being thrown off the EL, along with the usual reports of shooting, stabbing, and poisoning. I've never seen so much attention for a lousy reporter."

Jordan poked him in the chest. "He was a great reporter and he always searched for the truth, even if it got some people, like the police, into trouble they tried to cover up."

He narrowed his gaze at her, pursed his lips in thought, then gave her a smile. "You got guts, for a dame, talking to the police like that."

Jordan had to bite her tongue and remember what century she was in. She narrowed her gaze.

The man sighed, realizing she didn't appreciate his comment and wasn't going to leave until she got what she came for. "We've looked into leads. It was very foggy that morning and not many people on the platform. Someone found a scarf; someone else said they thought they heard what could have been a shot but they weren't sure."

"He said he thought he saw Tommy O'Connor. Have you looked for him?"

The policeman narrowed his gaze. "He disappeared years ago." When Jordan started to protest, he put up a hand. "You have to remember it's a train station, and people go about their business without paying too much attention to what others are doing. The only good to say is we didn't find a body."

Jordan shivered at his words, but at least he hadn't been found dead. Still, she was no closer to finding him. She thanked the man for his time and turned to leave.

"I'm sorry what I said about Henry," the sergeant called out. "He was one of the good guys, even if he did call us out on occasion. I hope he shows up."

"You're not the only one."

She stepped outside into swirling snow, having a hard time even finding Eddie, huddled against the side of the building. "Come on, we need to get home before this storm gets any worse."

"You didn't find out anything, did you?" he asked, and his crestfallen look made Jordan hurt. However Henry had befriended Eddie, this little boy looked up to him and Jordan hated breaking his heart.

"We're not done looking," she tried to sound perky as they hurried down the sidewalk. "But for now, you need to go home to your mom. Tomorrow is Sunday, then I don't want to see you again until the snow has stopped for two days."

"But," he started.

"No. We have to come up with a different plan and that will take a few days. Besides, we can't continue to run around in a blizzard."

They walked two blocks when Eddie grabbed her hand and pulled her to a stop. "I gotta go this way," he waved off to the left, seemingly reluctant to let go of her. She squatted in front of him.

"I know you miss Henry," she said softly. "I do too. We'll find him." She stood and squeezed his shoulders. "Remember, two days after the storm. Now scoot." She watched him scurry away before turning at the corner and hurrying to the EL stop to find her own way home.

* * *

Jordan would have forgone Sunday dinner but Beatrice insisted she attend, even though it was just with her and her father. She appreciated the fact they tried to lift her spirits with stories about people in town and what had been happening recently, but she couldn't summon any energy to respond in kind.

"I am sorry none of my inquiries have proven successful," her 'grandfather' finally broached the subject on all their minds. She gave him a weak smile. He did remind her of her real gramps, and the thought of him only made her more depressed.

"I just have to continue looking," Jordan said, even as she realized she kept talking about a new plan because she couldn't face the fact that Henry was really gone.

She excused herself early and crawled into bed to cry herself to sleep. That only managed to induce a terrific headache which kept her in bed the next day. When her brain finally relaxed enough for her to think, she actually did come up with a plan, although she had to keep it a secret. As congenial as Beatrice had become, she would never approve of what Jordan had in mind.

The sun was shining the next day with temperatures at least above freezing, so Jordan bundled up in wool trousers and a sweater, boots and the new coat Beatrice had ordered for her. The dark green wool was soft against her skin and the fur collar and cuffs were all the rage according to Beatrice. She might have hoped Eddie wouldn't be waiting for her when she left the house because she didn't want him going with her on this particular trip, but of course that wasn't the case. And to tell the truth, she felt better with him at her side, even though he was only a kid.

Maybe a kid in age, but with the soul of an old man. "You can't go in there!" he exclaimed when she told him where they were heading. "That's no place for a lady."

"We've been everywhere else, Eddie — where he lives, where he works. The only other thing to do is to ask people he would have come in contact with, and this is where we find some of them." The last was said as they stood in front of the Green Mill. Jordan remembered enough about Chicago history to know this was the hangout for Al Capone. Jordan didn't know what, if anything, Henry had written about Capone, but she knew he had investigated and written about gangsters and bootlegging. She also knew the man he had seen that morning – Tommy O'Connor – was a mobster, thus she felt Capone would have some kind of information. She only hoped bringing up Henry's name didn't get her killed.

"You'd better stay outside," she said to Eddie as she pulled open the door.

"No way. I gotta protect you."

It took a minute for her eyes to adjust to the dim interior of the lounge and by that time, two huge men were rapidly coming at her.

"This joint's not open," said one.

"I'm here to speak to Mr. Capone." She tried to stand up taller but the man towered over her.

"Mr. Capone don't talk to nobody without knowing them and he don't know you."

"Let her through," came a deep voice from the back. The two men parted and Jordan walked slowly toward the back booth, Eddie close to her side.

He looked like every picture she had ever seen of him, and yet not as scary as she would have thought. "What's a dame like you doing here?"

"Hey, she's no dame," Eddie spoke up, "she's a lady."

The two men to the side took a step toward them but Capone just laughed.

"Look at you, tough little man. Maybe you should come to work for me."

"I wouldn't..." Eddie began, and Jordan squeezed his shoulder tightly.

"I'm looking for Henry Douglas," Jordan said. "He's disappeared."

Even in the dim lighting, she could see his expression changed from bemused to angry. "You think I offed your boyfriend?" he growled.

Jordan tried not to be intimidated. "No, but you know everything that happens in this city. The day Henry disappeared he thought he saw a man named Tommy O'Connor, who—"

"Wait a minute." Capone held up a hand. "You're talking about the reporter; that Henry Douglas?"

"Yes!"

But he was already shaking his head. "I heard he'd gone missing, but it can't be because of O'Connor. That two-bit gangster disappeared years ago; probably trying to double cross his boss because he wasn't smart enough to do much except get in trouble."

"If Henry said it was O'Connor, then it was, but I don't care about that. I only want to find Henry."

"You seem like a nice person, but I can't help you. There's been no scuddle-butt about him, and I would know."

Jordan's heart sank. He had been her last hope, and now she didn't know what to do.

"Maybe," she started but Capone was already waving her off. The two burly bodyguards moved toward them and Eddie tugged her hand.

"We gotta scram," he whispered. She allowed him to lead her blindly out of the doors, tears obscuring her vision and the sobs she tried to contain choking her.

* * *

Jordan couldn't recall how she even managed to get home. Capone had been her last, desperate hope for a clue to what happened to Henry, and now she had nothing. She crawled into bed and refused to get up, even with Maddie pleading and Cook making her favorite foods. Beatrice let her be for two days but finally knocked on her door. When Jordan didn't answer, she let herself in.

"I don't need a lecture," Jordan mumbled into her pillow.

"And I'm not here to give you one," her aunt replied. She sat in the chair by the bed and for a moment didn't speak, but when she posed a question, it made Jordan sit up and take notice. "What were you and Mr.

Douglas pursuing when you left on the train the other day?"

"We were going after Harry Houdini," she said without thinking.

"And why were you doing that?"

Here's where it got sticky and she thought carefully before she answered, deciding to combine two truths. "He had a lock that was of value to us and Henry was looking for his brother's killer." Even to her own ears, that explanation didn't make sense.

Beatrice appeared to think as she studied Jordan until Jordan finally had to look away.

"I'm not sure I understand that, but ask yourself this. What can you do to finish what Henry and you started?"

Jordan swiveled back around, taken totally by surprise at her aunt's insight. Because she loved Henry, she had been more determined to find him and had forgotten about the lock. Now that he appeared to be gone for good, she had no reason to stay here if there was still a way to return to her own time. And that depended on the lock – her original quest.

"Oh my gosh, you are so right." She swung her legs over the side of the bed and bent to hug her aunt. "Thank you for making me see what was right in front of me."

She grabbed her robe and slid into her slippers, hurrying downstairs to the study. It was a longshot, but at this point she had nothing to lose.

"I need to call Mrs. Harry Houdini in New York," she told the exchange operator. She paced nervously about the desk, the telephone cord not letting her step far. After a series of connections, the phone was answered.

"Houdini residence."

"I need to speak to Mrs. Houdini," Jordan said.

"I'm sorry but she is in mourning and is not taking telephone calls or visitors."

"Please, this is important."

The connection broke and a buzz filled the air.

Damn.

Jordan waited a week and tried again. "Mrs. Houdini, please."

"I'm sorry but she is out of the country."

Double damn.

Jordan studied the items strewn across her bed. Her credit cards and driver's license did her no good in this century. The letter from the Masterlock creator that Henry had given her didn't do any good either but when she looked at it and the leather notepad with the lock impression, inspiration finally hit.

She remembered Henry telling her that Houdini didn't believe in seances and contacting people in the afterlife; in fact spent much of his life debunking mediums, yet he and his wife, Bess, had a pact to do just that when one of them died. Jordan decided to appeal to Bess's emotions. She hoped her love for her husband would make her sympathetic to Jordan's request. She had no idea how long the woman would be out of the country but there would be a letter waiting for her upon her return.

Jordan spent hours writing her appeal and she told Bess the entire truth and how they thought Harry's lock was the cause of her time travel. The woman would either embrace her or label her a lunatic, but every word Jordan wrote exposed her heart a little more. She concluded with an appeal to Bess's heart.

"If you believe in the magic of love, as you had with your husband, you will realize this may very well be his way of contacting you from beyond. I hope you will find it in your heart to help me try to return to my own century, as I can not bear to stay here without Henry."

Jordan carefully wrapped the letter, her notepad with the lock imprint and the locksmith's letter together and sent it off in the post. And she waited.

One week went by.

Another week with no mail other than Beatrice's magazines which Jordan couldn't sit still long enough to read. Although some days the weather was unforgiving, she started going for long walks along the lake front, bundled up with only a slit in her scarf to see. For some reason, it made her feel closer to Henry.

During week three, she seriously thought about going to work for Al Capone if it meant she could take out her frustrations on his minions. She had just returned home from yet another cold walk, stomping her boots on the front steps before entering the foyer to shrug out of her outer garments. She heard the telephone ring and knew Maddie would get it if Beatrice was gone.

"Miss, someone wants to speak to Jordan. I told them this was residence to a Jodelle, but she said it was definitely Jordan she needed to talk to."

Jordan's heart began to pound as she tripped over her boots trying to get to the study. She closed the door behind her, grabbing the telephone receiver.

"This is Jordan," she said breathlessly.

"This is Bess Houdini, my dear, and it is imperative that you come to New York at once."

Chapter 19
Chicago, 2022

It's raining.

Normally you would say that with a sigh and go about your business, knowing that within a few minutes; an hour at most, the weather tantrum would end and your day would again be sunny and bright.

Not in Chicago. We love a good storm, full of lightning and rolling thunder and raindrops big enough to drown a small animal. The wind roars in across the lake with such force it renders your umbrella useless, flipped inside out or literally ripped from your hands. For those who must venture forth -- perhaps because they have a job with a pain in the behind boss– be prepared for needle sharp pricks that feel as if they're shredding the clothes off your back.

I suggest you call in sick; chances are your boss has already done the same to his supervisor. I would caution you, though, to remain inside your warm little cottage and take a nap. Your boss might believe your excuse, but he also knows the name of your

Henry looked from the yellow pad he had been writing on to the window. It felt as if it rained harder here on the thirty-fifth floor than it did on the ground. The water rippled down the large panes in waves that obscured his view, which was just as well, he thought as he thumped his pencil on the glass dining room table he used as a desk. When the storm started, he had stood next to the window and felt he was about to fall right out and down thirty-five floors to the concrete below. The rain and the whistling wind he heard gave him the sense the building was swaying and when he looked down, the blowing trees only confirmed his acute sense of vertigo.

He pushed his notepad aside, putting his head in his hands as he recalled the day he and Jordan had gotten caught in the rain as they hurried down the street from a late supper. He hadn't had an umbrella so he quickly pulled them under the awning of a shop, but not before they had both gotten a bit wet. He remembered how she had laughed, not the least bit off-set over the fact the feather in her hat now hung down over one eye. Their laughter had died as her gaze slid to his. One dainty hand came up to cup his cheek, her thumb wiping the moisture away from his lips. He quickly nipped the pad of her thumb and her eyes flew wide; her breath a soft gasp as his lips met hers. It wasn't their first kiss; nor their last. But Henry had known then that she was the only woman with whom he would be sharing that pleasure from then on out.

He swept his arm to the side, the notepad sliding off the table and slapping onto the floor. Everything he did; everything he thought about, brought him back to Jordan.

With today's technology, you would think it easy to locate someone, but using the computer the best he could, he had gone down one rabbit hole after another. There couldn't be that many women named Jordan Foster in Chicago, but so far his research had come up empty. Perhaps she had gone back to using the name of the woman she impersonated – Jodelle Foster—or maybe she hadn't continued to live in Chicago. Had she remained in the twentieth century, or had she followed the path they had begun and managed to return to her place in the twenty-first century? If that were the case, why hadn't he been able to locate her? Maybe it was meant to be that she had traveled back in time and he had traveled to the future, their paths never to cross again.

He pounded his fists on the table, not wanting to believe that scenario. There had to be a reason they had met in 1926. All he had to do was figure it out. He looked again toward the windows where the rain had turned to sleet and he knew the snow would begin before long. Even so, first thing in the morning, he would start his investigations the only way he knew how, by pounding the streets and asking questions.

* * *

Henry found there were definitely advantages to living in this century. By the time he had eaten breakfast and dressed warmly, thanks to the other man's impressive selection of clothes, the city sidewalks had been swept clean and transportation was up and running. Still, he enjoyed walking the streets, amazed at the transformation of the downtown area of Chicago. Of course things would have changed in the last hundred years, but he still marveled at the skyscrapers and the large number of bizarrely shaped automobiles.

Especially impressive was what he had known as Municipal Pier, which now had a boldly arched gateway proclaiming it to be Navy Pier. As he walked the center promenade, he recalled the freighters and passenger ships that had once docked here, one of the original purposes of its construction. But it had also been used for expositions and pageants and other outdoor recreation, and that seemed to have evolved into its major purpose today, along with having many restaurants and shops.

He would not find the answers he sought in the souvenir shops, and he turned away from the waterfront to find his way to Graceland cemetery. He had decided last night that whether he liked the idea or not, he would start with the assumption that Jordan had lived out her life in his original time. Although stomping through cemeteries wouldn't bring her back, he needed to know what happened to her; he needed closure.

The cemetery was beautifully laid out but after looking at the map by the entrance, Henry realized he was trying to do the impossible. He couldn't walk through three hundred fifty acres, reading every gravestone; and this was one of more than six cemeteries, not to mention smaller church graveyards. Locating the administrative office on the map, he wandered that way, hoping someone was available to help point him in the right direction.

Luckily, Raymond Hill, director, happened to be in the office today and he assured Henry there was nothing he enjoyed more than to search for missing relatives.

"It's a hobby of mine," he told Henry as he ushered him into his office. "We get lots of requests from people doing their family trees, or from organizations like the ancestry one that puts together those family trees. Do you mind me asking if this is personal or are you researching for an article?"

Henry looked quickly away. "You recognize me?"

"Well, you don't look quite like your picture in the paper, but I guess close enough."

Henry shouldn't have been surprised. He would have to remember to keep a lower profile. Without answering the man's question, he asked, "What can you find if all you have is a possible name?"

Raymond shrugged. "With all the graves and family plots online nowadays, finding information has gotten easy. If all you have is a name, it will be harder, but I prefer a challenge."

"Ok. Her name is Jordan or Jodelle Foster and she lived in 1926 Chicago."

Raymond tilted his head. "Date of birth and death; married name?"

Henry shook his head. "I don't know." Now that he had to think about it, he didn't even know how old she was. "She wasn't married and may have been between twenty-five to thirty at that time."

"Wow. That will be a challenge," Raymond said as he jotted down the information. "I can give you the web addresses for some search aps, if you would like to have a go at it, or I can spend a little time looking and maybe narrow down known locations."

He couldn't explain his inaptitude on the computer, so accepted Raymond's assistance, especially when he said the search aps all interfaced so basically all the cemeteries in the city were linked. They exchanged phone numbers and Raymond said he would be in touch if he found anything.

If Jordan had stayed in his time, she would have no doubt continued her job with the telephone company, but when Henry walked to where the Chicago telephone Exchange had been located, he wasn't surprised to find the building had been repurposed.

In his research he had discovered his old employer, the *Chicago Daily Journal*, had ceased publication in 1929, so there was no reason to try and find that building. Even if it still existed, he couldn't very well walk in and ask if anyone knew him. Everyone he had known and worked with was dead now. A shiver raced down his spine at the thought. How had he even come to be here? The question was constantly on his mind with every day that went by.

When Henry got back to his apartment, he took a fresh notepad and tried to organize his thoughts. If Jordan had continued to live and then died in Chicago, Raymond might be able to find that information. He wrote that at the top of the page. At the bottom, he wrote that she had found a way to return to Chicago but it had been at some date other than when she had left and something had happened to her. And this was assuming it all happened in Chicago.

That left a whole lot of blank space for other scenarios, but he had no idea what they might be. His gaze kept bouncing between the top and bottom of the page –stayed and returned – stayed and returned. The words repeated like a jingle in his brain until they suddenly changed to "staying and returning."

"Sweet mother Mary," he exclaimed. At the time he had gotten shot and disappeared, they had been trying to find a way for her to return, following the lead provided by knowing the lock she had possessed belonged to Harry Houdini. They had been boarding the train on October 31, 1926, and he awoke in the hospital on October 31, 2022. Assuming their time ran parallel, although ninety-six years apart, it was late November in 1926, and she would still be in Chicago, perhaps trying to return.

This was certainly the best case scenario and Henry wrote it in the middle of the page in large letters. Beneath it he wrote the question: WHAT CAN I DO TO HELP?

He opened the computer and searched for Harry Houdini, only to find the man had died on the same day he technically had – October 31st. That could not be a coincidence, but he couldn't imagine how that had affected Jordan's search. How else was the magician connected to Jordan or to him?

Thinking back to when he had first encountered Jordan, he found his answer.

He had been at the Kirkland mansion to get information for an article on Houdini, who was performing at a social event. Jordan had magically appeared at that precise location because she had Houdini's lock, not that they knew it at the time. If there was any way to help Jordan from this point in time, he needed to start at the beginning where all three of them had been -- the Kirkland mansion of

* * *

Morning couldn't come fast enough and Henry spent most of the night pacing and drinking coffee, unable to sleep. He knew it was a long shot, but at least having a place to start gave him purpose. He hadn't heard from his editor, Harris, so assumed his PTO had been approved, but he wasn't sure he could go back to work at a newspaper, regardless of how his present circumstances turned out. He certainly couldn't continue to use another man's identity, especially without knowing whether that man was dead or alive; whether he would show up one day and declare Henry a fraud.

None of that concerned him as he hurried across town to the Kirkland mansion. The family had been part of Chicago's elite society at the turn of the century, so he hoped their residence had been preserved. He had been friends with them back in the day and Kirkland had advised him on investments. He wondered if those investments were still viable today, but without his stock certificates, there was no way to verify it. Regardless, it was a problem for another time.

He turned the corner and breathed a sigh of relief to see the large brick building right where it had always stood. He wondered who owned it now, but upon climbing the steps to the wide double doors, found it was now home not to a family but to several small businesses and city related offices. Jordan had been coming here for a reason that day, so he would start at the front and work his way through every single door, hoping he found answers.

No one in any of the boutiques on the first floor had heard of a Jordan or Jodelle Foster, so he climbed the stairs to the second floor, opening the door to the Chamber of Commerce.

Approaching the young lady at the reception desk, he asked politely, "Do you happen to know where I can find Jordan Foster, or perhaps Jodelle Foster?"

She looked at him strangely but shook her head. "No," she replied but Henry sensed her hesitation.

"What?" he prompted.

"I haven't worked here long," she said, "but when I started this past spring, there was talk about a woman named Jordan disappearing right in front of this building, but her last name was Barrister, not Foster."

Henry's heart skipped a beat. August and Beatrice's last name had been Barrister, of Barrister Brothers Furniture. Could it be that all this time, he had been looking for the wrong woman?

"Where do they; where did she live?" he quickly asked.

"I don't think I'm permitted to tell you that," she replied.

"Please. I've been away from here a long time and thought to renew an acquaintance. Places have changed over the years and I don't recall the address." He gave her what he hoped was a woebegone expression to enlist her sympathies.

She looked at him a long moment with pursed lips, then gave a sigh and reached for a booklet. "Please don't tell anyone I did this."

At his nod, she ran her finger down a column in the book and rattled off an address on Lakeview Drive.

Henry shook his head. "I went past there, but they're all businesses, not homes."

"As I understand my local history, that area was homes, but after the depression many people either lost or couldn't maintain their businesses downtown so started smaller shops out of their homes."

Henry remembered reading about the Great Depression of the 1930's when he gave himself a crash course via the internet about history since the time in which he had lived.

"You've been very helpful," he said with a genuine smile, feeling hopeful for the first time since his arrival here.

Although the day was warm enough to walk, Henry caught a cab and soon stood in front of the small antique shop on the corner of the street. It was the same address where he had visited with Jordan so often, yet the outside structure was different, the door now at ground level instead of having a set of steps leading upward. His stomach knotted as he turned the doorknob. Did he dare hope?

A small bell jingled as he came in out of the cold, his eyes adjusting to the light as he scanned the hodge-podge of furniture and knick-knacks that filled the small space.

"Good day," a male voice called from somewhere in the interior. "I'll be right with you."

Henry could see an elderly, white-haired man at a desk struggling to rise and hurried toward him. "Please. Stay seated and I'll come to you." A long, florescent light fixture cast a brighter glow over the back portion of the shop.

"Well, hello, Mr. Gallagher. To what do I owe this pleasure?" The old man had managed to stand and held out his hand.

"It's Henry Douglas, sir." He clasped the gnarled, slightly shaking hand. "Please; sit."

The man squinted at him. "Eh? You look just like that writer fellow."

"So I've been told," Henry muttered, looking around, wondering exactly how he was to start this conversation. A framed photograph sat on the top edge of the desk and when he looked closer, he sucked in a breath, his head spinning. He grabbed the edge of the desk to keep from falling.

"Looks like you're the one who needs to sit," the man grabbed his arm in a surprisingly strong grip.

Henry closed his eyes briefly and the dizziness passed. When he opened them again, his gaze flew back to the picture. "Who is that?" His voice came out as a squeak.

Although the man gave him a bemused glance, he picked up the photo and cradled it gently. "This is my granddaughter, Jordan, when she first came to live with me." He sighed. "That seems like an eternity ago and now she's gone." His voice wavered.

Henry's ears rang and his breath came in short gasps. The girl in the photo was definitely *his* Jordan. "She disappeared in June, didn't she? She had a blonde bob hair cut and wore a beaded, fringed dress like the flappers of the twenties wore."

The old man's eyes widened then narrowed in anger. "Young man, I don't know what you're trying to pull, but I suggest you leave right now."

Henry worried about giving the man a heart attack, but he had to convince him that he knew Jordan before he told him the whole truth. He searched his brain for something

Jordan had told him that wouldn't be public knowledge about her disappearance.

"The two of you went on a trip to Paris years ago and purchased a section of locks that had been on the pedestrian bridge called *Passerelle des Arts* when the city was taking down the locks because the bridge infrastructure was compromised. She told you she didn't know what to do with them but couldn't bear the thought of so much love being destroyed."

Tears flowed down the man's cheeks. "How do you know this? Do you know what happened to my granddaughter?"

"Mr. Barrister, I don't want to get your hopes up, but I believe I know where your granddaughter is."

"Tell me!" He gripped Henry's arm.

Henry looked around, knowing that at any time someone could come into the store and the story he had to tell couldn't be interrupted if it was to be believed. "Can I take you to dinner? Somewhere we talk privately?"

"I've got a stew and fresh baked bread upstairs," he replied, "if that will do." With more energy than Henry thought the old man had, he hurried to the front, locked the door and turned the sign to 'closed'. On his way back, he stopped at a doorway. "Alex, I'm closing shop for the day. I'll be upstairs if you need anything."

"Got ya covered," came a disembodied voice from beyond.

Henry looked more closely at his surroundings, trying to picture it as he knew it. The shop would have been the sitting room and dining area, the doorway to his left would have led to the study, and directly in front of him were the stairs. He watched as Mr. Barrister flipped down a small seat that appeared attached to the wall of the stairs. He buckled himself in and pushed a button, and the seat began moving upwards on a rail. His mouth must have dropped in amazement because the man chuckled.

"Lazy, I know."

"Ingenious," Henry said with a shake of his head.

The upstairs was laid out with an efficiency kitchen and small dining table, sofa and side chair and a television. Doors off to the side, though shut, were probably bedrooms. The decorations and pictures gave the place a homey feel, and Henry could almost feel Jordan's presence. The spicy aroma of the stew had him turning back to Earl.

Before he could speak, the man's questions began. "What do you know and why do you think Jordan is still alive? If she was, why wouldn't she come home?"

There was no easy way to tell this man what he wanted to know, but Henry didn't feel he could just blurt it out.

"Mr. Barrister, do you know much about your ancestry?"

"Call me Earl."

Henry nodded. "Did you have relatives in the 1920's by the names of August and Beatrice Barrister?"

The man paused in his actions, his gaze steady on Henry's for a time. He frowned. "I would have to check the family bible but as I recall, my grandfather had a brother by that name. They owned a furniture store but after the depression, they downsized and remodeled here, hoping to make ends meet. Through time, I inherited what remained of the business. Furniture from the beginning of the century, now considered antiques." He gave a rusty chuckle.

"I'm going to tell you an unbelievable story, but you have to listen to all of it and know that every bit is the truth, I swear on my blessed mother's grave."

"You're Irish," Earl said. "I can hear it in your voice."

Henry frowned, forgetting that his brogue sometimes emerged when he was stressed. "Is that a problem?"

"Not in this century." The last word trailed off and again he stared intently at Henry.

Before he lost his nerve, Henry blurted out, "As impossible as it will seem, I met your granddaughter on the steps of the Kirkland mansion in the spring of 1926."

Chapter 20

The spoon Earl held clattered to the counter, the sound echoing through the small space. Henry rushed around the counter, afraid the man would collapse onto the floor. Instead, Earl grabbed him by the lapels and ineffectively tried to shake him.

"You're telling me my granddaughter somehow is living in the last century?" Then his eyes widened in further astonishment. "You're saying *you* used to live in the last century but are now standing in my kitchen?" Every word grew in pitch until he was practically shouting. He was breathing heavily and Henry put his hands on his shoulders to hold him steady.

"Take a breath. I told you every word would be the truth, as incomprehensible as it might seem."

Earl gradually loosened his grip on Henry's coat. "Is she all right? Is she hurt?"

The man's concern for his granddaughter outweighed the incredulity of her having traveled through time.

"The last time I saw her, she was fine." He shook his head at the sound of such a mundane comment.

"The last time... How? What?" Earl continued to sputter questions. Much like Henry, he didn't seem to know where to start.

Henry looked around to find something that might ease the tension he could palpably feel in the room. "That stew smells delicious. How about dishing it up and we'll talk while we eat?"

That seemed to do the trick, until Earl sat a bowl of stew in front of him, then yanked it back. "How do I know you're not making this up, trying to scam me out of money? Everyone knows I would give everything I've got to have Jordan back."

Henry met his gaze unwavering. "I fell in love with your granddaughter; with her sense of humor, her determination, her kindness; and like you, I would give anything to have her back. I'm hoping somehow you can help with that."

Again, that unrelenting stare, sizing him up. "Talk," he finally said, sitting across from him and passing him a plate of crusty bread slathered in butter.

It was a long night, and in between bites of supper and even a beer, he laid the entire story out for Earl. He began with her falling into his arms that rainy spring day. He spoke about their developing relationship and her job as a telephone operator, but hesitated over the part when she had told him her secret, for he wasn't proud of the way he had first responded. Then he tried to explain how Houdini's lock came into play; how they had determined that was the cause of her time travel in the first place and how they had hoped getting the lock back would return her to the present.

"And you were just going to let her go?" Earl asked as he got up to fetch more beer. When Henry raised a brow, the old man chuckled. "I'm eighty-two years old. Besides, it's legal now."

Henry found it remarkable that Earl digested everything he had said with only a few questions about details, but with none of the disbelief he would have thought.

"Well, were you?"

"Very astute of you, sir." He raised his beer bottle in salute. "As a matter of fact, I had decided that if she did manage to get the lock, and it did manage to reverse what had happened, I would stick to her like glue."

"But something went wrong?"

Henry continued the story now with information about his brother and Tommy O'Connor and how it had all come to a head at the train station. "The next thing I knew, I was laying in a hospital bed in this present time."

Earl chuckled. "I can only imagine what you thought with all the new-fangled inventions."

"It helped that Jordan had given me some insight into the future, although this whole computer internet, google search thing is so far out in left field I have a hard time utilizing it as I would like. I know the answer is out there. I just haven't found it...yet."

"I understand how Jordan managed, luckily having been mistaken for a niece, but how are you getting by?"

"Remember when you called me Gallagher?"

Earl tilted his head and studied him, slowly nodding. "You do look like him. Did you stuff him in a closet somewhere?"

It was Henry's turn to laugh. "As luck, would have it, the 'other' Harry Gallagher is undercover for some reason. When I showed up at the hospital, everyone assumed I was him, and in fact, my real name is Henry Douglas Gallagher. I dropped the Gallagher at an early age because of the perceived taint of being Irish, as you have already surmised. Here, it was easier at first to assume his identity, but every day it gets harder because this Harry fellow is so well known in the city."

"And he may resurface one day."

"There is that," Henry agreed.

Earl sat quietly for a bit, twirling his beer bottle on the table, tugging at his ear in contemplation. When he brought his gaze back to Henry, there were tears glittering.

"So my little gal was an exchange operator, huh? I remember as boys, we used to make pretend calls just so we could hear their pretty voices." He snorted. "Can't say as I like all the automation of today. You could be on hold for a day before anybody thought to look for you."

Henry knew all too well.

"I don't understand how Jordan went back in time because of some lock and you came forward in time by getting shot. There's no common denominator there. But since you said you would have come with her if the opportunity had presented itself, let's not worry about sending you back. Let's figure out how to get Jordan back. That is, get her here. Damned if all that *back and forward* doesn't get a bit confusing."

Henry was amazed that Earl seemed to be taking all this in stride. "You believe me?"

"Son, I've seen men launched to the moon in a rocket ship and live in outer space. I've seen the miracles of science eradicate polio and smallpox. People disappear every day. It's not hard to imagine that maybe they're off having an adventure in another century. And it's better than thinking the alternative." He waved vaguely. "Go get me a paper from that desk and let's get cracking."

Henry walked across the room to the desk where a laptop sat, open to a blank screen. "Wouldn't you rather use this computer."

"You sound like my granddaughter. You can't teach an old dog new tricks," he replied.

Heny came back with some paper and a pencil, handing it to Earl. "You said you were shot on Halloween and you woke up here on Halloween, right? So that means time is running parallel."

Henry nodded. "Like grooves in a record."

Earl shook his head. "Record grooves go in circles," he spun his finger in the air, "and are continuous, one circle blending with the next. That would be like the line starting at the beginning of time and continuing to infinity. Railroad tracks, on the other hand, run parallel and never touch." He drew two parallel lines on the paper. "Here we are," He put an X on one line, then an X exactly opposite on the other lone. "...and here Jordan is. We will assume that since it is late November here, that is the same date in 1926."

Henry had thought the same, so was happy to see his surmise confirmed.

"You have disappeared and she has no way of knowing what actually happened to you. What would she do?" The man tapped the pencil back and forth between the two lines. Again, they were thinking along the same lines.

"I would hope she wouldn't want to stay there without me, so I assume she would continue the quest we had started."

"Exactly! What would be her next move?"

"Since Houdini died, I think that link is disconnected. Who knows what happened to the lock after his death. It could have transferred hands a dozen times. It could be anywhere." Henry couldn't think clearly.

"If Jordan came to that conclusion, too, she wouldn't try to find *people*," Earl said. "She would start at her beginning...where she got the *lock*."

"You have the section of fencing?" Henry asked.

"Downstairs in her shop." Earl rose. "Follow me."

Earl rode his little chair back down the stairs with Henry following. The antique store was in shadows, only a small table light giving the interior a gloomy glow as they slowly made their way to the open door where the study would have been when Henry visited the house. Earl reached around the doorframe and suddenly light filled the area.

The instant Henry walked through the doorway, scents assailed him and memories flooded back. Jordan had smelled of fresh rain and lemon when he first caught her on the sidewalk. The shop was filled with shelves and small tables, candles in glass containers sitting in small collections on every flat surface.

"Over here," Earl called and Henry walked across the small shop to an alcove.

The section of fencing was about four feet long and the same in height, covered with padlocks of every size, color and shape. He touched one after the other, nothing causing any kind of connection until he got close to one end and a small tingle shot up his arm. The sensation immediately disappeared, and he wondered if he had conjured it because he wanted so desperately to believe there was a link between Jordan and himself.

Henry said sorrowfully. "How will we ever know if she ended up in Paris?"

"I know someone who might be able to help. It's too late tonight, but I will make some calls and we can find out tomorrow."

Henry knew it was time to leave. "Thank you for believing me, Earl. You don't know how much it helps, having someone to talk to who understands." He put out his hand.

Earl clasped it warmly with both of his. "It is I who should be giving thinks. You have given me hope when there was none."

* * *

Another sleepless night and Henry arrived back at the antique store early, but Earl was waiting at the door and told Henry to wave down the taxi before it left. He locked the door behind them and they climbed into the taxi where Earl gave the driver the name of the Maritime Museum.

When they arrived, another man, equally as old as Earl, met them at the door and ushered them to a room in the back where a few computers sat at desks arranged among artifacts from various seafaring time.

"This is Jerry," Earl said by way of introduction.

"Sorry, we're at a pinch for space," Jerry said, setting himself in front of one of the computers. "Now, what do you have for me?" The man wasted no time getting to the point.

Henry must have looked surprised, for Earl spoke up. "Jerry has spent his retirement inputting ship passenger manifest data into the computer to create searchable databases on seafaring travel for, what, the last two centuries?"

Jerry shrugged. "I'm only back to about eighteen-fifty," he said.

Henry shook his head. "I thought you didn't use computers," he said to Earl.

"I don't," he replied, "but that doesn't mean I can't appreciate their capabilities, or that of people like Jerry, who do enjoy working with the technology."

"Gee, thanks," Jerry said with a grin. "Now, what do we know?"

Henry grabbed Earl's arm and turned his back on Jerry to speak in low tones. "Are you sure? We're going to sound like we're crazy."

"It's fine," Earl said and Henry decided he had to trust the man. He had already gotten a call from Raymond at the cemetery who had found no trace of Jordan in any registry or record. While that was a good thing, it had left Henry with no place to look until he had found Earl.

Earl turned back to his friend. "We're looking for a woman who might have traveled from here to Paris between, say mid-November to the end of the year in 1926."

Jerry typed. "Okay, so she most likely would have left from New York and sailed to the port of LeHavre, France. Do you have a name?"

"I'm not sure," Henry said. "It could be Jordan or Jodelle, and the last name is Foster."

"Let's assume she went back to her real name," Earl said. To Jerry, he said, "Use Jordan Barrister."

Jerry typed in the information, hit enter, and the computer did what Henry could only consider magic. While lines of data scrolled upward too fast to read, Jerry and Earl chatted about the latest gossip they had heard at canister club. After an incredibly short time, the scrolling quit and a single line was highlighted in yellow.

"A *J. Barrister* left the port in New York on December fifth and arrived at LeHavre on December tenth."

"Bingo," Earl said excitedly.

Henry looked at Jerry, who was typing more information into the computer, then back to Earl. "It was ninety-six years ago," he whispered.

"You forget the train track theory," Earl replied softly. "It's the same date then as here and she's just now trying to find her way."

Henry had read about the new records in which steamships were traveling across the ocean, but even so, a trip to Paris would be impossible in less than a week to ten days. He expresses his concern to Earl. "I can't get to Paris from here in five days. She might be there and gone before I can even arrive."

"You forget what century this is. You can fly directly from here to Paris in a day."

Henry recalled his long ago interview with the Wright brothers about their incredible, but very small and flimsy airplane.

"Fly?" His voice squeaked and his stomach knotted.

Chapter 21
New York, 1926

A trip that would normally have taken Jordan two hours on a plane was dragging on interminably aa she switched trains yet again. Even on the Twentieth Century Limited, one with the newest and most luxurious Pullman cars, fifteen hours might as well have been fifteen days. And of course, she hadn't gotten a first class ticket since she didn't know how long her money would have to last. She had gotten all her money from the bank before she left Chicago because she was pinning all her hopes on being able to return to her time in the twenty-first century, but she still needed to pinch pennies until that happened.

As the train rattled along the tracks, she reflected on the last two days. As much as she wanted to speak to Beatrice and August, she had been afraid she would spill the beans if she had, so although it was cowardly she had written a letter. She had thanked them for their hospitality and had simply said she was going home. Let them make of that as they will. She felt a little guilt, for if the real

Jodelle ever showed up, she'd have a lot of explaining to do.

It had been much harder to leave without seeing Eddie again. The poor kid had already lost Henery. She hoped it helped that she had written a letter to the bank, giving Eddie the contents of Henry's passbook by forging a letter and his signature. After all, the money wasn't doing Henry any good. She smiled, hoping he always had stuffed chicken for Sunday dinner.

When it came to packing, she took only a few dresses along with the original clothes she had materialized in. She didn't want to leave any trace of herself in this century, again assuming her plan worked. She did, however, take the meager contents of Henry's briefcase, tucking the stock certificates and family picture carefully in the side of her satchel. It was all she had left of him, and she cherished the article about the geese that remained on his notepad.

The whistle blew and steam hissed as the train began to slow. Mrs. Houdini had given her address, but it was in Manhattan and would require a taxi ride. Jordan took a few minutes in the ladies' room to freshen up, feeling as if she had slept in her clothes for days.

And now, here she stood in front of a small brick home, her stomach in knots and her palms sweaty even in the near freezing weather. A black wreath hung on the door, reminding Jordan that Mrs. Houdini was still in mourning, and she would have to be cautious with what she had to ask her. Regardless of how much Jordan wanted the lock, it had belonged to the woman's husband and she might not want to part with it. Still, she had invited Jordan here, so she took that as a good sign.

Her knock was answered by a young woman who took Jordan's hat and coat then led her into a sitting room where a small but cherry fire burned in the hearth. The woman sitting on the sofa to the side didn't rise to greet her, but Jordan assumed it was Mrs. Houdini.

"Hello," she said by way of greeting. When the woman vaguely waved a hand to the chair opposite her, Jordan sat primely down and folded her hands in her lap. The woman continued to stare at her intently and Jordan tried not to fidget.

"Tea?" she finally broke the silence and at Jordan's nod, she poured as she spoke. "I can see why Henry was taken by you."

"You knew Henry?" Her words surprised Jordan and her hands shook slightly as she accepted the cup and saucer.

"Not well, really. He was friends with the Kirklands, and the Kirklands were benefactors of my husband, so he was often in attendance when we were in town. He and my husband did not see eye to eye." She said this with a slight smile, as though fondly remembering.

"I didn't know that." Jordan did know, but decided to keep Henry's remarks about the magician to herself. She noticed Mrs. Houdini had her letter and the notepad on the sofa beside her and she wondered how soon it would be brought up.

"May I ask you one question?" the woman said.

"Only one?" Jordan said without thinking, given all the information she had written in that letter.

This made her smile. "Miss Barrister, your tale is too fantastical and absurd for anyone to make such things up, unless you are the likes of Mary Shelley. Besides, when one believes in magic, anything is possible."

"I am hoping that is true," Jordan replied, knowing she needed magic for sure. "Please, ask me whatever you want."

"In your time, close to one hundred years from now, what do people know of my husband?"

Realizing she wanted to know that her husband hadn't been forgotten, it wasn't hard to answer. "Harry Houdini is considered one of the world's greatest magicians and escape artist. There have been books written about him and movies made about his life."

"Motion pictures? Truly?"

Jordan nodded. "There are many who have tried to replicate his water torture escape with little success." She actually didn't remember all the specifics of

Houdini's life but it wasn't as if Bess would find out she had tweaked the truth.

"Thank you for that," She sat quiet for a moment, then reached over and picked up the notepad. "I know you did not come here to discuss my late husband, so how is it that I can help you?"

"As I tried to explain in my letter, I came in possession of a lock and it somehow caused me to appear in 1926, but in the process the lock disappeared. Henry and I discovered that it was a lock your husband had commissioned, and I believe the only way I can return to my own time is to regain possession of that lock."

"My husband had many locks," she said. "They were, after all, his stock in trade."

"I understand but this particular lock had a rather fancy façade of gold and silver on the front." She pointed to the notepad. "The pattern imprinted on that notebook." She watched the woman trace the pattern with a delicate finger.

"And you want to return to your own time because...?"

Jordan's heart squeezed as it did every time she thought of Henry. "I want to go home to my own people, because Henry is not here anymore, and I can't bare being here without him."

Bess looked across the small space with tears in her eyes. "I know exactly how you feel, but I'm afraid I can't help you."

"I don't understand. It was Houdini's lock. You don't need it anymore so what does it matter if you give it to me?" She sucked in a breath, not having intended to sound so angry. "I'm sorry; that was rude of me. It's just," she paused then continued. "I don't know how to explain my sense of loss."

"I do understand, completely, but I don't have the lock anymore."

Jordan gasped, not having thought of this scenario. "Where is it? Can I get it from someone else?"

The woman fingered a key that hung from a silver chain around her neck. "Have you ever heard of *Passerelle des Arts,* in Paris, where people often profess their undying love by locking a padlock to the bridge? My husband and I loved that city and so I took a lock to the bridge in honor of him." She looked at Jordan, again with tears. "The same lock to which you refer."

The lock had come full circle, back to the bridge in Paris. Jordan gasped. Or because of the difference in dates, it was *now* at the point where she had originally found it.

"They removed the locks from the bridge at some point in time," Jordan said, "and I purchased a section of grille with locks attached. That is how this all started."

Bess removed the chain from her neck, her hands trembling as she held the key out to Jordan. "Then perhaps this is how it should end. If this key to the lock actually returns you to your own time, it would truly be the greatest magic of all time, would it not?"

* * *

With the help of a friend of Bess's, Jordan was booked passage on an ocean liner two days later. As she walked up the ramp and onto the giant ship, all she could think of was the *Titanic,* and that was not a good thing. She went directly to her second-class cabin and didn't emerge for the first two days. By that time, her stomach rumbled with hunger and she realized that the ship would either make it to France or not, either of which was totally out of her control.

She spent the days walking the inside promenade as the wind and cold crossing the Atlantic in December was formidable. The size of the ship made it steady in the water and she rarely felt as though she were moving at all. The eloquence of the ship shouldn't have surprised her and she soon understood why this was considered the golden age of ocean liners. She had only begun to enjoy the meals and the camaraderie of fellow dinner passengers when supper announcements included that they would reach the port of LeHavre in the morning.

Since she'd been to France on more than one occasion, she knew basic geography, although she'd never visited LeHavre. It was only a short train ride into Paris, a city that she did know well. Of course, things looked different given the century, but the trains were familiar and her French, while rusty, was still serviceable, and she soon debarked near the Seine River walkway.

Paris in December was not Paris in the spring, and she shivered inside her coat as she walked along the river. Snow had begun, and the closer she came to the pedestrian bridge, the heavier the flakes. The path was almost obscured by the time she started up the slight incline. Bess had given her the approximate location of the lock, but the snow blew, making it even harder to see.

She felt along the railing to the light post, then crouched down to find the right row. Snow blew across her face and flakes stuck to her lashes. She fumbled for the chain in her pocket, sliding along its length to the key at the end. The swirling snow made her dizzy, but she pulled her hat lower on her forehead to block it as she searched for the lock. The ornate design made it easier to find and she grabbed it with one hand as she tried to insert the key. A tingle shot up her arm as her ears rang and her hands shook. The snow grew heavier, blinding her. The lock wouldn't turn. She swiped the lock face clear of snow and tried again, jiggling and twisting but to no avail.

"Jordan?" The shock of hearing her name made her drop the hold on the lock and she heard the key skitter across the bricks. She turned to the sound of a male voice calling her name again and instantly recognized the bare-headed man.

"Harry?" She jerked to her feet. "Harry Gallagher?" She took a step forward, then began to run. "Oh my god. It worked! I'm back!" She launched herself at him and circled his neck, holding on tight. She tilted her head to the side, the snow having slowed to allow the bright lights of the city to glow all around.

When she turned back, warm lips covered hers in a passionate kiss. Now, she knew Harry Gallagher but they had never dated and certainly had never kissed, yet the shock of his lips on hers instantly turned to familiarity and she melted into his embrace. She felt bereft when he slowly lifted his head after long minutes.

"Would it disappoint you to know I'm not Harry, but rather Henry Douglas?" He gave her a slight smile and her heart tripped as memories flooded her.

"Henry? That's not possible. You died." She shook her head even as she looked all around. "Didn't you?" She didn't give him time to answer but continued, "If you didn't die, that means..." she swallowed heavily, "that means it didn't work; that we're still back in 1926?"

He hadn't let go of her and now tugged her closer. "Would it matter if that were the case?"

She framed his face in her cold hands, staring intently at his features to assure herself that it was indeed Henry. Did it matter?

"I love you, Henry Douglas. If I'm with you, I don't care what century it is."

The End

Author Notes

"The proof that there will be no time travel in the future is that we are not being visited by travelers from the future."– Stephen Hawking

With respect to one of the greatest physicists of our time, who studied our universe and had much to say about it, I have to disagree with him in regard to time travel. Perhaps we *do not know* we are being visited, for much the same reasons that Jordan and Henry wanted to keep quiet about their travels. It is more than likely that unscrupulous people would try to take advantage of the knowledge and technology that someone from the future would hold. But maybe some of today's most inventive and brilliant people are actually from a time far in the future, and had they not stopped during our time, we would not be enjoying the technology we currently use.

Conjecture, of course, but here are some real facts. According to the National Missing and Unidentified Persons (NamUS) database, which is funded by the U.S. Department of Justice, more than 600,000 people go missing annually. The majority are found quickly, but as of December 31, 2021, the National Crime Information Center's (NCIC) database contained 93,718 active missing person records.

In this story, Tommy O'Connor, a two-bit gangster in Chicago, actually did disappear in the 1920s. He was by no means the only one during this turbulent period of our history with prohibition, bootlegging and mob takeovers. Where are those people? Is it possible that they traveled through time and lived an entirely different existence far into the future, or far into the past? I like to think so, but then, I do write fiction.

Also by Barbara Baldwin from BWL Publishing

Her Scottish Legacy
Loving Charlie Forever
An Interlude
Hold On To The Past
Spinning Through Time
A Game of Love
Always Believe
Prospecting for Love
If Wishes Were Magic
Love in Disguise
Prelude and Promises
Dreamcatcher
Tenderhearted Cowboy

Barbara was born in California and now resides in the Midwest. She loves to travel and explore new places, which usually means each of her novels is set in a different locale. She has been published in formats from poetry and short stories to full-length fiction. She really loves writing romance, whether it is contemporary, historical or time travel. She has an MA in Communication and has taught every grade from Kindergarten to college. Visit her website at http://www.authorsden.com/barbarajbaldwin.